THE FORGOTTEN GIRL

DAISY CARTER

CHAPTER 1

he West Country, England - 1852

MARGARET SCOTT STUMBLED ONWARDS, walking blindly across the common without paying much attention to her surroundings and oblivious to her aching legs from the miles she had covered. There was a sheen of dew on the grass, and the bottom of her gown was damp from it, but she didn't care. The sky was starting to turn pearly pink in the east as the sun rose over the distant hills. In the other direction, where the sinuous river carved through the land-scape, the silvery crescent moon still hung in the midsummer sky, glowing eerily amid wisps of cloud.

The rational part of her mind thought about the

hot day ahead. The farmers would be busy in the fields, scything the grass to make hay. Farming never stopped, especially when the weather was good. All too soon, the seasons would turn, and the land would be cold and barren again, so they needed to gather in the crops to keep the animals fed during the long winter months.

Wildflowers studded the rough grassland around her, their colours like tiny jewels: the blue of hare-bells, pale pink milkwort, sunny spires of yellow rattle, and the occasional purple flash of an orchid. It was the time of year when everything in the West Country felt lush and abundant, but it gave Margaret no pleasure on this particular day. Her mouth pinched resentfully as she pondered the mockery of all the young animals in evidence all around her. In their rural setting there was no escaping it. The sheep had lambed a few months earlier, and now the curly-coated lambs frolicked in the fields, leaping off grassy banks and racing in riotous gangs as the ewes bleated in consternation. The spring calves had also been born, and they hurried after the cows as they ambled slowly across the common land with swinging udders to the next patch of good grazing. The hedgerows were alive with the chirping of nesting birds and their newly fledged chicks, and a speckled brown skylark fluttered ahead of her, feigning injury to draw her away from its nest.

The next generation of all creatures is blossoming except for me. The bitter thought felt like grey fog seeping into every corner of her mind, blocking out all beauty and happiness. There had been a new moon a few days earlier. It was supposed to herald a time of new beginnings, but for Margaret, the night the lunar cycle turned had brought only death and disappointment. The baby she had carried for so many months had arrived early and unexpectedly, carrying her on a shocking tide of red-hot pain like an iron fist gripping her back and belly. When the little boy had slithered out, there had been no lusty newborn cry, just silence, followed by the sound of her own weeping.

Since then, Margaret hadn't been able to sit still or stay in the house. Some primal urge drove her to keep walking, which was why she was exhausted as she stumbled to the edge of the common, where the land fell away sharply in front of her, and the village lay nestled below. She hadn't told anyone what had happened. It was a secret shared only by her and her husband, Bill, because the words felt too unwieldy to utter. She didn't want well-meaning condolences and folk making a fuss. She wanted her baby.

A long sigh came from deep in her chest as she stood at the edge of the escarpment, gazing over the patchwork of fields and toy-sized cottages below her, with the soft outline of the Welsh mountains in the distance across the border. She held her arms wide and tipped her head back. The breeze made her shawl flutter like wings. She wished she could float away from all her cares, circling on the thermals like the buzzards, but what would be the point? Her sadness would follow her.

As the sun rose higher, Margaret's tears dried on her cheeks, and she gradually became more aware of the view, which had always been her favourite. She and Bill had used to walk on the common when they were courting, and before this terrible event, it had always brought her comfort. But not anymore.

Perhaps we need a fresh start somewhere else? She looked bleakly at the village that had always been her home. There was a cluster of honey-coloured cottages at the centre surrounding the village square, and the lanes fanned out in a higgledy-piggledy fashion as it had grown over the decades. A grand manor sat imperiously at one end with a sweeping driveway lined by horse chestnut trees, and there was a scattering of farms with cattle, sheep and pigs.

As her gaze wandered from east to west, she could see the cobbled bridge that crossed the stream near the duck pond. A lone horse pulling a cart clopped along the lane on its way to market. On the outer edges of the village, there was the mill and a tidy row of mill cottages. The church spire glinted in the rising sun, and Margaret felt a faint sense of peace for the first time in days that soothed her weary soul. She attended church every Sunday, like all the villagers, but her faith had been sorely tested. She hoped it would return soon to help her get over losing her baby.

Looking down at the churchyard made her think about Bill. He was fifteen years older than her and a kindhearted man. When he wasn't working as a gravedigger, he helped out on the local farms and was well-regarded by their friends and neighbours. She could see the gravestones in neat rows, some aged with lichen and others still clean and new. Generation after generation of villagers laid to rest. At the end of the row, there was a dark hole in the ground. It was old Mrs Lynch's funeral in a couple of days, and she knew that Bill would be spending the afternoon in the churchyard, making sure that the grave was perfectly dug with the solemnity and attention it deserved. What he had done with the lifeless body of their baby, she couldn't yet contemplate. All she knew was that he would be buried on consecrated ground, not in a pauper's grave. Bill had promised her that.

"I'm sorry I couldn't provide you with the son you wanted," she murmured, plucking and twisting the edge of her shawl. Even though there was nobody nearby to hear her words, and she had already said it to Bill dozens of times, she still felt the need to say it again as some sort of penance for what felt like her failure. Bill had done his best to reassure her, telling her firmly that it wasn't her fault. It was a tragedy, but God-willing, there would be other children, and they would have the family they yearned for.

Logically, Margaret knew he spoke the truth. It was all too common for babies and infants to perish when poverty was so rife, but with her body still heavy with milk and no baby to cherish, it still felt like a cruel blow.

"What if I never have another baby?" Her words came out in a hoarse groan, carried away on the morning breeze. She fell to her knees and fixed her gaze on the church below. "It's so unfair," she cried. Tears pooled in her eyes again and rolled slowly down her cheeks, but she dashed them away. She couldn't hide away in self-pity forever, and Margaret prided herself on being a practical person. She took a shuddering breath and clenched her hands together to stop her resolve from crumbling.

The moon had almost disappeared as the morning sun got stronger, and mist rose around her, giving the land an ethereal feel. She glanced at the church, but then her gaze was drawn to the moon like so many women before her, seeking strength from the beliefs that were rooted in more ancient times. "All I ask...pray...is that I might have a child sometime in my life," she murmured.

* * *

THE BREEZE STRENGTHENED, rustling the grass around her and pulling Margaret out of her troubled thoughts. She wasn't the first woman to experience loss, and she wouldn't be the last. Bill needed his breakfast, and then she supposed she would have to start facing the villagers and explaining what had happened. She wasn't looking forward to it, but life went on. She had been distracted from her button-making business, but they couldn't live on Bill's income alone. She would set up a table under the apple tree in their small garden and hope that the sharp ache of misery would slowly ease and that her body would soon readjust to not being in the family way.

In spite of trying to talk herself into feeling better, Margaret still wasn't quite ready to face some of the village ladies, who loved nothing more than to gossip about other people's misfortune, so she stuck to the narrow, dusty back lanes as she quickly made her way home again. Every now and then, she could hear shouts from the farmers as they called their dogs to bring the cows in for milking. Swallows whistled as they swooped overhead, catching insects, and cobwebs glistened in the hedgerows as the morning dew burnt off.

She looked down at her gown and shook the dust

from it as she slipped through the wooden gate at the end of their long, narrow garden. She was pleased that they didn't live in the row of mill cottages with a shared privy out the back where everyone would be queuing and chattering at this time of the morning. Bill's job as a gravedigger meant that they rented a small cottage near the vicarage. There had been times when she missed having immediate neighbours, but today, it was a relief to get home without bumping into anyone. Glancing up at the small window under the thatched roof, she was surprised to see that the faded curtains were still tightly closed. She stepped into the kitchen and was struck by how quiet it was. Bill must have set off early for work. She missed his strong arms pulling her into a hug and decided to make him a hearty breakfast. It would only take her a minute to walk to the churchyard and call him home when it was ready, and she knew it would please him to see her getting back to some sort of normality.

Margaret left the kitchen door open and stoked the range. It wouldn't take long for the kettle to start whistling merrily, and she added a pinch of tea leaves to the brown teapot and swept some old bread-crumbs off the table to scatter on the back doorstep. A blackbird hopped down immediately, giving her a beady look before pecking at the crumbs and then fluttering back into the apple tree. Two sparrows were squabbling in the dust beneath the tree, and then three more fluttered down to join in, and to her surprise, Margaret found herself almost smiling. *Life really does go on.*

She added oats, water, and a pinch of salt to a saucepan and started stirring, still watching the birds. Bill liked a splash of cream and a drizzle of honey on his porridge, and she was glad he'd had the foresight to fetch some from the farmer rather than her having to go to market.

As she turned to fetch Bill's bowl from the dresser a few minutes later, an unexpected sound drifted through the open door that made the hairs on her arms stand up. It sounded like a whimper. The sort of noise a newborn baby would make. Her hands trembled slightly, and she tilted her head to one side, straining to listen. Had she imagined it? Was she going mad? All she could hear was the chirping of birds and the sound of distant voices as the village came to life.

The garden gate clicked shut, and heavy footsteps announced Bill's arrival. He filled the doorway, and her heart lifted at the sight of his broad shoulders and kind face.

"That's good timing," she said, putting her fanciful notions from her mind. "I'm sorry I haven't been myself these last few days or cooked anything." She gestured towards the range. "I made porridge. That cream and honey you got from Moorend Farm will go lovely on top."

Bill glanced furtively over his shoulder into the garden and shut the kitchen door firmly behind him. It was only as he did so that Margaret registered he was wearing his coat draped over one shoulder like a cloak. It seemed incongruously out of place on such a hot day, and his cheeks were ruddy. She felt a pang of alarm. The doctor had always said that Bill needed to watch his health because his father had died young from heart congestion and that it might run in the family.

She brought the bowl to the table and raised her eyebrows. "Have you been out? I hope you're not overdoing it, Bill. I couldn't bear it if something happened to you as well. You don't look yourself if you don't mind me saying."

"It's nothing to worry about," he said. His voice sounded slightly breathless, which worried her even more. "I couldn't sleep, so I went out for a walk. I hoped I might find you."

She shrugged, feeling guilty for her absence. "I wanted to be alone, so I went over the common. I won't do it again, but I couldn't bear to be at home these last few nights." Margaret stepped forward to take his coat and hang it up behind the door, but as she did so, he pulled the coat to one side and revealed that he was carrying something concealed underneath. It looked like an old lace shawl all bundled up.

Suddenly, the whimpering sound came again, and Margaret gaped in astonishment as the shawl fell away to reveal a baby.

"Who...? What...?" Her words came out in a croak, and before he could reply, she snatched the baby from his arms and looked down at it.

"'Tis a little girl." Bill could barely tear his eyes away from the sight of her in Margaret's arms.

"She looks so ill and frail...a newborn, surely..." A torrent of emotions crashed over Margaret as she cradled the tiny infant. Confusion tinged with a fierce longing. Almost without thinking, she unbuttoned the front of her dress and pressed the baby to her chest. Its cheeks were cold in spite of the warm morning, and it felt limp. For one terrifying moment, she thought it might have perished and that she was caught up in some terrible nightmare she couldn't wake up from. But then the baby latched on and started suckling, and her heart soared with sheer joy.

Silence fell in the kitchen, other than the tiny snuffling sound of the baby feeding, and relief washed through Margaret as some colour returned to its cheeks.

"What a beautiful little one you are," she whispered. The infant's translucent eyelids fluttered open at the sound of her voice just as Bill pulled a chair out and placed it next to the range. Margaret sank grate-fully into it. She didn't think her legs could have held her up for much longer; she was so shocked.

"Where is she from?" She hardly dared look Bill in the eye. The baby's hand rested like a starfish on her chest with fingernails like exquisite tiny shells, and Margaret's heart melted as she looked down into her dark eyes framed with delicate lashes. She knew at that moment she could never go back to being child-less again.

Bill reached out and gently stroked the baby's head before giving Margaret a look that was hard to read. She wondered whether he was going to refuse to answer, but then he squeezed her hand and took a deep breath.

"Losing our son was difficult for both of us and when I was out walking, I felt drawn to go past Hayton House."

Margaret couldn't hide her surprise. Hayton House was at the end of a long lane, shrouded in a thicket of ancient rhododendron bushes and from what she'd heard, not many people knew about it. Mrs Lowell, the owner, was an eccentric old lady who was rumoured to accept foundlings and cared for them before they went to the orphanage or were adopted by a family. "You mean this baby is one of Mrs Lowell's?"

Bill shook his head. "No, the place was all closed

up. I don't even know if she was there." His gaze slid away for a moment, and he looked evasive. "I saw a bundle on the steps outside the gates," he continued in a rush. "It wasn't moving, but something made me look…and…I discovered this baby. She was so cold, Margaret, and I couldn't bear to see her left for dead like that. I had it in my mind I'd be burying her before the morning was out, but when I picked her up, I realised she was still alive, so I came straight home with her. It was like a miracle."

"But…who would do such a thing?" Margaret's head was spinning with Bill's revelation, but then a painful thought occurred to her. "What if Mrs Lowell finds out you took her? Surely, we'll get into trouble." Her arms tightened protectively around the baby as if she already belonged to them. "Did anyone see you?" She darted a look towards the window half expecting to see the constable striding up the path to hammer on the back door and demand they should return her.

"You know as well as I do that Mrs Lowell has her hands full already if the rumours are to be believed. She has all those stray cats and dogs, plus unwanted children."

"Who left her?" Margaret wasn't sure she wanted to know.

He shrugged. "I expect it was just some travelling folk passing through. Hayton House looks like it belongs to a wealthy owner from afar, and perhaps they thought leaving the baby with a well-to-do family would mean she would be cared for better than they could manage." He looked slightly shifty again. "All I know is that it must have been someone who fell on hard times and didn't want her, Margie."

Even as Bill said the words, Margaret doubted them, but she would never say it out loud. At least not yet. "Are you sure they won't be back for her?" She could hear the longing in her own voice, and the soft weight of the baby in her arms just felt so right.

Bill squeezed her hand again and smiled, looking deep into her eyes. "Maybe this is the answer to our prayers," he said softly. "Our own boy didn't live, but surely the fact that I found her shows that it was meant to be. We can give her a better home than if she ended up in an orphanage."

The baby had finished feeding, and Margaret carefully lifted her up to rest on her shoulder and rubbed her back to wind her. Part of her wanted to press Bill for more details. *Did he see the people who abandoned her? Is he telling me the truth?* She decided to push her worries aside and realised that although she would always mourn the loss of her little boy, this new baby, who had come unexpectedly into their lives when they most needed it, must have happened for a reason. *Didn't I ask for a child only a few hours ago on the common?*

She remembered that nobody in the village knew they had lost their son. It would be simple enough to tell the neighbours that they'd had this little girl. She was still so tiny it was clear she was a newborn, and nobody need ever know any different.

Margaret shook her head in wonder and astonishment. "I can't believe she was just left abandoned and forgotten." She cradled the infant again and looked at her husband. "We can give her a happy home, can't we, Bill?"

"Of course we can." He stood up and put the teapot in the middle of the table, reaching for two mugs. "The first thing we need to do is give the poor little mite a name," he said happily.

Margaret sipped her tea and started to feel normal again for the first time in days. "We did think about Suzanne if she was a girl, but I think Nancy suits her perfectly."

"Nancy." Bill tried it out and nodded. "I'm sure I heard someone say that Nancy means favoured one."

"Well, that's perfect." Margaret stroked the baby's downy, brown hair and sighed with contentment. "I think you must have been favoured for Bill to find you this morning, my love. We'll call you Nancy, and maybe one day you might have some brothers and sisters, but for now, having you is just perfect."

CHAPTER 2

ancy rubbed her knuckles in her eyes to banish the last remnants of sleep and tugged the curtain over her bed open. Daylight already? She sprang out of bed and shivered as she scampered down the narrow wooden staircase of the redbrick two-up, two-down cottage, pulling her dress over her head as she went. She had overslept, which was most unlike her. "Luke should have woken me," she muttered to herself, almost tripping over in her haste. Her brown hair fell in unruly curls over her shoulders, and the sharp ripping sound as her elbow poked through the threadbare sleeve made her frown. *Too late to hide that from Ma.* She would just have to patch it later, she thought ruefully. The ragged hem of the dress flapped high on her shins, and it had already been patched so much that there wasn't much of the original fabric left showing. What she really needed was a new one, but she knew better than to ask.

"Morning, Ma," she cried as she burst into the kitchen. "Sorry I'm late…promise it won't happen again, but it's probably Luke's fault for sneaking downstairs without waking me up…has he gone to work on the farm already? He told me they were giving him a shilling a week for planting potatoes if he could keep up with the men." Nancy spoke fast to distract from the rip in her sleeve, tiptoeing across the flagstones to stand in her favourite spot by the hearth to warm up. There were no warming orange flames, just grey ash. She stopped abruptly and gave her mother a puzzled look. "Why isn't the fire lit?" Even though it was late spring, their house was in deep shade on the steep side of the valley, and the sun had yet to rise, so everything felt damp and cold.

Margaret pushed a lock of dark hair back from her forehead and eyed her eldest daughter wearily. "Give the questions a rest, will you," she snapped testily. "I've never known a girl talk so much about nothing in particular. You're too clever for your own good." She hitched Primrose higher on her hip and scowled as she started to howl and chewed on her pudgy fist.

Nancy danced from one foot to the other, trying to keep warm, although her bare feet were already tinged blue from the cold floor. "Our Primrose is hungry, Ma," she said without thinking, raising her voice over the rising wail from her younger sister.

Margaret rolled her eyes, plonked Primrose unceremoniously in her wooden high chair and threw her hands up. "I don't need you stating the bleeding obvious, Nancy. Everyone is always hungry, but I can't make a decent breakfast out of thin air, can I."

Primrose's blue eyes brightened, and she grabbed a spoon, banging on the table. "Bekkfast?" she parroted hopefully. At two years old, she was picking up words fast, but all it did was irritate Margaret even more. "Bekkfast, Mamma?" The words were more insistent.

"Shall I run down the lane and see if Gertie can spare a jug of milk?" Nancy was smart enough to recognise when her ma's patience was stretched thin, and now that she was ten years old, she was becoming more adept at keeping her happy. "I can scrounge a couple of lumps of coal as well and light the fire. I think there are a few twigs in the wood-shed." She reached for her boots and tugged them on, wincing as they pinched her toes. The holey soles wouldn't keep her feet dry on the muddy farm track, but they were better than nothing.

To Nancy's alarm, instead of her suggestion making her ma happier, Margaret's eyes suddenly filled with tears. "How are we going to manage without neighbours like Gertrude helping us out?"

"What do you mean?" Dread curled in Nancy's belly. *Please don't say it's happening again, just when I made some new friends.*

Margaret dried her tears on the corner of her apron, and her face settled into harsh lines of resignation. It seemed to be her permanent expression lately. She jerked her head towards the window. "Take a look for yourself, Nancy. There's no point in me keeping it a secret from you any longer. You're old enough to understand." She grabbed the stale loaf of bread at the centre of the table and started slicing it with a savage sawing motion, mumbling a steady diatribe of complaints under her breath but not caring if the children heard. "It's one job after another...no sooner do we put down roots than it's onto the next...why does nothing ever work out...I should never have married him..."

Silence stretched for a moment. Then, the final cutting comment. "I rue the day my darling Bill died, and Ezra Burton swept me off my feet with his handsome smile and promises. So much for marrying a soldier. I should have known better."

Nancy tried to close her ears to the mutterings, thinking they were rather unfair. Her stepfather, Ezra, wasn't as terrible as Ma made out. They had just fallen on hard times, hadn't they?

She could still vaguely remember when her ma's cheeks dimpled with laughter, and the days seemed to be full of hazy golden sunshine, but sometimes she wondered whether she had imagined it. She darted around the kitchen table and pressed her nose to the window. Sure enough, there was Papa Ezra guiding a horse and cart down the narrow lane, with Luke perched on the seat next to him. The scrawny pony came to a halt outside their house and whinnied, stamping a hoof impatiently.

"Is it...are we...?" She could barely bring herself to ask the question, especially with Margaret's face growing more thunderous by the moment.

"Yes," Margaret cried bitterly. "The fire isn't lit because we're leaving Eaton Cottage today, Nancy." She folded her arms across her ample bosom and sniffed. "The farmer said Ezra spent too much time malingering. So here we are. Another job he can't hold down for longer than a year, and another home we can't afford the rent for."

Before Margaret could continue railing against her second husband, Luke came bounding in. He was three years younger than Nancy, and she was struck again by how different she looked compared to them. Luke and Primrose both took after Ezra with fine blonde hair and blue eyes, unlike her brown curls and green eyes.

"Pa said it shouldn't take us long to pack up," he said brightly.

"Of course it won't," Margaret harrumphed. "We've had that much practice I could do it with my eyes closed. I sometimes think we should just leave everything in our carpet bags to save the effort of unpacking. It's never long before we have to move again." She scraped a thin layer of butter on the stale bread and passed some to Primrose. There was no jam, but Nancy's tummy rumbled loudly, making Luke snort with laughter.

"Don't be rude, I can't help being hungry," Nancy said, giving him a good-natured prod. "Anyway, you should have woken me."

Luke tipped his head back and made a loud snoring noise. "I tried, but you were fast asleep and snoring louder than one of the farm pigs...looked like one, too, with your mouth open catching flies."

Nancy pounced on him and gripped his head under her arm. "Take that back, Luke. You're not so charming yourself when you're asleep, snuffling like an African warthog." She didn't really know what a warthog was, having only read it in one of the books at Sunday school, but it sounded fitting for her annoying brother. She was still taller than him and could wrestle him into submission, but it wouldn't be for much longer.

"For goodness sake, do I have to give you two a

clip around the ear?" Margaret's voice rose in exasperation. "Nancy, behave more ladylike, will you? And Luke, stop teasing her. You're both as bad as each other."

Primrose thumped her pudgy hands on the wooden table, scattering breadcrumbs on the floor and babbled with excitement as Ezra came into the room, sweeping his cap off and bowing with a flourish. "Papa." She strained to be lifted out of her chair, and Nancy obliged, jiggling her up and down.

"Your carriage awaits, my dear." He grabbed Margaret around her waist and smacked a kiss on her cheek, which went some way to thaw her bad mood.

"Don't think you can get round me that easily, Ezra," she scolded. "I'm not happy about leaving, and you know it. We can't keep moving on every time things get difficult. It's not fair on the children."

Ezra's expression clouded momentarily, but then he turned to Nancy instead for support. "It won't be so bad; we have each other, and it will be nice to have a new start. I expect you'll make more friends in no time."

"Are you sure about that?" Margaret said, looking unconvinced. "I thought you said this new job working as a navvy on the railways meant that we might have to carry on moving every time they need you to work on a different part of the track."

Ezra frowned but then shook his head and smiled cheerfully again. "Some of the workers are in transitory roles, but I'm sure with my skills from being in the army, I'll soon get a promotion. I know navvying doesn't sound like much of a job, but I'll do my best to keep the money coming in."

Margaret sighed and relented slightly. "I suppose you do your best," she conceded grudgingly. "Nancy and I will have to work faster on the buttons." Her brow furrowed with worry as she continued packing their meagre possession into an old tea chest. "Every time we move, I have to find new customers for the buttons we make, Ezra. It's hard enough making a bit of extra money on the side as it is, let alone having to start from scratch every year." The pans clattered, emphasising her annoyance. "Maybe Luke might be able to do a few jobs as well."

Luke stuffed a piece of bread in his mouth and chewed it hastily, not bothering to sit at the table. He grinned at his ma's words. "Does that mean I won't have to go to school or carry on with boring book learning?"

"Certainly not," Ezra shot back. "Getting an education is the way out of poverty. Just because we're hard up, I'm not going to let you skive off school. Our Nancy is a bright girl, and you're smart too, Luke. Who knows, you might even get a job as a clerk when you're older, and Nancy could be a governess."

"Can we stay longer at the new place we're moving to, Pa?" Nancy bit her lip, trying not to show her disappointment. "The thing is, we only just made friends with the other children in the village school, and I suppose we won't see them again after today. Where exactly are we moving to?" She wondered momentarily whether it might be somewhere local, except then she realised there were no railway tracks nearby.

"Lower Amberley, up yonder past the canal and through the valley." Ezra ignored the way Margaret's lips pinched with disapproval and beamed at them all. "They don't just take anyone on as a navvy, you know. It was lucky I happened to call at The Dancing Bear for a pint of ale and got chatting to that fellow who told me about the job."

"It would have been luckier if you'd carried on working for Farmer Derwent," Margaret muttered under her breath.

"Shall we start loading the cart, Pa?" Luke's eyes were bright with eagerness. "Nancy and I can start bringing things downstairs if that would help."

Nancy grabbed the last slice of bread before her brother took it and trudged back up the stairs. There would be no hot cup of tea or porridge that morning, and she could sense an argument brewing between

Ma and Papa Ezra, which she didn't want to be part of.

"Cheer up, Nancy," Luke said once they were back in their bedroom. "Pa told me he has high hopes for this job working out."

He said that last time. She bit the words back and perched on the edge of her narrow bed, trying hard not to feel upset as she looked through the window and watched Roland Derwent ambling across the fields to fetch his cows in for milking. She had enjoyed living at Eaton Cottage and had even allowed herself to start to believe they would stay put.

"Don't you get fed up, always having to start anew?" Nancy had protected Luke from the spiteful comments about their family when they first started at the village school the previous year, but she wasn't looking forward to having to do it all over again. She had never even heard of Lower Amberley and wondered what it would be like.

"It ain't so bad," Luke said cheerfully, starting to roll up the blankets on his bed. "I'm hoping I might be able to work with Pa building the railway tracks. School is boring, and Ma will be happier if I'm bringing in a few extra coins every month." He stuck his chest out, trying to look older than his years, and Nancy chuckled.

"There's no chance of that, Luke. You heard what

Pa just said. He always tells us he had a decent education when he was growing up, and it was only his bad experience in the army that stopped him from working in an office since then."

Luke glared at her stubbornly. "I don't want to be stuck behind a desk poring over ledgers."

"It's a while away yet." Nancy shrugged and dragged the two battered banded trunks out from under her bed, sliding one towards Luke so they could pack faster. She wasn't sure why they needed to leave so quickly, but it wasn't her place to ask.

As they folded their bedding, the sound of raised voices from downstairs was impossible to ignore.

"I know you said this time would be different, Ezra, but every time we move, life seems to get harder. It's never a step up, no matter how hard you try to persuade us that it is." Margaret's tone was still irritated. "We had that lovely cottage when you worked at the piano factory. But that barely lasted a year until we had to move here. Surely you should be starting to feel better with each year that passes since you left the army, not worse?"

"It's not that simple." Ezra's tone was so apologetic that Nancy felt sorry for him.

Her thoughts drifted back over what she could remember of Ezra since he'd married her ma and become her stepfather. He was a kindhearted pa, but she had seen with her own eyes how the black mood crept over him when they least expected it, laying him low for weeks. The last time the doctor visited with a tonic to revive Ezra, Nancy had pressed her ear to the door, listening to the murmured conversation between the doctor and her ma to try and glean more information about what was happening.

"It's not a condition that we really know much about, Mrs Burton. I've only seen two other cases of it, and both times, it was in soldiers who served under the Commander-In-Chief General Sir Hugh Gough or in the 24th Foot." There was a pause as he rummaged in his leather bag for the medicine. "They were fighting in the Punjab for the British East India Company and suffered with their nerves afterwards because of experiencing such heavy losses during battle."

"An attack of the vapours, you mean?" Margaret sounded surprised. "Like highly-strung ladies have?"

"Similar, but in many cases far worse," the doctor had said sympathetically. "More like nervous exhaustion. It seems to linger in the mind and show up when something reminds them of the past."

Nancy had thought it sounded rather fanciful that Pa would be affected by something so many years later, but there was no other explanation that made sense. Most of the time, he was cheerful and hard-working, but when the black moods descended, Ezra became a shell of a man, his hands trembling and his eyes haunted by things he could never explain to them because he said they were too awful for anyone to behold.

"I'm sorry, Margaret, I really am." His heartfelt apology snapped her back to the present, and Nancy really did hope that this might be the last time they would need to move. "I can't promise I'll never be unwell again, but I'll always do my best for you and the children. Just give me a chance, that's all I'm asking."

Much to Nancy's relief, after a brief pause, she heard her ma agree, and a few minutes later, she even heard laughter drift up the stairs as they started packing up the kitchen together and were entertained by Primrose's antics.

Nancy folded their clothes and stuffed them into the trunk, pressing them down hard so that they could squeeze everything in. "You're right, Luke," she grinned. "As long as we stick together, things aren't so bad. Maybe Ma will find some wealthier customers for our buttons, and things will take a turn for the better."

Luke nodded sagely. "Pa said Lower Amberley is near the canals and that more well-to-do folk live over that way. We'll make a success of it, I'm sure."

They snapped the lid of the trunk closed and dragged it out of the bedroom to the top of the stairs. Nancy could only hope that Luke was right. She felt a flutter of anticipation and excitement in her chest at the thought of the day ahead. If nothing more, it would be a new adventure.

Who knows where this move might take us? She was usually optimistic by nature and decided the only way to tackle their change of circumstances was to make it fun. "Race you to the bottom of the stairs," she said, nudging Luke behind her and clattering down ahead, chuckling at his look of outrage at coming second.

CHAPTER 3

"I think that's almost everything," Ezra said. He unwound a rope and twisted the end to loop it to a hook under the cart before throwing it over their belongings to secure them for the journey ahead.

They had received some curious stares from the neighbours as they loaded up all their worldly possessions, but now the cobbled lane was deserted. The men had headed off to work, and the women were busy with their household chores.

Nancy slipped upstairs again to check that nothing had been left behind in the two bedrooms. Her boots echoed loudly on the floorboards now that the rag rugs had been taken out, and the house already had a forlorn, empty feel about it. She couldn't help but wonder who would live there next.

Would they stand at the window and watch the farmer gathering in his cows every morning like she had? Would the next family spend many happy years together living in Eaton Cottage, making a success of things where they had failed?

She leaned out of the window and waved to the widow, who lived on the other side of the lane. "Goodbye, Mrs Godfrey." The old woman paused from pegging out her washing and fluttered her handkerchief.

Will anyone even remember us in a few months? The thought began to make Nancy feel sad, so she pushed it aside and tightened her shawl. She was determined to make the best of their change of circumstances to keep Ma happy. After another lap of the two bedrooms, she ran out to the cart. "I checked upstairs, and there's nothing left behind."

"It's just this banded trunk to go on the back now, and that's it," Luke said. He was standing behind the cart, with his thumbs tucked into his waistcoat, looking more excited than anxious.

Margaret paced up and down by the front gate, jiggling Primrose every so often. "What about the downstairs rooms? Will you just have another look around them for us, Nancy?" Primrose was starting to fidget impatiently in her arms, and Margaret looked flustered. "I would do it myself, but you'll be quicker than me. Mind you check in all the nooks and crannies; we can't afford to leave anything behind."

Nancy rushed back in again, knowing that Ezra was eager to get going. It was already an hour later than they had intended to leave. She crawled on her hands and knees and looked under the old dresser, which belonged to the landlord, pulling out an old bobbin of cotton, which had rolled underneath, and putting it in her apron pocket. It barely took her two minutes to check all the rooms again, but then she noticed that the pantry door was ajar. At first glance, she could see it was empty, but she wasn't tall enough to see the top shelf. That was where Ma liked to hide food that she wanted to last, hidden from Luke, who had a habit of helping himself when he was particularly hungry.

The chairs had all been packed, but there was a rickety old wooden orange crate which Ezra had chosen to leave behind. She fetched it from the kitchen and upended it, steadying herself as she climbed onto it. "This had better be worth my while," she muttered.

She balanced on her tiptoes and smiled as she spied something in the dusty corner of the top shelf which had escaped Margaret's eagle-eyed gaze. It was a glass jar full of plums in syrup that Gertrude had given them for Christmas. Her stomach rumbled as she thought about the delicious combination of the tart fruit and oozing sweet syrup. It would be perfect to go on top of their morning porridge, and she knew her ma would be pleased she'd found it.

"Hurry up, Nancy!" Ezra yelled. "We haven't got time to wait any longer. I want to get there before nightfall."

Nancy wobbled slightly and lifted herself on her tiptoes again, poking her tongue out with concentration. "I...just need to...get this," she grunted under her breath. Stretching every sinew, she was just about able to hook her fingertips around the side of the jar, and she slowly pulled it towards her, already imagining everyone thanking her with delight. The plums were like ruby jewels, and her stomach rumbled again. *Nearly there.* She nudged the jar towards the edge of the shelf and grasped it firmly with both hands. Suddenly, a mouse scuttled out from the shadows and ran down her arm. "Get off!" Nancy shrieked. The crate wobbled, and the jar tilted perilously above her head. She felt the mouse skitter down her leg and across her ankles and kicked it away, making the crate rock alarmingly. "Help!" It was too late to regain her balance, and she shrieked again as the heavy jar tilted. The cork lid popped out, and the thick fruit and syrup concoction poured over her head and down her dress, closely followed by a crashing sound as she fell off the crate completely, and the jar smashed on the flagstones, shattering around her.

"Nancy? What's going on in there?" Ezra sounded alarmed.

"I…just dropped something."

Nancy's heart sank as she wiped the fruit out of her eyes and saw her ma striding across the kitchen with a face like thunder. She scrambled to her feet and hastily tried to scrub the thick, syrupy mixture from her hair with her shawl, but all it did was make it worse. Her hair hung like dripping, rats' tails around her face, and her gown was sodden with splatters of fruit.

"Trust you to get yourself into trouble right when we should be leaving." Margaret stood over her with her hands on her hips and shook her head in annoyance. "We haven't got time to sort this mess out now." She gripped her shoulder and marched her back outside. "Look what she's done, Ezra. I take my eyes off the children for one minute, and this happens. What are we going to do now?"

"Blimey, our Nancy," Luke chuckled, "you smell like a fruit crumble, and you look like you've been dragged through a hedge backwards. I ain't going to sit next to you on the cart all the way to Lower Amberley."

The corners of Ezra's mouth twitched slightly as he tried to stop himself from laughing. "Don't fret,

Margaret," he said jovially. "We can stop by the pump in the middle of the village and wash it all off."

Margaret shook her head dismissively. "It will take more than cold water to get this syrup out of her hair. It's all stuck together." She looked Nancy up and down, and two red spots of anger appeared on her cheeks. "And don't think I didn't notice that you ripped your dress this morning, either. You look like something the cat dragged in."

"I was only trying to get the plums down off the shelf," Nancy mumbled. Her ma's anger felt unjustified, and she surreptitiously licked some of the mixture off her hand, enjoying the sweetness of it. "It would've gone lovely on our porridge when we have breakfast. I wasn't expecting a mouse to jump out and frighten me. It made me lose my balance."

"Honestly…if it's not one thing, it's another." Margaret sighed with exasperation and reached into her carpet bag on the back of the cart. "There's only one thing for it." She whipped out her scissors and hurried back to Nancy. "Turn around and stand still. It won't take a moment."

Before Nancy could utter a word, Margaret lifted a handful of her matted hair and snipped it off in one decisive movement. She watched in horror as her curls landed on the floor. "Don't do that, Ma," she pleaded. "Stop. Let me wash it instead. I'm sorry I made us late."

A stubborn glint came into Margaret's eyes, and she pursed her lips. "That'll teach you not to be so careless."

Nancy blinked back her tears, noticing that even Luke looked slightly aghast at their ma's drastic actions.

"It will soon grow back, Nancy," Ezra said, trying to look on the bright side.

With a few more snips, the worst of the sticky syrup had been dealt with, and she shivered as she raised her hand and ran it over the short tufts of hair that remained. Her neck felt exposed in the cold wind, and she wished she'd never attempted to get the jar down.

"What are we going to do about this dress?" Margaret said, speaking to herself and not expecting an answer. She rummaged in the back of the cart again and pulled out one of her old grey cotton gowns, but when she held it up in front of Nancy, it puddled on the floor, clearly far too long.

"I haven't got a spare dress," Nancy said in a small voice. She blushed as a couple of women gossiped at the end of the lane, leaning over the fence and enjoying the spectacle.

"What are you lot gawking at?" Margaret snapped, waving them away. "The sooner we get out of here, the better," she muttered.

"Do you have something smaller she could change

into? How about one of your nightgowns?" Ezra started to open another trunk.

"Don't be daft. Do you want us to look like a travelling circus?" Margaret rolled her eyes and turned back to look at Nancy. The plums had stained her dress in garish purple splatters, and the syrup had soaked into the thin cotton. "I was hoping this dress would have lasted a couple more months until we could afford something better for you."

Ezra flushed guiltily. "I'll buy you a new one as soon as I've saved up a few coins from the new job." He shot Nancy a smile. "I know you were only trying to be helpful today, and it was just an accident."

"You'll just have to wear some of Luke's clothes for now," Margaret said briskly. "I put some by for him to grow into, which should fit you. And you can wear one of his caps to hide your hair until I can do a better job to make it tidier."

"What, dress her like a boy?" Luke spluttered with laughter, and Primrose joined in, clapping her hands together.

"You can't do that," Nancy cried. "What if someone sees us?" Her voice cracked at the humiliation of it all.

"What of it? It's better than being filthy and wet." Once Margaret had an idea in her head, there was no stopping her, and she dug through the clothes in one of the trunks, finally smiling with satisfaction as she held up a pair of trousers, a flannel shirt, and an old jacket with patches on the elbows. "We're not going to make a new start in Lower Amberley with you covered in plums and syrup, my girl, or we'll be a laughing stock before we've even spent one day in the village. Put your brother's clothes on, and try not to do anything else to draw attention to yourself. Ezra's right; your hair will soon grow back, and we'll make sure you have a nice gown in a few days, even if it is secondhand."

Nancy knew there was no point in arguing and went back into the kitchen again for one last time to get changed.

Half an hour later, they were on their way. The pony trotted along at a smart pace, and the cart rumbled over the cobbles. The sun was warm, and Ezra whistled jauntily, full of hope for their new start. As they rolled past the village school, some of the children rushed to the fence, pointing and giggling. Nancy clenched her hands in her lap, and her cheeks burned with indignation, but she kept her eyes fixed firmly ahead and didn't wave goodbye. She might look strange, but she wasn't going to give anyone the satisfaction of seeing how upset she felt, that was for sure.

CHAPTER 4

"Tell us more about the work you'll be doing on the railways, Pa?" Luke fidgeted between Ezra and Nancy. They had been in the cart for four hours already, and Nancy hoped they would stop soon for something to eat and to give Luke a chance to run around.

"Can't you sit still," she said, jabbing him in the ribs with her elbow. "You wriggle around more than a ferret in a sack. Maybe you should just get down and run along beside the cart for a while." Nancy grinned at her brother to show that her comment was meant in jest.

"We should get to Thruppley soon," Ezra said, meeting Nancy's gaze over Luke's head. He chuckled. "With this much energy, I'm sure they'll be pleased to find some jobs Luke can do with the navvies."

"What exactly will you be doing?" Margaret asked. "You were rather vague when you sprang it on me." Primrose was perched on her lap, playing with the fringe on her shawl, and they both turned to look at Ezra.

He cleared his throat. "Well, I'm not exactly sure, but the fellow I spoke to at The Dancing Bear seemed to think I would be best suited to manage one of the gangs. He mentioned I might be keeping note of the hours the navvies work and tallying supplies, that sort of thing."

Margaret's face brightened. "So you won't be labouring on the tracks and getting all grubby?" She pointed out a speckled thrush pecking at a snail for Primrose to look at. "I'm glad they recognise that you're worth more than working your fingers to the bone on construction. Perhaps that means we'll have a nice cottage to go with the job after all."

Ezra nodded, but Nancy noticed that he wouldn't quite meet her ma's eye and quickly looked away. "We'll stop at the bakery in Thruppley and buy a pie to share," Ezra said, changing the subject. He patted his pocket, where a few coins jingled.

"We're never going to get there at this rate," Margaret sighed a few minutes later. A dozen woolly sheep were blocking the lane, bleating balefully. Every time their pony walked a few steps closer, the sheep circled in a tight bunch and eyed them with confusion as though they had completely lost all sense of direction. "Daft beggars," Margaret muttered. "Hop down and open the gate, children. They must belong to the flock in that field over yonder. We'll be sitting here until sunset waiting for the farmer to arrive, otherwise. Anyone would think we had all the time in the world."

At first, Nancy felt self-conscious, chasing the sheep back into their field, wearing Luke's trousers. It felt strange not to have her legs hidden by her dress, but by the time she climbed back onto the seat at the front of the cart, she was more used to it. "Everything is so much easier wearing your clothes," she remarked.

Luke knocked her cap off her head and ruffled her short hair. "Don't go getting any ideas, Nancy. It ain't very ladylike, and I don't want our new friends to think you're the boy in the family. You're my big sister, and don't you forget it."

"Give it here," Nancy grumbled, putting the cap back on again. She felt like a shorn sheep without her long curls. "I'm just saying it's easier clambering in and out of the cart, that's all."

"Stop squabbling," Margaret scolded, clipping them both on the back of their heads. "We'll all be hard at work again soon enough, so you should sit politely and admire the view while we've got the chance."

As they wound their way through the West Country lanes, Nancy's spirits started to rise. Yellow primroses and cowslips dotted the grassy verges, and some of the blackthorn trees were just coming into blossom in a froth of white. It was always a relief to put winter behind them, and she felt a sudden surge of optimism. The first honey-coloured stone cottages of Thruppley came into view, and her mouth watered as she thought about tucking into a pie with buttery pastry and a tasty meat filling. Perhaps there would even be enough money for them to buy a wedge of sticky lardy cake dotted with dried fruit for afterwards.

"Look at that big house over there," Luke cried. He pointed towards an elegant Edwardian manor house in the distance. The drive was flanked with mature trees that would soon burst into leaf, and a russet-coloured herd of Hereford cattle grazed in the pastures beyond it. "It looks so grand. The owners must be proper toffs."

"I wonder who lives there?" Nancy allowed herself to drift off into a daydream...one where she was sitting in a gleaming carriage pulled by four matching bay horses. She imagined them trotting past the ornamental fountain and stopping at the bottom of the wide steps, where a footman was already waiting to help her down. *Welcome to the midsummer ball, Miss Burton,* a handsome gentleman in a smart tail-coat would say, brushing his lips to the back of her gloved hand, eager to introduce her to the other guests...

A sharp nudge from Ezra tugged her back to the present. "I happen to know who lives there," he said, giving them a wink.

Margaret's eyebrows shot up in surprise. "How would you know folks who live somewhere that grand?"

Ezra smiled and shook his head. "I don't know them personally. I just said I know who lives there. One of the men who used to drink at the Dancing Bear, Roger Postlethwaite, used to work in the stables. It's Chavenhope House, owned by Horace Smallwood." He looked expectantly at Margaret as though she would know what that name meant. "You must have heard of old man Smallwood? Horace Smallwood's pa. He's a self-made man who made his fortune setting up and improving some of the businesses around these parts. There a mill in Nailsbridge, I believe, and a brewery."

A thoughtful look came over Margaret's face. "If Lower Amberley isn't too far away, perhaps your friend Roger could arrange some introductions. I need to get new customers for my buttons."

Nancy eyed their threadbare clothes and privately thought that the Smallwoods would surely only deal with some of the finest dressmakers in the county.

"Perhaps," Ezra said eagerly. "Roger told me that Horace Smallwood's wife, Lillian, takes great satisfaction in doing good work for the needy." He pointed towards another grand building with manicured gardens, which ran all the way down the river on one side and the canal on the other. "That building over there is the Rodborough Hotel. Horace Smallwood owns that as well, and he's doing very well for himself by all accounts. The well-to-do folk from London come and stay to take the country air."

Nancy saw a hint of newfound respect in Margaret's eyes as Ezra regaled them with more tidbits of information about the grand businesses and wealthy families in Thruppley. *How does he know so much about these people?* Nancy could only assume it was from acquaintances he drank with at the village inn. It gave her more confidence that perhaps he really was hoping to pull them out of their dire situation by bringing them to live in this part of the county. She brushed her hands over her trousers and wondered what sort of new gown she might be allowed once they reached Lower Amberley. If she and her ma were going to be hobnobbing with wealthy folk, she would need something that fitted properly and wasn't patched to within an inch of its life.

"Imagine if we lived in a cottage in their grounds, Ma," she said wistfully. "All the grand ladies would travel from far and wide once they heard about your buttons. We might even have ladies from Paris coming to order buttons from us, especially for dress fittings to go to the opera."

Luke burst out laughing and rolled his eyes. "Chance would be a fine thing."

Nancy felt deflated as her ma's lips pursed disapprovingly. "For goodness' sake, Nancy, it's time you stopped all this ridiculous daydreaming. You know as well as I do that life isn't like that. I only meant that we might get an introduction to some of the ladies in Thruppley village, who are a little more well-to-do than us, not a grand family like the Smallwoods."

"Leave her be, Margaret," Ezra said as he saw how Nancy's face had fallen. "There's nothing wrong with daydreaming and hoping for a better future."

Margaret looked away. "You're a fine one to talk," she muttered. "Life's just one disappointment after another, and Nancy would do well to remember that. Otherwise, she'll only have her hopes dashed."

Ezra sighed, and Nancy felt sorry for him again. Her ma had a sharp tongue and rarely praised him.

"What sort of good works does Lillian Smallwood do, Pa?" Luke yawned, bored of the journey now.

"Last I heard, she was going to start fundraising to set up a new orphanage in Thruppley."

Nancy felt the blood rush to her cheeks, and a prickle of awkwardness shiver down her back as always happened whenever orphans were mentioned.

"Like the sort of place that Nancy came from, you mean?" Luke's remark held no malice, and he stated it matter-of-factly. He didn't seem to be aware that Nancy didn't like it being talked about, although her family had never made any secret of the fact that she was adopted.

"Oh no, I expect it will be a bit grander than where Bill got you from, Nancy," Ezra said. "If the Smallwood family are involved, 'tis bound to be the sort of place folk will admire."

Of course it will be. Nancy couldn't help but feel hurt, although she knew that wasn't Ezra's intention. *They just don't understand what it's like.*

"Tell us again where Nancy came from, Ma," Luke asked, pressing for more details.

Margaret coughed and fussed with Primrose's dress for a moment, but Luke was still looking at her expectantly. "I've told you before," she said bluntly, "my first husband, Bill, found Nancy abandoned on the steps of a house where the woman used to take in foundlings. She was a bit eccentric but meant well."

Luke lifted his cap and scratched his head. "It all sounds very mysterious and exciting."

"We thought we weren't going to be blessed with children of our own." Margaret glanced down at Primrose on her lap, and her expression softened, which didn't go unnoticed by Nancy. "After I was widowed and then I married again, I could hardly believe my luck when I had two more children. If I'd have known..." She bit back whatever she'd been about to say and bounced Primrose on her knee.

Does she wish she hadn't adopted me? Nancy pushed the horrible thought away. *Surely not?* Ezra gave her a kind smile, and she realised she was imagining things. Her ma loved her just as much as Luke and Primrose.

Luke fidgeted again. "That must explain why you look so different from us, Nancy, and why you think you're smarter," he added with a wry smile. Nancy caught a glance between her ma and pa as if there was more to it. She noticed they did it whenever the subject came up, but she couldn't explain what it meant.

"I'm not different," she said hotly, glaring at Luke.

"Well, someone at school said that if you're an orphan, it's like being a cuckoo in the nest," Luke continued, blithely unaware that his words were hurtful. "It doesn't matter, though. We still think you're one of us, our Nancy."

"Of course we do," Ezra said, patting her hand. "Margaret always told me that finding you was one of the happiest days of her life, and I know you don't remember your pa, Bill, but I'm sure it was a special day for him as well."

Nancy lifted her chin and wished that, just for once, her ma would agree wholeheartedly so she didn't feel like the outsider of the family, but the silence stretched between them.

Ezra looked at Margaret and raised his eyebrows. "Maybe it's time to tell—"

"Tell me what?" Nancy demanded. Her ma frowned at Ezra.

"Nothing. Well...I don't know about you, but I think we should pull up for a rest," Margaret said briskly. "Of course, Bill and I were lucky to adopt Nancy, but we don't need to keep harking back to the past like this, not when we've got so much to think about today."

"Can we stop down there by the canal, Pa?" Luke asked. "I've never seen a narrowboat up close before." He leaned forward. "Look at all them posh folk getting out. Proper la-de-dah, they are in their fancy duds."

"That's a good idea." Ezra pulled the reins lightly and steered the pony and cart down the lane that ran alongside the canal. "We can hitch up here for a little while and stretch our legs before heading into the village to find the bakery."

Nancy perked up as she looked at the scene in front of them. The long, narrowboat had been deco-rated in traditional folk art, and a sturdy draft horse waited patiently on the towpath as a group of well-dressed gentlemen and ladies disembarked. There was a field nearby, awash with nodding, golden daffodils, and a young lad was holding the gate open so they could go and stroll among the flowers.

"Isn't it charming," Nancy said breathlessly. She had never seen so many grand people up close. The ladies wore ruffled silk gowns and fur-trimmed coats, and several were holding silk and lace parasols over their heads for fear of the spring sunshine marring their creamy complexions. The gentlemen were dressed in finely tailored suits and chivalrously offered their arms for the ladies to hold as they wandered side-by-side. It was quite the most delightful thing Nancy had ever seen.

"I thought narrowboats were only used to haul goods from village to village," Margaret said as they all climbed down from their cart. Even her interest was piqued by the unusual sight.

A broad-shouldered man, wearing a jaunty spotted neckerchief, jumped off the front of the narrowboat and patted the horse before strolling to the aft, where he coiled a thick rope and buffed the brass bell with a rag. He caught sight of them watching. "Good morning," he called, giving them a warm smile and tipping his cap. "Don't be shy. You can come and have a closer look if you like."

Nancy and Luke needed no second invitation, and they ran along the towpath. "It's so smart and colourful," Luke said. He looked longingly at the velvet-covered seats inside the narrowboat, but Nancy tugged him back.

"We can't afford a go on that," she whispered. "It's not like a ride at the travelling fair, Luke. We'm too dirty. Just looking is good enough."

The man shook hands with Ezra and Margaret. "Looks like you're on the move," he said, jerking his head in the direction of their laden cart. "Are you settling in Thruppley? My name is Joe Granger, by the way."

"No, we're just passing through, heading for Lower Amberley." Ezra gave the narrowboat an admiring glance.

"That's not far...'tis just yonder a bit further up the valley." Joe followed Ezra's gaze. "You like the narrowboat? She's called *The River Maid.*" There was pride in his voice. "My wife's family used to use her for carting grain down to Nailsbridge Mill and Frampton Basin, but that was before the steam trains started to take over. I run her for leisure cruises now, taking the well-to-do folks from the hotel for a little jaunt out."

"It looks popular." Ezra doffed his hat to a genteel lady who stared at them.

"It is. I never thought it would work, but I was happy to be proved wrong. We were lucky to be offered the job by Mr Smallwood." He waved towards the boy holding the gate open, telling him to stay there. "That's my son, Albert. He loves nothing more than helping me out, although Dolly, my wife, will probably say he should been in school." He cocked his head and looked at Nancy. "He's about the same age as your son," he said, smiling at Margaret.

"I'm not a b—" Nancy's words were cut off by a sharp jab from Margaret.

"Yes…well, we'd better get going, Mr Granger. It was nice to meet you, but we still have a fair distance to travel, and the children are hungry." Margaret chivvied Luke back along the tow and gave Nancy a pointed look.

Nancy suddenly felt resentful about the way her ma had dressed her. It was all very well saying there hadn't been time to wash the plum syrup out of her hair but being mistaken for a boy with her short hair under Luke's unsightly cap was humiliating. She lingered by the horse and picked a handful of grass, smiling as his whiskery muzzle tickled her palm. She wished they could live here. There was something about Mr Granger's open expression and generous smile that felt welcoming, like the sort of place they could make new friends easily. She watched the light breeze rippling the water and the birds chirping in the nearby willow trees. Everything was so charming.

"If you're ever passing through again, come and say hello." Joe gave Nancy a curious look that lasted slightly longer than was polite. "What's your name, lad?" he asked. "You're about the same age as my Albert. Perhaps you could be friends." He seemed puzzled and stared at her more closely. Nancy saw a look of alarm flash across her ma's face as she hurried back to her side.

"I'm called N—"

"Ned." Margaret's voice was loud and firm. "He's called Ned, and we have to go." She gripped Nancy's arm and bundled her back towards the cart.

"Sorry, I didn't mean to be rude," Joe Granger called after them. "Your son, Ned, looks remarkably similar to someone I know…a distant relation of my wife's called Maisie."

Margaret nodded politely and shoved Nancy onto the cart seat, where Ezra and Luke were already sitting. "Good day to you, Mr Granger," she said curtly, not replying to his previous comment. "I doubt we'll be back in Thruppley, so I'm afraid Ned and your son won't be able to make friends." She gave Ezra a sharp look, and he hastily picked up the reins and urged the pony to trot on.

As their cart rumbled away, Nancy twisted in her seat to look back at Mr Granger. He had thumbed his cap to the back of his head and was still staring at her with a puzzled expression, as though he hadn't quite believed what her ma had just said.

"Why did you tell that man that Nancy is called

Ned?" Luke looked confused. "He was only being friendly, but you sounded cross."

Margaret sniffed disapprovingly. "You might think he was being friendly, but I would call it nosy. I don't want folk knowing our business, especially when it doesn't concern them." Her lips pressed together into a thin line to indicate that that was the end of the matter.

Ezra grinned at Nancy. "More like your ma doesn't want people to think she dresses her daughter like a boy," he chuckled.

"Is it far to the bakery, Pa? I'm starving." Luke had forgotten the incident already, but Nancy felt a lingering sense of unease.

Maybe it was the talk of her adoption earlier or the fact that Joe Granger had looked at her so curiously as though he already knew her. Whatever it was, she couldn't help but think it was all rather strange. *Is Ma ashamed of me?* She turned in her seat again to try and catch another glimpse of *The River Maid*, but they had rounded the corner, and she could no longer see the canal. *Who is this woman that Mr Granger thinks I look like?* The question swirled troublingly through her mind, and Nancy wished she could find out the answer, but it was too late.

CHAPTER 5

*N*ancy stuffed a rag into the bottom of her boots before pulling them on to block the holes. They still pinched her toes, but thankfully, the spring weather was warmer now, so at least her feet wouldn't get wet. She nudged Luke awake, and he sat up on the thin, lumpy mattress, still tousle-headed from being asleep. He yawned loudly and stretched.

"I hope we've got porridge for breakfast," he mumbled. "I'm so hungry. I've been dreaming about food all night."

Nancy opened the threadbare curtains and peered through the small window of the wooden hut, which was now their home. There was no rolling farmland to see or charming rural view. Instead, there was just a row of identical wooden huts to their own. They all had a ramshackle, temporary air about them, and she thought longingly back to Eaton Cottage, which had been positively luxurious in comparison.

"Hurry up and get dressed, otherwise Ma will only get cross." She lifted Primrose out of the little wooden cot in the corner of the bedroom, and her heart melted as she kicked her legs and fastened her arms around her neck. She was a sunny-natured toddler, thank goodness. It wouldn't have been much fun to listen to a grizzling child in such confined quarters.

"Hello, my poppet." Margaret smiled as Primrose toddled ahead of Nancy coming out of the bedroom. "You're late getting up." Her tone was not quite as warm for Nancy.

"Morning, love." The front door creaked open, and Ezra slipped in, shrugging off his jacket. He pulled something from the pocket and handed it to Margaret, looking guilty.

"At last, you got paid." She inspected what he'd just given her, and her smile faded. It looked like coins but different. "This isn't real money. How am I expected to buy food and clothes?"

Ezra's hands shook, and he sat down heavily on the wooden chair next to the small stove. "They're tokens," he said with a defeated air. "Because I haven't been able to work this past week, I think the manager believes it's because I've been drinking. It's company policy. The Gloucester Railway Company issues tokens instead of coins, so they can't be spent on ale."

Nancy was gripped with worry as she saw her ma's expression darken. Their new start at Lower Amberley Railway Camp was not living up to Ezra's promises of a better life. If anything, they were sliding closer to poverty and destitution with each week that passed. And it was true that many of the navvies and railway construction workers were unruly drunkards come nightfall. She'd heard the carousing and swearing only the night before as they stumbled home, and some nights, it was so raucous she wondered how any of them managed to put in a proper day's work the following day.

"And what exactly am I meant to do with these tokens?" Margaret pursed her lips and shoved them in her apron pocket. "You expect me to drag the family to stand in a queue at the meal caravan for a bowl of soup and a crust of bread, is that it? We're barely faring better than the poor wretches who have to rely on charity and soup kitchens down at the docks." She threw up her hands, blinking back tears. "Has it really come to this?"

"It's not Pa's fault he hasn't been feeling well." Nancy couldn't help but leap to Ezra's defence. His gaunt cheeks and dead-looking eyes filled her with pity but also fear for their future. It didn't seem fair that he had been tarred with the same brush as the other drunk men when, in fact, he rarely had more than one pint of ale.

Ezra leaned forward in his chair, with his elbows on his knees and his shoulders hunched around his ears, looking at a spot on the floor instead of his wife's accusatory glare. "I'm sorry I've failed you again, Margaret. I told Cecil Fernsby that working as part of the gang of navvies in the tunnels wouldn't be good for me, but he wouldn't listen."

"I've got a good mind to tell Cecil Fernsby what he can do with his bloomin' tokens," she harrumphed. "We've only been here a month, and he's already taken a dislike to you." Margaret paced back and forth, working herself up into a fury. "What about the position as a clerk that the fellow at the pub promised you? Or was that just another case of wishful thinking?"

Ezra dragged a hand through his fair hair and folded his arms defensively. "It was never a definite promise, and perhaps I was too quick to trust him. I wasn't to know that they would use explosives in the tunnel, Margaret. You know how unexpected noises like that play on my nerves...bring the bad dreams back again and make it hard for me to do anything."

"Yes, I know only too well." She sniffed with annoyance.

Nancy crept across the kitchen, wanting to get on with the morning chores but mindful not to do anything else to annoy her ma. She lifted the kettle to check it was full and put it on top of the small pot-bellied stove in the corner of the room that served as their kitchen, parlour and dining room. She and Luke had stocked up with sticks the day before, so she put a few more in the stove and riddled it with the poker to get it going. Before long, the kettle was whistling merrily, and she made a pot of tea, then turned her attention to something to eat. There was half a loaf of bread, which wasn't yet blue with mould, so she grabbed the frying pan and put a dollop of beef dripping in. Bread and dripping with a mug of tea would keep them going until lunchtime.

Her stomach rumbled as the grease started to sizzle, spitting fat and filling the room with the smell of cooking.

"Lawks, Nancy, can't you remember to open the window when you're cooking?" Margaret suddenly blanched and stumbled outside. The sound of retching from behind the back of the hut was impossible to ignore, and when she returned a couple of minutes later, looking whey-faced, Ezra stood up and rushed to her side.

"Is this what I think it is?" His expression was a mixture of tenderness and surprise. "That's the third morning this week you've been sick."

Margaret nodded miserably and pressed a handkerchief to her nose so she wouldn't smell the frying fat. "I kept telling myself it couldn't be true..." She gagged slightly and fanned herself. "Yes, I suppose you may as well know because it will be obvious soon enough...I think I'm in the family way again."

"Another baby!" Ezra grinned proudly, but Nancy could see her ma didn't share the sentiment.

"Yes, another baby." She closed her eyes for a moment and shook her head in disbelief. "How on earth will we manage, Ezra? Four hungry children to feed, and you not able to work. We can't risk losing the roof over our heads, even if it is just this cramped wooden hut."

"If I could only get my hands on some tonic like I used to take, I'd probably be alright again."

"We don't have enough money to buy laudanum," Margaret stated matter-of-factly. "I haven't had a chance to drum up any new customers for our buttons, and you know how ill I was when I was expecting Primrose."

Nancy cut several slices of stale bread and laid them in the frying pan, darting a look at Luke as he emerged from the bedroom to warn him that Ma was in no mood for any nonsense.

"I'll just have to try and plead with the company to give me some different sort of work," Ezra said. A violent tremor gripped him, and he sank back onto the wooden chair. "I can't work with the explosives in the tunnel again, Margaret. It will be the end of me. I'll just have to hope that Mr Fernsby shows me some mercy."

"There's not much chance of that," Margaret said bitterly. "He strikes me as the sort of man who delights in being spiteful for the sake of it."

"Have a heart. Can't you say something nice for once?"

"Shall Luke and I go and fetch water from the pump?" Nancy could tell that another argument was brewing, and it would be best for them to be out of the way.

Her ma waved them away absentmindedly and trudged across to the wooden drawers where the cutlery was kept to start laying the table for their meagre breakfast. "You may as well. Mind you don't get into any trouble with the other families."

Nancy picked up one of the buckets and handed the other to Luke.

"Lord knows how I'll be able to hold my head up when we're waiting in line for lunch to be doled out." Margaret sighed loudly and Ezra sank lower in his chair. "We'll need a bleedin' miracle to get out of this mess...but when was the last time one of those happened? Never, Ezra...that's when."

"WHAT DO you think will happen if Pa doesn't get offered a different job?" Luke trotted to keep up with Nancy's long strides as they hurried across the camp.

"I don't want to think about it." The truth was, she was dreading being told that they might have to move again already. Although they hadn't really made any new friends yet, it was the fact that it felt so unsettling. She thought longingly of the canal and Thruppley village again, recalling how everything was awash with golden sunlight and how everyone seemed happy.

Nancy had already discovered that the locals regarded the navvy community with suspicion, likening them to gypsy travellers because they were transitory. It felt unfair. It wasn't their fault that the camp was like a shanty town with poor sanitation. The only nice building was the stone cottage Mr Fernsby and his family lived in as a perk of being the manager. It was set well away from the wooden huts, though, she noted.

"I don't like it here." Luke looked glum, which was unusual enough to make Nancy stop in her tracks.

"Why not?"

He kicked a stone and put his bucket down. "It feels as though they're looking down their noses at us. Everyone else has been here longer than us, and I overheard one of the men saying that Ma has too many airs and graces." His mouth turned down, and for a moment, Nancy thought he might be about to cry. "They said that Ma was stuck up because she prefers to stay in our hut making buttons instead of mixing with the other ladies in the camp."

Nancy gave his shoulder a reassuring squeeze. "What do they know," she exclaimed. Just because we want to try and better ourselves, it isn't something to be ashamed of."

It didn't take much to cheer Luke up, and he grinned and grabbed his bucket again. "How come you'm always right, our Nancy? I'll ignore them next time." He already had a smattering of freckles across his snub nose from the spring sunshine, and Nancy realised with a shock that he was nearly as tall as her now. In spite of always being hungry, he was shooting up like a weed.

"Do you think Ma's new baby will be a girl or a boy?"

"It had better blooming well be a boy," Luke chuckled. "Imagine me having to put up with three sisters twittering in my ear all night long about all sorts of nonsense." He ducked out of reach of Nancy's playful prod.

As they rounded the corner and got closer to the water pump that served their end of the camp, a brisk breeze tugged at Nancy's dress. She hadn't bothered to put her bonnet on, and she suddenly felt self-conscious as she spotted Elmer Fernsby making a beeline for them across the grass with two other boys hot on his heels.

"Oh no, that's all we need," she muttered, catching Luke's eye. The camp manager's son was like a chip off the old block and went out of his way to be as spiteful as his father.

"Well, well, if it isn't the newcomers strolling across the camp as though they own the place," he called. "For a moment there, I thought it was a couple of tramps on the scrounge for some clothes."

Elmer was tall and big-boned, with lank ginger hair and a pasty complexion. Even though he was only sixteen years old, he was running to fat and sported a garish chequered waistcoat as though he was a London dandy. In spite of his size, his voice sounded strangely high, which struck an odd counterpoint as he lumbered clumsily towards them.

"Watch your mouth," Luke shot back. He thrust his narrow chest out and lifted his chin, determined not to be bullied.

"'Ooh, watch your mouth'," Elmer echoed, mimicking Luke's remark. Like all bullies, he was nothing without his entourage, and the two scrawny boys standing behind him laughed obligingly when he turned to include them in the conversation. "Did you hear what he said, Jim and Danny? Why should I watch my mouth, you little runt? It ain't as though you hold any sway around here." His small eyes were like two dark currants sunk in dough, and he regarded them sourly. "Do you know who I am?"

"Of course we do," Nancy said, quickly stepping in front of Luke to stop him from saying something that might get them into trouble. "You're Elmer, Mr Fernsby's son."

"Correct. So that makes me a person of influence. My pa runs this place, in case you haven't noticed, so that little squirt shivering behind you should speak to me with more respect."

"Y...y...you lot can't just swan in here like you own the place," Jim stammered with a scowl.

Elmer rubbed his plump hands together as though he was just warming up to his sport of taunting them. He smirked as he looked at Nancy's short hair. "You're not much to look at, are you? Everyone's saying you have nits really badly to have your hair all chopped off like that."

Nancy bristled, and all her thoughts of keeping the peace vanished. "Of course I haven't got nits, you ignorant boy. A jar of syrup spilt on my hair, and Ma cut it off. Not that it's any of your business."

"Nits... fleas...bedbugs. I bet you've got them all. But if that's the story you're telling everyone, you must be a clumsy oaf as well." Elmer sniggered as Jim and Danny started hopping from foot to foot and scratching their heads as though they were being eaten alive. "Don't get too close to her, lads. Who knows what you might catch."

"And they stink like old tater peelings on a hot day." Danny screwed up his nose as though there was a foul stench in the air.

"You're a fine one to talk, you smelly urchin." Luke sprang out from behind Nancy with his fists clenched, much to her alarm. "You can't speak about my sister like that. You'd better watch yourself, or I'll tell my pa."

The two boys hooted with laughter, but Nancy noticed that, although they were behaving like a pair of buffoons, it was Elmer who had a glint of genuine cruelty in his eyes. His aim was not to be amusing but to belittle and pour scorn and derision on the people he picked on.

"Hush, Luke," Nancy said quietly. She laid a restraining hand on his arm. Her brother was whip-thin compared to Elmer and wouldn't last a minute if they squared up to each other.

"Yes, run along, little boy."

She chuckled, trying to diffuse the situation. "You're quite right, Elmer; these are my oldest clothes." She pointed out a couple of the purple splotches on the soft cotton. "It was plums in syrup that fell on me, and we haven't managed to get into the village yet for Pa to buy me a new dress." She couldn't resist a small dig. "Perhaps, if your father paid a bit more generously for all the hard work the navvies do, I could have had something better to wear by now," she added smoothly.

An angry flush stained Elmer's cheeks, clashing with his ginger hair. "Are you being rude about my pa?" He stepped closer to Nancy, and his voice was laced with venom. He smirked again and glanced back towards his two sidekicks to make sure they were listening. "If we're talking about fathers, perhaps we should discuss yours? Everyone here knows that Ezra Burton is nothing but an idle layabout."

"Lazy old Ezra Burton, with his shaky hands... jerking like a puppet on a string," Danny said in a sing-song voice.

Elmer spluttered with laughter, but it held no humour. "Who does this remind you of, Jim and Danny?" He pressed his hands to his cheeks in a cruel parody of someone upset. "'Ooh, Mr Fernsby, I'm scared of the explosions in the nasty dark train tunnel. The loud bang frightened me, so I can't work.'" He grinned, and the two boys doubled over, laughing so hard that there were tears in their eyes.

Without thinking, Nancy lowered her head and charged with an angry roar. Her shoulder smashed into Elmer's plump belly, and she heard a whoosh as all the breath was driven from his lungs. She'd had the element of surprise, and he toppled over like a tree being felled in a storm, and Nancy sprang on top of him as they wrestled in the dirt.

"Take…that…back," she grunted, raining blows on him.

"Help!" he squawked.

"You don't know anything about my pa." All the injustice of how Ezra suffered with his nerves filled her head like a swarm of angry wasps buzzing so loudly that she couldn't think straight. "He can't help being unwell…you should be more sympathetic instead of spreading rotten lies and rumours about us when we've only just arrived."

"Don't just stand there, lads," Elmer shrieked, "get her off me!" He tried to thump Nancy back, but she was too quick and rolled away out of his reach.

Before the two boys had a chance to rush to Elmer's aid, Nancy heard the sound of running footsteps. A hand clamped on her shoulder and dragged her upright. "What are you doing?" Margaret hissed in her face. "Don't you know that's Mr Fernsby's son? Are you determined to completely ruin Ezra's chances of getting a different job in the camp?"

"He was saying horrible things about Pa," Nancy said hoarsely. Her mouth was full of dust, and she noticed a new rip in her dress. "I was trying to defend our family name. He's just a mean bully."

The two boys had hauled Elmer into a standing position, and he nonchalantly brushed the dust off his waistcoat and trousers, giving Margaret a cool look. "Your daughter has the manners of an alley cat, Mrs Burton. I said no such thing, and I'm sure you wouldn't believe such a wicked lie against me, the son of the camp manager."

"That's not true. I'm not lying, Ma—"

Margaret held up her hand to silence Nancy and gave her an icy glare before turning back to face Elmer. "My daughter can be a little hotheaded, so please accept my apologies. I've heard nothing but good things about you and your family. I expect Nancy was just hungry and misheard what you said."

Elmer shot Nancy a triumphant look, and his plump face creased into a self-satisfied smile. "I'm sure I can overlook it this time as long as it doesn't happen again." He jerked his head to Jim and Danny, and they trotted after him as he strolled away.

"Why did you say that, Ma?" Nancy burst out a moment later. "He was nasty about all of us and called Pa a layabout."

Margaret picked up the bucket and thrust it at Nancy. "I've never known such a troublesome child as you, "she said wearily. "If you had an ounce of common sense, you would know that we have to be nice to Cecil Fernsby and that lazy, bullying son of his. Otherwise, we'll be thrown out on our ears with no job and nowhere to live. Now run along and fetch that water before I tell Ezra to give you a good hiding."

Nancy walked away, biting back the emotion that was clogging her throat. In the distance, she could see Elmer and the boys watching her and chuckling among themselves. "Laugh all you like," she muttered to herself. "One day, I'll be more than just a scruffy girl who doesn't even know her real parents." In their troubled new life at the camp, she knew she had made an enemy, but she had to cling to hope. It was all she had.

CHAPTER 6

*T*wo weeks had passed since the incident with Elmer, and with a bit of ingenuity, Nancy had managed to avoid him and his lackeys and was hoping that might be the end of it. It was a warm spring Saturday afternoon, and her spirits lifted at the thought of having a couple of hours free from work. Her ma had managed to find one new customer for the buttons and, in a rare good mood, had promised Luke and her an afternoon off from chores and work.

"What shall we do this afternoon?" Ezra said after waking up from his lunchtime snooze in the armchair. He yawned and stretched and stood up to smack a kiss on Margaret's cheek. "Did I sleep for long? I think it's just what I needed because, at night, my mind is whirling with too many memories from the past to sleep well." He stretched again. "Judging by your gentle, ladylike snoring, being in the family way isn't keeping you awake."

Margaret swatted him playfully with the clean shirt she was folding after fetching the washing from the line strung between their hut and next door's. "I'm glad to hear you feel rested. Hopefully, you'll be well enough to speak to Cecil Fernsby again on Monday morning." Her eyes clouded momentarily at the mention of the hardhearted camp manager. Ezra had pleaded with him several times to be allowed to leave the gang of navvies working in the tunnel, but Cecil had stubbornly refused to entertain the idea. He insisted Ezra's nervous exhaustion was a figment of his imagination and that he would be perfectly fine if he just got on with the work like everyone else. On each occasion, Ezra had sunk into an even deeper black mood, but today was the first time he had started to look a little more like his old self.

"Monday...possibly." Ezra sounded worried again. He didn't want to dampen the mood and picked up Primrose, swinging her around and making her giggle. "Shall we tell your ma what I found in my winter coat yesterday, Primrose?"

Nancy looked up from the mending she was doing. This sounded promising. "What is it, Pa?"

"Yes, Papa...cuddles." Primrose patted Ezra's bushy beard, enjoying the happy moment.

Ezra bounced Primrose up and down as he walked across the room to where his coat was hanging behind the door. He reached into the pocket and pulled out some coins, holding them up with a flourish like a magician. "I must have left these in my pocket the last time I wore this coat, and I forgot all about them."

Margaret's face lit up at the sight of real money again. She had reluctantly got used to the unusual system of being paid in tokens and fetching their meals from the food caravan the railway company provided. In a strange way, it gave her one less thing to worry about, knowing that everyone would have at least one hot meal to fill their bellies each day, even if it wasn't as nice as her own cooking. But they all knew she was still annoyed at Ezra being labelled as a drunk when he wasn't. "How much is it? That's a wonderful discovery to make. It's quite cheered me up."

"I thought it would," Ezra said, smacking another kiss on her cheek. "It's not much, I'm afraid, but enough for us to treat ourselves to something nice to eat. What do you say, children? Shall we have a stroll into Lower Amberley village and buy something from the bakery? There might even be enough to stretch to a twist of mint humbugs from the sweet-shop as well."

Luke jumped up from where he had been

polishing his boots and whooped with excitement. With the money and an afternoon off, there was a celebratory air in the wooden hut, and Nancy hurriedly packed away her sewing.

"Are you sure we shouldn't save it for a rainy day?" Margaret eyed the coins in Ezra's palm again.

"Please, Ma, please let's go into the village." Luke knew how to get around her. "You've been working hard ever since we arrived here, and it might be a good way to meet a few more locals to sell your buttons to."

"That's the idea," Ezra chuckled, winking at Luke. He unhooked Margaret's bonnet from the back of the door and handed it to her, as well as her shawl, not taking no for an answer. "Luke's right, my dear, we all deserve a little treat. I promise I'll try harder with Mr Fernsby on Monday morning if you'll humour us with this outing. Look what a lovely day it is outside. It will do us all good."

THE WALK into Lower Amberley made Nancy realise that she had been wrong to dismiss it as nowhere near as nice as Thruppley village. There were several large mills, their water wheels turning ponderously, and she could hear the weaving looms clattering loudly through the open windows. Many of the houses were made of the same honey-coloured stone that was so distinctive to the area. The hawthorn trees and horse chestnuts were in blossom, and in the distance, she could see farm labourers working in the fields, which reminded her of where they used to live. Two carts rumbled past them on the lane, and the drivers waved cheerily to wish them a good afternoon. Everything felt more normal away from the overcrowded railway camp. It was a sharp reminder of how much their lives had changed, but she didn't want to dwell on that.

Luke was carrying Primrose on his shoulders, and they paused to watch a duck with a gaggle of fluffy ducklings paddling through the reeds on the edge of the river. The swallows had arrived a couple of weeks earlier from their long migration north from the sunnier countries they had overwintered in, and sand martins swooped in and out of their nesting burrows on the steep sides of the opposite riverbank. Nancy couldn't remember the last time they had all felt this happy as a family. *I wish it could last forever.* She imagined being able to preserve the moment in aspic jelly and then shook her head at the absurd idea. *But it would be nice to remember this moment like a keepsake.* She turned around slowly, watching Primrose chattering on Luke's shoulders and her ma and pa walking arm in arm as though they didn't have a care in the world, and tucked it into the corner of her mind. It would be a treasured memory she could return to when the inevitable harder times returned.

"It's a quaint place and busier than I thought it would be," Margaret remarked as they came into the village. The cobbled streets fanned out from a market square, and families bustled past, intent on running errands or gossiping with friends and neighbours.

Nancy felt a pang of envy as three girls about the same age as her skipped past, rolling wooden hoops and talking loudly about having a pot of tea and buttered crumpets in one of the tearooms. Two matronly ladies followed behind and smiled indulgently, barely registering Nancy and her family. The girls all wore crisp, sprigged muslin gowns, and their hair was styled in ringlets held back with velvet ribbons that matched the lace trim on their dresses.

"Didn't anyone tell you it's rude to stare?" The tallest girl had circled back, and she poked her tongue out before hurrying after the other two.

Didn't anyone tell you it's rude to be so bossy? Nancy pressed her lips together to stop her reply from popping out. She was acutely aware of the ragged hem of her dress, which was far too short, and the fact that her hair had barely grown enough to cover the nape of her neck. Her bonnet was battered and grimy, and no amount of polishing could conceal the fact that her leather boots had come from the secondhand shop six months ago and were starting to make her limp; they pinched so tightly. There had been no mention of any new clothes since Ezra had been suffering from his nerves again. Even hand-me-downs from the church ladies would be preferable to the plum-stained dress.

How will I ever make friends looking like this? The upsetting thought cast a shadow over the day, but there was no denying that she felt lonely. Elmer had spread his poisonous rumours about the family throughout the railway camp, so the girls there gave her a wide berth, refusing even to speak to her. And even if Ma allowed her to attend the village school, Nancy already had a sinking feeling that the children there wouldn't want to befriend her either because the navvy families were seen as troublemakers, one and all.

As if reading her mind, Luke nudged her with his elbow and gave her a cheerful grin. "Don't worry, our Nancy, them stuck-up girls probably wouldn't be much fun anyway."

"Look...doggy...doggy..." Primrose wriggled excitedly on Luke's shoulders, providing a welcome distraction, as she pointed at the bow window of the toy shop. A stuffed toy dog on wheels had pride of place behind the window, along with a set of wooden soldiers and a doll's house so intricate Nancy could scarcely believe it. *What would it be like to have my very own bedroom with a doll's house to play with?* Her thoughts drifted back to the grand country home Ezra had pointed out to them in Thruppley. She wondered whether the Smallwood family had a daughter. If they did, she was bound to have every luxury a girl could desire: her own pony, piano lessons, and a gown for every day of the week. Nancy was not by nature someone given to jealousy, but there was something about that doll's house that fascinated her; the miniature furniture had been exquisitely carved, and there were even tiny plates of pretend food in the dining room. *I wish I could close my eyes and step into it.* She smiled at her fanciful imagination, but then the waft of freshly baked bread snapped her out of her daydreams.

"Are we allowed to go and look in the bakery window, Pa?" Luke asked. "My stomach's rumbling so loudly, I'm surprised all the folk in the village square can't hear it."

"You can look, but don't touch anything," Margaret said, clutching her bonnet as the breeze picked up. "And don't press your nose to the window like some sort of beggar child. We don't want the villagers looking down at us for having no manners."

"I'll be on my best behaviour." Luke handed Primrose to Margaret and bounded across the cobbles, making Ezra chuckle and shake his head. Even though Nancy was hungry, she was enjoying watching all the people around them too much to want to hurry after her brother. She knew him well enough to realise that he would want to spend at least fifteen minutes agonising over which treat to buy, no doubt changing his mind many times. She grinned to herself, knowing that he would still alight on what he always chose in the end: an iced currant bun.

"Excuse me, Miss, can I get past," a friendly voice said behind her. It was just as a drayman with a large cart rumbled by, taking up the whole width of the lane.

"Oh, yes, of course?" Nancy spun round with surprise as none of the other villagers had spoken to them. Was it someone from the camp?

"Afternoon." A boy with curly brown hair that stuck up in a cow's lick and the brightest blue eyes she had ever seen tipped his cap. "You're new to Lower Amberley, aren't you?" His face was tanned with freckles across his cheeks as though he worked outside, and the question sounded genuinely curious. She was reassured to see that he didn't look well-off. His shirt cuffs were slightly frayed, and his boots were scuffed. An early white campion flower was tucked jauntily into the top buttonhole of his waistcoat, and she noticed he had a twig caught in his hair, which made her laugh. His eyebrows shot up. "I didn't think I was that amusing, saying good afternoon."

Nancy bit her lip, groaning inwardly, worried that she had probably offended the only person who had bothered to be friendly. "Sorry. Don't tell Ma I laughed, or she'll be cross with me for being rude. It's just..." She gestured to his mop of curls. "You've got a twig stuck in your hair."

The boy was a couple of inches taller than her. He grinned and hastily pulled it out. "I'm not meant to be in the village. I'm supposed to be looking after the little 'uns back home, but they were reading quietly, so I slipped out through the hedge."

"A hedge? That would explain the...ah, twig." She wondered how large his family was and why he was meant to be in charge of his brothers and sisters, but before she had a chance to ask, he tipped his hat again and started to walk away.

"Nice to meet you," he said over his shoulder, "I'll see you around, no doubt. What's your name, by the way?" He turned and walked backwards, watching her and not caring that he might barge into someone.

"Nancy Burton." She hesitated, not wanting to spoil the moment by explaining she lived at the railway camp.

"Don't tell anyone you saw me here, Nancy Burton." The boy tapped the side of his nose, and his blue eyes twinkled with amusement. "You'd better get going. Otherwise, your brother will eat all of that currant bun without sharing it with you."

"Wait…what's your name—"

It was too late. The boy had loped away, and Nancy's words went unanswered.

She shook her head with a wry smile. Had he been watching them for a while to realise she was Luke's sister, she wondered? She was annoyed that she hadn't discovered who he was or his name, but Lower Amberley was a small village. They were bound to cross paths again, she hoped.

Just ahead of her, a wealthy couple rounded the corner, deep in conversation, as they strolled through the village. The gentleman was wearing a smart frock coat and a top hat and was listening to his wife with a doting look on his face. Their words drifted towards Nancy.

"…Must you really go up to London again so soon, Felix? I know your new position in the company means that you have to travel, but I wasn't expecting you to be away quite so soon." The woman's brow furrowed with a frown, and he smiled tenderly, tucking her hand in the crook of his elbow.

"I'm sorry, Trudy, I wasn't expecting it to be this soon either. Some of the managers have been rather lax in how they've been running things while old Mr Mulligan was ill. Costs have been spiralling out of control, so they expect me to get them reined in quickly. The investors in London are worried about their money being frittered away, so I have to go to reassure them that things will improve very soon." He lowered his voice. "Between you and me, The Gloucester Railway Company should have noticed sooner, but standards slipped while they were busy expanding."

Nancy's ears pricked up at the mention of the railway company. He looked far too grand to work for the same people as her pa. She stood back, politely waiting for them to pass, even though she could see Luke beckoning her from outside the bakery.

"Oh, no!" Another sudden gust of wind surged through the village, stronger than usual because of the way it funnelled between the buildings. It snatched at the woman's elaborate bonnet and tugged at the fine silk shawl around her shoulders.

"Look out, my dear," her husband cried. He caught the bonnet as it blew off her head, and the woman coughed as dust eddied up into her eyes, making her stumble. As she retied her shawl around her shoulders, Nancy saw that the ruby brooch on the lace collar of her gown had come undone. It dropped into the gutter, rolling away, and in their haste to rescue the bonnet, neither of them had realised.

Nancy glanced around furtively to see if anyone else had noticed, but the wind had caught everyone else by surprise, too, and they were busy picking up dropped parcels and scurrying for shelter in case it happened again. The brooch glinted enticingly. She wondered how much it might be worth. *Would a posh lady like her even miss it?* A tempting thought slid into her head. If she gave it to her ma and they took it to a pawnbroker, it would probably be worth more than Pa earned in a whole year...more than enough to lift them out of their dire circumstances.

"We mustn't be much longer," the woman said to her husband. "I don't like leaving Rosie at home with the housemaid for too long. Especially now that she can't get around very easily since the accident."

Nancy immediately felt guilty for even entertaining the idea of claiming the brooch for herself. Just because the couple looked well-to-do, it didn't mean that they were immune from worries of their own. She darted forward and picked the brooch up in one swift movement, unnoticed by anyone except one person standing in the shadows and watching with interest.

She gave it a quick polish on her sleeve before running after them. "Excuse me, Sir...Miss...this brooch fell off your dress when you lost your bonnet. You didn't see, but it would be a terrible shame for you to lose it." She held it out and bobbed a small curtsy as they both turned to stare at her.

"Oh, my dear," the woman exclaimed. Tears filled her eyes. "You have no idea how precious this brooch is to me. It belonged to my grandmother, Rosemary. Our daughter, Rosie, is named after her, and she loves it almost as much as I do."

"There, there, Trudy, don't upset yourself." The gentleman pinned it back on her collar and gave Nancy a grateful smile. "Our daughter fell down the stairs. It was a terrible accident, but nobody's fault. She has to use a bath chair to get around, but we hope she'll walk again one day." His expression clouded with sadness for a moment.

Nancy felt a renewed sense of guilt for the few seconds she had considered stealing the brooch and was glad she hadn't succumbed to temptation. "I'm sorry to hear that, Sir."

"I'm Felix Harrington, and this is my wife, Trudy."

Nancy was shocked when he reached out and shook hands with her. He didn't seem to notice her tatty clothes, or if he did, he was gracious enough not to let it stop him.

"We must give you something to say thank you," Trudy Harrington said. "Most people would have pocketed the brooch for their own gain. Your parents should be proud of you for being so thoughtful and considerate."

Nancy suddenly realised that Margaret was hurrying towards them, her lips pursed with disapproval.

"What are you doing hob-nobbing with these fine people and wasting their time," she grumbled, pulling Nancy away. "I'm sorry. My daughter has no sense of social etiquette. Not for lack of trying to drum it into her," she added, rolling her eyes.

"Actually, your daughter was being an upstanding citizen of good morals," Felix said, not put off by Margaret's brusque manner. "My wife dropped her brooch, and we would have returned home none the wiser if it wasn't for your daughter returning it to us."

Trudy nodded. "I was just saying we should give her a little something to say thank you." She extended a gloved hand and patted Margaret's arm. "You've raised her well...Mrs...?"

Now that the compliment was directed at her, Margaret beamed. "Mrs Burton. My husband Ezra works at the railway camp, except he's ill at the moment...he suffers terribly with his nerves ever since serving in the Punjab under General Gough, especially with Mr Fernsby being so unkind about it." She flushed slightly, remembering herself. "Sorry, I shouldn't bore you with such trivialities. But what I meant was that a small reward for Nancy's good deed would be a great help."

Felix Harrington pulled some coins out of his pocket and pressed them into Margaret's hand. "Your husband works for Mr Fernsby, you say?" he asked curiously.

"In a manner of speaking." Margaret's expression became closed and wary again. "Like I said, he hasn't been well. Lord knows if he'll even have the job next month if Fernsby gets his way." With that, she bobbed her head again and pulled Nancy away.

"What was that all about?" Ezra asked as he emerged from the bakery. Luke was already biting into his iced bun with a sigh of blissful happiness.

"I was just—" Nancy began.

"Nothing," Margaret said, cutting her answer off. She had already pocketed the money Mr Harrington had given them, and Nancy realised she wanted to keep it.

"Are you going to let me have a bite of that bun or scoff it all yourself?" she asked Luke.

As they strolled away, she was unaware that Felix Harrington was watching them all with a thoughtful expression. But he wasn't the only one. The boy with the blue eyes had also overheard the exchange, and as he turned on his heel and hurried through the back lanes an idea was forming in his mind that had the possibility to change Nancy's life forever.

CHAPTER 7

"*You* ou promised you would go and speak to him again, Ezra."

Nancy grimaced as she pulled her boots on and prodded Luke to get up. It was clear from Ma's voice that all the good cheer of the Saturday outing was long forgotten.

"Don't you remember," Margaret continued in a shrill voice, "you promised you would speak to Mr Fernsby again on Monday morning, which is today."

Nancy picked up Primrose and edged out of the bedroom, sliding past the scrubbed wooden table to put the kettle on the stove.

"Don't start nagging me again," Ezra snapped in a rare display of bad temper. Usually, he managed Margaret's sharp words with good grace and humour, but this morning, his face was etched with exhaustion, and he had dark circles under his eyes again. "I didn't get a wink of sleep last night, thinking about having to face Cecil Fernsby. He's got it in for me, Margaret, and I just have to accept it. He's never going to change his mind. A man like him prides himself on managing us navvies by threats and force."

Margaret planted her hands on her broad hips and looked around the modest room with a scathing glare. "So that's it, is it? You're just going to hide in the hut all day, refusing to work. I can't stand the man either, but how can we expect Mr Fernsby to let us keep living here if you're not doing any work, Ezra?"

"Would it help if I went to speak to him, Pa?" Nancy's heart thumped in her chest at the thought of having anything to do with the Fernsby family because she knew that Elmer would delight in seeing her grovelling for kindness. But if it meant they could keep their home, she would do it.

Her question seemed to make Margaret realise that she had been unusually sharp. "There's no point," she sighed. "I'd go over there myself if I thought it would help, but Fernsby is a bully. I think he actually takes pleasure in demeaning you, Ezra. I expect that's why you haven't been given the sack yet, truth be told."

The kettle started to whistle, and Nancy reached

for the tin of tea leaves. She opened the lid and pulled a face. There was barely enough for two pinches to add to the teapot, and after that, there would be none left. She hurried to the cupboard, where they kept the used tea leaves in a jar, and tipped them back into the pot to stretch the fresh ones a little further.

"Maybe it's time…" Ezra's voice was strangled, and the words fizzled out. He sank into his armchair and rested his trembling hands on his knees, looking even more haunted than usual. "Maybe it's time for me to try and look for work elsewhere," he suggested cautiously.

Margaret turned her back to them and walked to the window to peer outside. Her shoulders drooped in defeat, and she rested her hand protectively over her belly as though to shield the new baby from more misfortune.

"I thought this would be our new chance," she murmured quietly to herself. When she turned back to look at Ezra, she no longer seemed angry but resigned to their fate. "I'm tired of moving, Ezra," she said softly. "If Fernsby makes us leave, he's hardly likely to give you a reference to help you find another job. We'll have no money coming in, and we won't even have the camp's food caravan to provide our meals."

"Won't you let me try and speak to Mr Fernsby?" Nancy pleaded. She couldn't bear to see her ma and pa looking so wretched, and even Primrose had started to grizzle, chewing hungrily on a dry crust bread that was left over from the previous day's lunch.

A sharp knock at the door made them all jump. Margaret hastily looked into the mirror and patted her hair to make herself look presentable. "Answer it, then, our Nancy, don't just stand there."

Nancy opened it cautiously, half expecting it to be Cecil Fernsby, demanding that they should pack up and leave immediately. "Oh, it's you, Mr Harrington!" She couldn't keep the shock from her face, and she blinked, wondering how he knew where they lived and why he was there.

"Lawks...Mr Harrington, the toff from our day out?" Margaret straightened her apron and bustled to the doorway. "Good morning. How may we help?"

Felix Harrington was dressed in a more practical suit than the one he'd worn on Saturday, and he took his hat off and inclined his head in a polite nod of greeting.

"I hope you'll forgive me for surprising you like this, but Trudy was most touched by what your daughter did for us on Saturday. I've been giving some more thought to something that you said to me, Mrs Burton."

Margaret's expression was wary, and she glared at the two women who were standing outside the wooden hut next door, making no secret of the fact that they were trying to listen to the conversation. It was unusual for someone as well-dressed as Mr Harrington to be at the railway camp, and Nancy knew that everyone would be gossiping about this visit within minutes, speculating even more about the Burton family and their strange ways.

"You'd better come in," Margaret muttered reluctantly. "It's nothing grand, but it will save those two busybodies getting a crick in their necks trying to find out why you're here." She nudged Nancy, darting a pointed look towards the tangle of dirty clothes in the corner of the room, waiting to be washed, and Primrose's wooden blocks, which were scattered across the floor.

Nancy sprang into action and scooped up the clothes, bundling them hastily into her bedroom and deftly tidying up the wooden bricks with her feet as she passed. She half expected her ma to tell her to wait in the bedroom, but much to her surprise, she called her back in.

"Mr Harrington wants to say thank you to you again, Nancy," she said.

"Thank you for what? Is anyone going to tell me what's going on?" Ezra levered himself out of the armchair and struggled to his feet, looking puzzled.

"Nancy noticed that Mrs Harrington had dropped her brooch when we were in the village on Saturday, my dear," Margaret explained. She reached out absentmindedly and straightened Ezra's shirt collar, which was sticking up on one side. "She picked it up and gave it back to them before some other ne'er-do-well had the chance to steal it. Mr Harrington was generous enough to give us a little reward for her quick thinking."

"That's good to hear." Ezra beamed proudly at Nancy and smoothed his hair down, wanting to make a good impression.

Felix Harrington cleared his throat and gave Ezra a kind smile when he noticed how much his hands were trembling. "Your wife mentioned that you served in the Punjab," he said casually.

"Yes, under Commander-in-Chief, General Sir Goff. We were fighting in the Chillianwala area."

"I fought in the Crimea myself," Felix replied.

"Oh, I see." Sensing their visitor's seniority, Ezra stood to attention and held his hands behind his back.

"When I got back from fighting, I wasn't myself for a while," Felix continued. "I had terrible nightmares and couldn't bear loud noises." He smoothed his moustache and gave Ezra a direct look. "Something your wife mentioned made me wonder if you're experiencing the same sort of challenges as I did." He put his shoulders back and paced up and down several times as though the memories were uncomfortable. "Of course, the doctors don't really understand much about it, but that doesn't mean it's not a genuine ailment. I was lucky; my wife nursed me back to better health, but I know that Cecil Fernsby takes a dim view of any sort of illness that isn't easy to explain."

"I...I'm not quite sure I understand why you're here talking about this," Ezra stammered. He looked between Margaret and their guest, aghast that Margaret had discussed it with a complete stranger.

Felix stopped pacing and chuckled. "I completely forgot to introduce myself. I'm Felix Harrington, one of the general managers for the Gloucester Railway Company."

Ezra gulped nervously. "I suppose you're here to send us packing. I wouldn't blame you. I haven't been much use since we arrived, but it's the explosions in the tunnel, you see. I can't bear the sound of them. I've pleaded with Mr Fernsby to allow me to work on a different part of the railway line where they're not using explosives, but he keeps telling me I'm making a fuss about nothing."

"Yes, I thought that might be the case," Felix said dryly. "The truth is, he has something of a reputation for the rough treatment of the navvies at this camp, but he's been working for the company so long, they are reluctant to reprimand him."

"It's not that my husband is workshy," Margaret

said, unable to hold her tongue for a moment longer. "He should be doing a better job than labouring, but nobody will give us a chance."

Mr Harrington smoothed his moustache again and rocked on his toes. "I don't like to see a fellow soldier being punished after fighting for Queen and country. Also, I feel rather indebted to your daughter. My wife would have been very upset if we'd lost that brooch." His eyes twinkled as he looked at Nancy, and she felt her cheeks redden. "I'm sure for a moment or two you might have been tempted to pocket it and get some money for it?"

It was the truth, but she didn't want to admit it.

Margaret looked affronted. "Certainly not. I like to think I've raised her right, even when times have been hard."

"Exactly, Mrs Burton. That's why I think I may have a suggestion that could help you and your family. I can offer you a job as an assistant clerk at one of the different railway camps, Mr Burton. Do you think that would be more suitable for your recovery?"

"What? You mean we can leave here?" Ezra's voice held a note of hope that Nancy hadn't heard for a while.

"Yes, but before you say anything more, there are a couple of things I'll need to make you aware of. It's in a village some way from here, and the living quarters might be tight. The hut will be smaller than this, but at least you won't be working with explosives. If you do well, I can put in a good word for you to be considered for a promotion in the future."

Ezra grabbed Felix's hand and pumped it up and down, looking relieved. "Thank you, Sir. You won't regret offering me the position, Mr Harrington, I promise."

Felix held up his hands and chuckled. "There's no need to say right away. I'm sure you might like a day or two to discuss it with the rest of your family, Mr Burton."

"Will there be room for all of us?" Margaret asked. "I'm in the family way. We'll need a hut that's big enough for me and Ezra and four children." She looked around their current accommodation with a doubtful expression.

"As I said, you should weigh up everything I've said for a couple of days. In fact, I insist upon it."

Nancy didn't know whether to be excited about the offer or worried about the fact that they would be moving again, and she exchanged a glance with Luke as her ma showed Mr Harrington out.

"You two can run along and fetch some water while Pa and I discuss things," Margaret said a moment later.

Nancy knew that when they wanted them out of the way, important things would be divulged, so she put her finger to her lips and beckoned Luke around to the side of the hut so they could listen in on the conversation.

"This is exactly what Pa wanted," Luke whispered.

"Yes, but if there isn't room for us in the living quarters that go with the job, how can they agree to it?" she whispered back.

Luke was about to start speaking again, and Nancy frowned and shook her head as Margaret threw the window open, unaware that they were nearby.

"The job sounds perfect, Ezra, but you heard what he said. I was already worried about how six of us would squeeze into this hut when the baby arrives, so goodness knows how we'll manage in a smaller one." She stuck her arm out of the window and shook a duster with brisk efficiency. "Now that our Nancy is ten, maybe it's time for her to go into service as a maid. It's a bit sooner than I'd hoped, but it's the only thing I can think of for us to be able to accept Mr Harrington's offer of a better job."

Nancy's stomach lurched at the suggestion, and she saw Luke's eyes widen with surprise.

Ma wants to send me away. It must be because I'm not her real daughter. It was a painful thought.

Ezra's voice drifted out through the window. "What about her education? She's a bright girl, and

I'm sure with a bit more book learning, she could do better than being a maid, Margaret."

"We can't afford the luxury of coddling Nancy in the hope that she'll make something of herself in the future."

"But she's only ten. She'll miss Luke and Primrose dreadfully. We always vowed we would never split the family up, no matter how difficult things became."

Nancy held her breath, praying that Ma would agree, but her hopes were dashed with brutal speed.

"We can't be sentimental about things, Ezra, and you know it. I've done my best for her all these years, but now we have to think about what's right for the rest of the family, especially with the new baby coming. Plenty of orphans go into service in a live-in position at her age."

But I'm not an orphan. Tears burned in Nancy's eyes as she picked up her bucket and stumbled away. She had never allowed herself to wonder whether Ma loved Luke and Primrose more than her, in spite of Pa's protestations that being adopted didn't mean anything of the sort. *But if they loved me, they wouldn't want to send me away.*

"Wait for me, Nancy."

Luke hurried after her, and she dashed her tears away and raised her chin. Hadn't she wanted Pa to get a better job? This was his opportunity to get well again, and as much as it hurt her, she knew her ma's mind was made up. She could only hope that perhaps she would be working close enough to visit the family regularly and that they wouldn't forget about her.

CHAPTER 8

"Stand still, Nancy," Margaret scolded, "how am I meant to make you look presentable if you're wriggling like a dog with fleas?"

Luke sniggered as he finished his last few mouthfuls of porridge. "Are we all coming with you today, Ma?"

Nancy winced as Margaret dragged a comb through her hair and snagged a knot. It had grown back long enough now to become curly again, and it didn't take much to tangle, but at least she was grateful she didn't look like a boy anymore.

"I hope you will all come with me." Nancy's eyes watered, and she wasn't sure if it was from feeling sad or Ma's vigorous combing. "What if someone says they want me to start immediately? I wouldn't even have the chance to say goodbye."

Ezra spat on the toe of the boot he was polishing and buffed it to as much of a shine as he could. "There you are," he said, lining them up neatly for Nancy to put on once Margaret had finished brushing her hair. "I think it's best if we all come with you into the village, Margaret. We don't want any potential employers to think that Nancy is just an unwanted waif. She's more likely to get a position as a housemaid if they realise she's had a good family upbringing."

"I suppose so." Margaret stepped back to assess whether Nancy looked clean and smart enough for her liking. She whipped out her handkerchief and scrubbed the corner of it on a dark smudge on Nancy's cheek, which had appeared after she brought wood in for the stove. "That will have to do," she added with a satisfied nod. "But if I catch you misbe-having. Luke, and spoiling our chances of finding Nancy a job, I won't be best pleased."

"I wonder what sort of family you'll end up working for?" Luke pondered. "You'll probably have a smart new grey dress and mob cap and three hot meals a day with the other servants." He picked his bowl up and surreptitiously licked it clean while nobody was looking. "I bet you'll have your own bedroom as well," he said, sounding rather envious.

"How about we ask if they want you as a chimney sweep then, seeing as you make it sound so much fun?" Nancy blurted out mutinously. Ever since Ma and Pa had come clean about their plans for her the evening before, she had tried to be brave about it, but deep down, she was feeling scared and alone. It was as if she was being cast out from the family. *I expect they'll all be too busy settling in at the new camp for Pa's job to miss me.* She gulped, determined not to cry. If her eyes were red, Ma would get annoyed.

"You ain't going to send me away as well, are you, Pa?" Luke asked in alarm.

"Of course not," Ezra said, ruffling Luke's tousled blonde hair good-naturedly. "You're still far too young to work for the gentry. Besides, I'll need you to be the man about the house and help your ma out on the days when I'm busy with my new job. Nancy's a sensible girl, and her employers will be lucky to have her working for them," he added, trying to boost her spirits.

Nancy felt as though she had carthorses gallivanting in her stomach an hour later; she was so nervous. They had walked through Lower Amberley, and she stood in front of an imposing house, looking up at its elegant, red brick frontage. She counted the chimneys and wondered how many fireplaces one family could possibly need. Her ma had decided that the best approach to finding her a position as a maid was to call at all the poshest looking houses in the village and speak to the owners. Nancy had hoped they would just make a few discreet enquiries instead, but it seemed Margaret had other ideas.

"Now then, Nancy, make sure you curtsy politely and smile when they welcome us. We might not be the smartest-dressed folk, but nobody wants a maid with a sulky expression. Let me do the talking; otherwise, you're bound to speak out of turn and put your foot in it." She glanced around at the others. "Ezra, you and Luke can stand behind the two of us. Keep Primrose quiet and make sure nobody sees your hands shaking if you start having a funny turn."

"Wouldn't it be better for us to go round the back to the servants' entrance?" Nancy grumbled. She adjusted her bonnet. It was Margaret's and was slightly too big for her, but her ma had insisted she should wear it.

Margaret sniffed and lifted her chin defiantly. "Certainly not. Why should we slink around to the back, looking apologetic, as though we don't belong here? Just because we're down on our luck doesn't mean we don't deserve a fair chance."

With that, she gripped Nancy's arm firmly and pushed open the wrought iron gate, marching purposefully through the manicured front garden and up the steps to the large, black front door. Before Nancy had even had a chance to catch her breath, Margaret lifted the shiny brass knocker, which was shaped like a dolphin, and rapped sharply three times on the door, squaring her shoulders as though she was preparing to do battle.

The knock echoed in the grand hallway behind the door and was quickly followed by the sound of ponderous footsteps. Bolts were shot back, and the door creaked open. A tall gentleman with grey hair looked down his nose at them. "Yes?" he snapped, eyeing their clothes. His lip curled with disdain. "We're not giving away anything for charity today, and we don't have anything for rag and bone collections. Be on your way."

He started to close the door, but Margaret hastily stepped forward and put her foot in the crack. "Hold on a minute, are you the butler?"

"I am indeed, madam. And as such, it is my job to send vagrants away." He pulled a crisp white linen handkerchief from his pocket and dabbed his nose.

"We're not vagrants," Margaret bristled. "My daughter, Nancy, is available to work as a housemaid. She's very polite and a quick learner. We just wanted to know whether the lady of the house is at home to see if there's a position for a hard-working girl."

The butler's supercilious expression thawed a fraction, and he shook his head. "The master and mistress are entertaining guests at the moment, but we have no need of any additional servants. They took on two new maids earlier in the year, and they have settled in well."

Nancy bobbed a curtsy. "Thank you for letting us know, sir."

"Your daughter seems a little young to be sent into service, madam, if you don't mind me saying."

"It's just that she's small for her age," Margaret said firmly. "She's nearly fourteen years old and quite capable of working in a house like yours."

The butler arched one eyebrow, clearly not believing that Nancy was that age for one moment. "As I said, we don't have any positions in the household that need filling. The master doesn't like tradespeople calling at the front of the house, so all I can suggest is that you try some of the other places in the village." He gave them a curt nod. "Good luck to you, and good day." The door was shut firmly in their faces, and Nancy breathed a sigh of relief.

"Come along, dear," Ezra said cheerfully as they retraced their steps. "They seemed a bit stuck up for the likes of our Nancy, so how about we try at those couple of grand houses on the far side of the village instead?"

The next house turned out to belong to an elderly couple who spent most of their time up in London, staying with their daughter. Although the housekeeper wasn't as snooty as the butler they had just encountered, she, too, shook her head regretfully.

"Master Pendle only likes to 'ave a couple of maids working for me...and then only when they'm here in the country instead of up in yon city," she said, folding brawny arms across her ample bosom. She leaned closer and pinched Nancy's arm, checking how strong she was, and looked disappointed. "The mistress doesn't like new folk much. They've had the same servants working here nigh on twenty years. I doubt they'll 'ave a vacancy until one of us is pushing up daisies, ducky." She wheezed with laughter at her own joke. "Most of the gentry won't entertain the idea of taking on a young girl like your lass without a personal recommendation. Do you have a letter? Per'aps I could pass it on to someone."

Margaret mumbled that they had lost the letter of reference as Nancy did her best not to look embarrassed at the lie.

By the time they got to the third house, their high spirits were starting to flag. It was a hot day, and she wished she didn't have to wear her ma's thick shawl, but without it, her prospective employers would see just how scruffy her dress was.

"This looks more promising," Luke said, trailing along and kicking a stone. An elegant, honey-coloured house was ahead of them, with a well-kept garden. Nancy could see the family taking tea on the lawn in the shade of a willow tree. It looked charming, and she imagined herself bustling out to serve them with plates of cucumber sandwiches and dainty cakes. Her stomach rumbled, and she lifted her bonnet and dragged the back of her sleeve across her forehead, where her hair stuck damply to her head.

"Third time lucky, perhaps," she muttered.

"Stand up straight and look like you're interested," Margaret snapped. She had already said she was feeling nauseous, and clearly, her patience was wearing thin.

"Are you sure we shouldn't go round the back, dear, and speak to the housekeeper? I'm not sure your plan of speaking to these well-to-do families is for the best." Ezra tried to steer them away from the front gate, but Margaret was having none of it and shrugged his hand away.

"Don't be silly. I know what's best, and you can see that the mistress of the house is just over there. I'm sure if we go into the garden, she'll see us, and we will be able to speak to her directly without some stuffy butler stopping us."

Margaret bundled Nancy through the gate, and they started weaving their way through the symmetrical rose beds instead of up the wide stone path that led to the front door. "Cooee, Miss," she called, waving as they headed directly to where the family were dining outside.

Suddenly, the air was split by a volley of barking, and Margaret shrieked with fright. Two large hunting dogs came bounding across the grass; their hackles were raised, and their bared teeth looked terrifyingly sharp.

"I say, what do you think you're doing trespassing on our property?" The young man, sitting at the table, jumped up and strode towards them, his face red with anger. "Heel Zeus...heel Jupiter," he shouted.

"I...we came to see whether you had need of a new maid to join your household," Margaret stammered. She shrank back from the dogs who had gone to sit next to their master, and Ezra came to her side and put his hand on her shoulder to comfort her.

"We didn't mean to intrude," he said jovially, trying to reassure the well-to-do gentleman. "We're just trying to find work for our daughter, Nancy, here." He tipped his hat to the elegant woman who had stood up and was looking most affronted at being disturbed in such a way. "Good day to you, miss," he shouted. "Our Nancy would make a wonderful addition to your household as a maid if you happen to have a position she could be considered for." He stepped forward, and the dogs growled again.

"Stay where you are."

Nancy wasn't sure whether the man meant his dogs or them.

"Are you lot from the railway camp?" he drawled, looking faintly amused.

"What if we are?" Ezra replied defensively.

"I should have guessed." The man rolled his eyes, and Nancy was shocked to see the woman clutch her hands to her neck as though she was scared of being attacked. "We employed people from the navvy families in the past, and both times, we ended up regretting it. They stole from us, and you look like you're cut from the same cloth. Even if we did have a position, we certainly wouldn't offer it to the likes of you."

"There's no call for being that rude," Margaret cried, elbowing past Ezra again. She put her hands on her hips and glared at the gentleman, quivering with indignation. "You shouldn't judge us by other people's actions. We've never stolen a thing in all our lives, thank you very much."

The gentleman shrugged. "That's as maybe, but you're trespassing, and our guard dogs don't like it, so you should leave immediately before I have you chased off the property."

Margaret tossed her head and propelled Nancy back between the flowerbeds. "I wouldn't let my daughter work here for a master with such rude manners," she called as her parting shot over her shoulder.

The dogs growled again, and Nancy trotted the last few yards to the gate, not knowing whether to laugh or cry at how outraged her ma looked at the way they had been treated.

"You certainly told him, Margaret," Ezra chuckled once they were all safely back out in the lane and out of earshot.

"Maybe it's a sign that Nancy is meant to stay with us," Luke said. "None of the toffs in Lower Amberley seem to want a maid. Can we go and have something to eat now? I'm starving."

Nancy gave her brother a grateful smile, pleased that he wanted her to move to the new village with them even if Ma and Pa didn't.

"Nonsense," Margaret said briskly. She patted her hair back into place after their hasty exit and started walking back towards the village centre. "I'm sure we'll find someone who can take Nancy on. We just haven't looked hard enough yet."

"Perhaps we should rest for a while," Ezra suggested. "You're looking a bit pale, my dear, and I don't want you to overdo it now that you're in the family way."

Margaret waved Ezra's concerns away and walked purposefully along the lane. "We have to find something for Nancy today, especially if you're going to visit Mr Harrington this afternoon and accept the new job."

"What about that house over there?" Luke pointed towards a stand of trees. Beyond them, they could just make out the outline of a house which had been hidden from view when they had passed by earlier.

Now that Nancy looked more closely, she realised that the thick hedge on the eastern side was the boundary to a garden, and a set of rusty iron gates between two ivy-clad gateposts was indeed the entrance to a house.

"Well spotted, Luke." Ezra swung Primrose onto his shoulders, and they continued further along the lane. "Do you think anyone is at home?"

They stood in front of the gates, peering through. The gravel driveway was dotted with weeds, but there was a certain faded splendour about the house itself. Unlike many of the traditional honey-coloured stone cottages of Lower Amberley, this one had an air of exoticness. There was a long veranda across the front of the house with criss-crossed wooden railings, a rocking chair, and an ornate roof jutting over the top of it. The grounds were overgrown, and Nancy wondered if it was uninhabited until she heard the sound of children's laughter in the distance from the garden beyond the house.

Margaret pursed her lips as she took in the ivy rampaging up the brickwork and the peeling paint on a wooden summerhouse. "It looks pretty neglected if you ask me, not the sort of place that would be looking to hire a maid. I think we're wasting our time. Let's try some of the big houses on the eastern side of the village instead." She started walking away, expecting everyone to follow, but before she had got a few steps, she swayed and stumbled.

"Margaret, wait," Ezra cried, hurrying to her side. "That's enough now. It's a warm day, and I insist that we find somewhere to sit down so that you can rest for a few minutes." He looked around, hoping to see a bench, but there was nothing.

"Ask that boy up there," Luke said, pointing towards the figure running towards them.

Nancy's heart lifted as she realised it was the same boy who had spoken to her in the village a few days earlier.

"Nancy!" the boy cried. "Fancy seeing you here. I've just been to the railway camp looking for you, with some good news."

Margaret's face creased in puzzlement as she looked between Nancy and the boy. "Who are you, and how do you know my daughter?"

"Oh, sorry, I'm Arthur Pittman. I met Nancy in the village." He politely removed his cap. "I wasn't eavesdropping, Mrs Burton, but I overheard what you said to those toffs when Nancy found their brooch. It seemed to me that you're having a spot of bad luck, so I had to find Nancy to see if she wanted to come to Kingsley House." He jerked his thumb towards the rusty gates. "I see you've already found it...that's Kingsley House right there." He grinned at Nancy, his blue eyes dancing with intrigue.

Margaret still looked puzzled. "You mean the family is looking for a maid?"

"Is this where you live?" Nancy asked, interrupting her ma. She felt a glow of gratitude that he had remembered her, and even though he didn't look well-to-do, the thought of working for his family didn't seem so bad compared to the other places they had tried.

Arthur's face creased into a smile, and he chuckled. "No, they're not looking for a maid, and this isn't my grand family home." He chuckled again. "This is Kingsley House. You must have heard of it?"

"I wish you would stop speaking in riddles," Margaret said. "Do they need a maid or not? We'll consider anything. Even a position as a scullerymaid will do."

Before the boy could reply, Margaret swayed again, and Ezra grabbed her around her waist. "Never mind that...my wife isn't well. Is there somewhere she can sit down and have some water?"

"Of course." Arthur gestured towards the gates. "Follow me. As I said, I was looking for Nancy anyway. Miss Kingsley is expecting you," he added mysteriously.

CHAPTER 9

"Oh, you poor thing, you look absolutely done in. I'm Cressida Kingsley; you must come inside immediately and let me give you some refreshments."

From the moment Miss Kingsley laid eyes on them, after a hasty explanation from Arthur, Nancy felt as though they were in safe hands. She had wispy grey hair tucked into a rather haphazard bun, and her brown eyes twinkled as she stood back and urged them to come into the hallway. The motheaten heads of stuffed animals mounted on wooden plaques lined the walls, and a parrot squawked from where it sat on the bannister at the top of the stairs.

"Goodness me…is that a bird…inside?" Margaret flinched as the parrot squawked again and flapped its wings, looking down at them with inquisitive eyes.

"Don't mind Mr Popinjay," she said, gesturing vaguely in the bird's direction. "He gets rather talkative when we have visitors." Silver bangles jangled on her wrists, and her silk shawl billowed behind her in colourful swirls so bright it was quite unlike anything Nancy had seen before, not to mention the feather pinned to her dress.

"We don't want to put you to any trouble," Ezra said, "just a glass of water and somewhere for my wife to sit down for a moment would be perfectly fine."

"I'm sure we can do better than that." Miss Kingsley ushered them into the front parlour. The furniture was scuffed and faded, clearly well-used, but it looked comfortable, and Margaret sank gratefully onto the sofa, heaving a sigh of relief. "Arthur, will you ask Moira to bring tea and cakes; enough for all of us, please."

Nancy stood nervously between the sofa and window, wondering what Arthur had meant by the fact that Miss Kingsley was expecting them. Outside, she could see a gaggle of children chasing each other around a pond which was congested with reeds. The oldest one looked to be about eight years old, and after a moment, they all trooped over to the edge of the woods and started collecting sticks. Miss Kingsley followed her gaze and nodded approvingly.

"It takes a lot to heat this house in the winter, so I always encourage the children to collect sticks for the wood store. Arthur is a good boy and saws up the big logs for us."

A timid-looking maid appeared a moment later and put a tray of cherry cakes and cinnamon buns on the table in front of where Margaret was sitting. She bobbed a curtsy. "I'll be back with the tea in just a minute, Ma'am." She bustled out again, and Arthur returned to the room, giving Nancy a warm smile.

"They thought this was my family home, Miss Kingsley," Arthur said. "I didn't have time to explain everything yet."

"Well, I suppose it is in a manner of speaking." Cressida gestured for everybody to sit down and then settled herself in the chair nearest the hearth that had a bag of knitting perched precariously on the arm. She placed it next to the chair and absent-mindedly tucked a wisp of hair back into the bun. "I expect all this seems rather mysterious, Arthur saying that I was expecting you? He said you had no knowledge of Kingsley House."

The colour had returned to Margaret's cheeks, and she sat up straighter. "We haven't been living in Lower Amberley for long. We've just been calling at some of the posh houses...I mean, where the well-to-do folk live, trying to find work for Nancy."

"Arthur caught us staring through your gates, but we didn't mean to be rude," Ezra added.

Margaret nodded. "We were just leaving because we thought that nobody lived here. It's just that it looks a little different from some of the other houses we went to."

Miss Kingsley's skin was as dark and lined as a walnut, as though she had spent many years in a hot climate, and her eyes crinkled as she laughed. "That's a very polite way of saying that my family home looks a little bit rundown. I should probably explain everything..." She paused as Moira returned and poured cups of tea for everyone.

"My mama and papa purchased this house as an investment many years ago. Papa made his money in India, but we never really lived here much."

Nancy's ears pricked up at the mention of India, and she saw her pa's eyebrows rise as well. "India? That's where Pa was. Is that where your beautiful shawl came from? And that feather?" Nancy couldn't help herself and blurted out the questions without thinking. She bit her lip as Margaret turned to frown at her.

"You're very observant, Nancy." The old lady seemed completely unperturbed by the questions. "The silks in India are beautiful, and Mama had many clothes made by the skilled dressmakers out there."

She gave Nancy a conspiratorial wink. "I refrain from wearing most of the gowns because I'm not sure the good ladies of Lower Amberley would think they're appropriate, but I can't resist wearing some of her shawls. It's nice to be reminded of her since my parents passed away."

"Nancy, hush. You must excuse my daughter," Margaret interjected. "I'm always telling her she should think before she speaks, but she forgets more often than I would like."

"Oh, I don't mind. I like to see a girl with a lively imagination and a sense of curiosity, don't you, Mrs Burton?" Miss Kingsley touched the feather as if it was some sort of talisman. "There's quite the story behind this, I can tell you."

Everyone leaned forward, eager to hear more from this unusual woman with her exotic past.

"Not long after my sister, Marigold, and I returned from India to start living in England again, a strange old lady stopped me in one of the local villages. I had dropped my handkerchief, and she gave it back to me. We got talking, and she told me she was a fortune teller. Ava Piper was her name."

Nancy caught Arthur's eye, and he winked. It looked like he had heard the story before.

"There were plenty of soothsayers in India, but I didn't expect to meet one here in the West Country.

Of course, I told her I was a regular churchgoer and didn't believe in such things, but she didn't seem offended. She told me I would have many children and plucked this feather out of her hat and gave it to me."

Margaret's eyes flickered towards the window, where all the children were in clear view. "I reckon she must've been right, judging by your brood out there."

"Oh, they're not mine," Miss Kingsley chuckled.

"Who do they belong to?"

"Well, that's where it gets even stranger. For a while, I was convinced the old fortune teller was wrong. I never married, you see. But after Mama and Papa died, and Marigold and I inherited this house, we had to decide what to do with the place." She glanced around the room fondly. "We could have sold it for a lot of money, but Papa brought us up to try and do good where we could. I decided to set it up as a charitable home for needy children, and Marigold was quite happy to go along with the idea. I always wanted a family of my own, but it wasn't to be. So instead, I've put my efforts into this." She smiled as she caught sight of the children outside. "They might not be my flesh and blood, but I suppose the fortune teller was right...I do have many children in my care."

"I was the first one here," Arthur piped up.

"Yes, poor Arthur had become embroiled in a

gang of pickpockets, and I could see that if I didn't step in, he would probably end up in prison one day."

"It was my lucky day when I was told to steal something from Miss Kingsley." He grinned as he saw Margaret's shocked expression. "She caught me red-handed, but instead of calling the constable, she paid the master of our gang and brought me to live here. My ma and pa died when I was a little 'un, and the neighbour took me in. But Bernard Doyle turned out to be a wrong 'un." He shrugged. "I had to do as I was told, or I'd have been sent to the orphanage. I was good at it...the best dipper he had, Bernard used to say. I could steal a fob watch off a gentleman's waistcoat and a silver compact from a woman's reticule without ever being noticed."

"Until I caught you helping yourself to my locket," Miss Kingsley shot back goodnaturedly.

Arthur scratched his head. "I dunno what happened that day. Perhaps I was tired and off my game. But I'm grateful nonetheless."

Nancy could tell that her ma was struggling with this information and didn't know whether to disapprove of what Arthur had done in the past, or approve of how he had turned over a new leaf with Miss Kingsley's help. "And what about all the other children?" Margaret asked faintly.

"Some were orphaned, through no fault of their own, a couple were abandoned by families who couldn't afford to feed them, and several were heading into a life of crime like Arthur was." Cressida's expression was sympathetic. "I didn't want to be like some of the larger orphanages, where the children sometimes suffer terribly. I set up Kingsley House so it would feel almost like a family, but where the children could receive an education, plenty of good food, and escape from the clutches of pickpocketing gangs or toiling away in the factories and suffering ill health."

"It sounds like a very worthwhile endeavour," Ezra said. He cleared his throat awkwardly. "I'm still not quite clear why Arthur said you were expecting us if you're not looking for a maid."

Miss Kingsley paused for a moment to sip her tea and, for the first time in their conversation, looked slightly uncertain of herself.

"I never usually approach parents directly about their children. Word gets around about what I do, you see. In the past, when families have fallen on hard times, they came to me to see if their children could live here."

"How did you know about us hoping to find work for Nancy?" Margaret still looked mystified.

"It's like I told you, Mrs Burton," Arthur said. "I saw Nancy give those toffs their expensive brooch back when the lady dropped it, and in my eyes, that showed that she's an honest sort of girl. And then I overheard what you said to them, and it sounded like things were a bit of a struggle."

Ezra shifted uncomfortably in his seat. "I don't like to make too much of it, but I've suffered with my nerves since fighting in the Punjab when I was in the 24th Foot. Poor Margaret has the patience of a saint, but the job I had working for The Gloucester Railway Company was impossible for me to do."

"He's tried his hardest." Margaret patted Ezra's hand.

"I've been beside myself with worry about how to make ends meet, but thankfully, Mr Harrington...the gentleman whose wife dropped her brooch, works for the company, and he has offered me a job as a clerk. The problem is that we'll only have a small wooden hut to live in. It's better than nothing, but Mr Harrington was quite clear that it wouldn't be big enough for all of us, which is why we wondered about finding a position as a maid for our Nancy." He took a deep breath, looking embarrassed. "I don't want you to think that we don't care for her, Miss Kingsley. It was a difficult decision. My wife is expecting another child, you see."

Cressida Kingsley nodded slowly, giving Ezra a sympathetic smile. "I quite understand. You seem like caring parents, but sometimes life can be unkind. And it must be hard for Nancy, too, I don't doubt.

What with the thought of being separated from her family."

Nancy felt the knot of anxiety, which had been present in her chest all day, start to loosen slightly. This was the first time that anyone had mentioned that she might be sad about what her parents had decided.

"I can't offer your Nancy a position to work as a maid, but how would you feel about her becoming one of our merry band?" Miss Kingsley folded her hands in her lap, not wanting to rush anyone with an answer. "I know that perhaps you were hoping Nancy would earn a wage and possibly even contribute to your family's finances, but if she stayed here, she could continue with her education."

"You're right. We had hoped that Nancy would earn a wage," Margaret said bluntly.

"I would happily provide some recompense for the loss of earnings," Miss Kingsley said gently. "And I expect you would like to visit her when time permits. I always encourage family visits with the children who still have parents nearby."

She's paying for me to stay here instead of me working for a family of toffs? Nancy wondered if she was dreaming.

"You'd like it here, Nancy," Arthur said cheerfully. "I thought it would be like living in one of the orphanages that my neighbour used to talk about to put the fear of God into me, but Kingsley House is nothing like it. We do our lessons, and we have three square meals a day and help with chores to keep the house running. And when I'm older, Miss Kingsley says she's going to help me find a proper job."

Nancy looked at her parents. Ma still seemed hesitant, but Pa looked as though he wanted to jump up and shake Miss Kingsley's hand to agree on the deal immediately.

"Don't you find it too much managing all these children yourself, with just your maid Moira?" Margaret sounded as though it would be the last thing she'd want to do.

Miss Kingsley looked out of the window for a moment, watching the children running back and forth across the lawn with the firewood. "I can understand you asking that, but it's not just me. My sister, Marigold, helps."

"Shouldn't we meet her?" Margaret asked. "What if she doesn't like our daughter? Nancy might be a chatterbox, but I want her to be happy."

Nancy was surprised that her ma had admitted such a thing, and it made her feel a bit better about being sent away.

"I can assure you that Marigold will find your daughter just as delightful as I do, Mrs Burton." Miss Kingsley gave a tinkling laugh and shook her head. "We always thought the two of us would live here as a pair of old spinsters just looking after the children, But then the strangest thing happened."

"Go on." Margaret was drawn in by another story.

"We decided to sell one of Mama's emerald necklaces to help repair the roof after the winter storms. Marigold is much better at that sort of thing than me, so we agreed that she would go and stay in Bath to take the waters for a few days for her health and show the necklace to one of the jewellers there at the same time for a valuation. The first shop she went into was run by a gentleman called Dorian Holt." She shook her head and laughed again. "Marigold's first impression was that he was a bit of a rogue with the ladies. But blow me down if he didn't sweep her off her feet. They had a short courtship, and now they're married." She looked slightly wistful for a moment and touched the feather as she gazed outside.

"So there is a man of the house?" Ezra sounded relieved.

"They're away in France on their honeymoon at the moment, but when they return, they plan to settle in Lower Amberley. So I shall have more than enough help running Kingsley House, and I expect they would be delighted to meet you when you come and visit Nancy. I hope that puts your mind at rest."

Margaret exchanged a glance with Ezra and then stood up and gestured for Nancy to do the same. "I think this would suit our daughter very much. What do you say, Nancy?"

Nancy took a shaky breath, realising that this was it. If she agreed, she would be living at Kingsley House, away from her family and everything she had ever known. "I...I suppose so. Thank you for your kind offer, Miss Kingsley."

Arthur sprang forward and shook Nancy's hand. "I'll look after you and help you settle in. If you're anything like me, you might be feeling a bit scared at the thought of joining us, but there's no need to be. We'll be your new family, and you'll see your folks as well."

The tears, which had pricked at the back of her eyes, receded, and Nancy nodded, for once finding it hard to speak.

"I don't know how we can thank you," Ezra said, jumping to his feet. "Our Nancy is a bright girl, so I always hoped she could have a bit more book learning. I'm not sure exactly how often we'll be able to visit, but your ma will write you a letter with our news now and again, Nancy, won't you, Margaret."

"That's all settled then." Miss Kingsley stood up with a jingle of bangles. "Why don't you and I go and discuss money while Arthur introduces Nancy to the other children."

"What about us?" Luke asked. He was still holding

Primrose and looked as though he didn't want to miss out.

"Arthur can take you as well, young man," Miss Kingsley said. "I'm sure you're a great help to your parents, and I don't want you to worry about your big sister. She'll be perfectly happy here."

CHAPTER 10

*N*ancy jerked awake and blinked her eyes slowly, wondering why she couldn't hear Luke snoring. Looking sideways, she saw dappled light playing on the floorboards and rag rug next to her bed, and she remembered where she was. *Kingsley House.* Lifting her head off the pillow, she looked across at the other three beds in the room. She had been at Miss Kingsley's charitable home for children for a week, but still, in that moment of drifting between sleep and wakefulness, her mind hung onto the past, deluding her and making her think she was still back in the wooden hut at the railway camp. She wondered how much longer it would continue to happen until her previous life was slowly relinquished like a leaf floating away down a river.

She stretched her toes out under the faded, patch-work quilt and realised that this was the first morning her stomach hadn't lurched with shock and homesickness for her family. Rubbing the sleep from her eyes, Nancy examined that thought. Did she still miss her family? Yes, without a doubt. Should she feel guilty that she was relieved she was starting to settle in at Kingsley House and view it as home? She stretched her toes again and pushed the thought away. It was what her family had wanted, after all. And she was sure that homesickness would return now and again, tapping her on the shoulder and giving her a dull ache of loss in her chest when she least expected it.

Her gaze roamed around the bedroom, taking in her unfamiliar surroundings again. The dappled light on the floor was caused by the large oak tree growing right outside their bedroom window. The leaves were a soft, verdant green, having not long unfolded in the late spring, and every now and then, one of the branches tapped and scratched against the window in the wind. Birds fluttered in the leaves and chirped noisily with their dawn chorus. She liked having the tree outside the window, standing like a guardian and wondered what its gnarled branches had witnessed over the years before Miss Kingsley's family had bought the house. Had there been elegant tea parties in its shade on hot summer days? Perhaps couples had stolen a kiss or agreed to marry beneath the rustling leaves.

Luke would say I'm soft thinking of such romantic notions. She smiled to herself. There had never been time to lie in bed for a precious extra five minutes and let her mind wander in her previous life. Not with Primrose needing breakfast and water to be fetched.

The figures in the other three beds started to stir, snapping her back to the present. Closest to Nancy was Tess. She was eight years old, had raven-dark hair, and had been rescued from one of the cotton mills down Bristol way. She still bore the scar on her hand from when it had been snatched into one of the weaving looms, making her a useless liability to the overbearing manager, who'd had no qualms about throwing her out onto the streets because of her disability.

In the other two beds, tucked up against the far wall of the bedroom, Anne and Sophie sat up, both with a tangle of coppery-coloured curls which Nancy knew would take some taming. They were sisters, aged six and five. Their parents had left England on one of the mighty ships at Liverpool docks several, heading to America to find their fortune. They had begged Miss Kingsley to take them in, saying that it was too much of a burden to take the two little girls with them when they barely had enough money to cover their own passage. Arthur had told her that the sisters had cried every night for two months straight when they first arrived, but now they could scarcely remember their ma and pa.

I pray that I'll never forget my family or they forget about me. Nancy grimaced and hastily told herself that, of course, that would never happen. She was only here until Pa got back on his feet again and to get a better education than she would have in the railway camp with the other navvy children.

"Wake up, you lazy lot." Arthur's comment was accompanied by a chuckle as he poked his head around the bedroom door. He and the other boys, Blake, Robert, and Rick, were split between two bedrooms further along the hallway, but Arthur was usually first up. Nancy had discovered that he was a bundle of energy, champing at the bit to start the day and always with a smile on his face. She wasn't sure she would have managed her first week at Kingsley House without his good cheer sweeping her along.

"I'll be downstairs in a minute," Nancy said, quickly throwing her blankets back. She hated for anyone to think she was idle but knew that he didn't mean it that way.

"I ain't never known anyone so chirpy as you in the mornings, Arthur Pittman," Tess grumbled as she slowly sat up and pushed her dark hair out of her eyes. "Can't you give us a minute to come to our senses without thumping on the door and yelling as if the sun has already been up for five hours?"

"You know what they say, Tess, the early bird catches the worm." He grinned again, and his blue eyes glinted with mischief. "What I actually mean is that the early bird catches the rabbits. I set a couple of snares in Farmer Thompson's fields last night, so I'm going to slip out and see if we caught anything."

Anne and Sophie sat bolt upright, both looking alarmed. "What did you go and do that for? You know he can be a grumpy old so-and-so if he thinks anyone's been trespassing on his land. Folk will think you're a thief if they see you."

"I'm like a will-o'-the-wisp," Arthur said, tapping the side of his nose. "I'll be in and out of his fields before he even knows it, and hopefully, you lot and Moira can cook us a tasty rabbit stew for dinner."

Sophie and Anne exchanged a look and shivered. "But if you get caught, and Miss Kingsley finds out, who's going to look after us little 'uns when you get sent to jail by the constable?" Anne looked close to tears.

"Jail? Sent to Australia on one of them plague-ridden convict ships, more like," Tess added darkly. "Just because you used to be a dipper, picking pockets for a living, doesn't mean you have nine lives, Arthur."

"Surely it won't come to that," Nancy said hastily.

"They're only teasing me." Arthur winked to reassure her. "Bernard Doyle always said I was the best dipper he had, so I'm not going to get caught snaring a couple of rabbits, don't you worry." He jammed his cap on his head and hurried away, clattering down the stairs and making Mr Popinjay squawk.

"I'm surprised Miss Kingsley would need rabbit meat to feed us," Nancy said. Her voice was muffled as she pulled her nightgown over her head and reached for the new dark Linsey-woolsey dress and petticoat she had been given on her first morning. It was a relief not to have to worry about poking her elbow through her sleeve or wondering whether the seams would split like she'd had to with her old dress. The much-patched gown had since been banished to the bin, too ragged even to make dusters.

"It's not that she needs the meat or that we're poor, but I think things are a little bit harder than they used to be." Tess yawned and stretched her arms above her head, clearly in no hurry to get up. "When I first came here after being at the cotton mill, it felt like having a banquet every evening when we sat down to eat. But I've overheard Miss Kingsley talking to her sister about the cost of keeping the house up together many times."

Sophie nodded solemnly, sucking her thumb. "That storm we had last winter was terrible," she mumbled around her thumb. "It felt like the devil was hammering on the roof, trying to get in, and when we saw the damage at daybreak the following morning, Miss Kingsley cried." Her eyes clouded at the memory. "The slates blew off the roof, and they were scattered all over the lawn. And it rained for days afterwards. It was like a river of water running through the old bedroom the boys used to have, and it even went through the floorboards and into the back parlour."

"Kingsley House isn't run like the big orphanages in Gloucester and Bristol where the dignitaries donate money," Tess explained. She winced slightly as she caught her hand on the bedstead as she was getting out of bed. Although her accident had been a while ago, thanks to the mill manager's miserliness, he hadn't deemed it enough of an emergency to send for the doctor until her wound had become infected. And now the scar where she had lost two fingers was still sensitive and probably always would be.

"So who pays for all of this? Is it just the money Miss Kingsley inherited from her family? That's what she told my parents." Nancy pulled her boots on, quickly tied the laces, and then picked up the brush from the dressing room table. She enjoyed doing Anne and Sophie's hair every morning, even though they did yelp if she happened to snag a knot. "Are you ready, Sophie? I'll do you first."

"We don't know," Tess said, glancing towards the

bedroom door and lowering her voice. "I suppose some of the charitable toffs in the village help out, but the truth is, we try to stay clear of listening anytime Miss Kingsley and her sister talk about money."

"Or better still, we do something to interrupt them." Sophie looked at Nancy in the mirror and grinned. "The boys are good at that. They pretend they're fighting or doing something troublesome, and Miss Kingsley soon comes running to sort them out."

"You pretend to do something troublesome?" Nancy shot her a puzzled look. "Why would you do something that means you get told off?" She thought back to all the times her ma had walloped her and Luke on the backs of their legs for being naughty.

Sophie giggled as though it was obvious. "It's not that we like being told off. It's because Miss Kingsley always looks worried and upset when they're talking about money, so we do it to distract her. "

"I see, "Nancy replied, still puzzled as she tackled Sophie's curls with the brush. She tied them back off the little girl's face with a ribbon and gestured for Anne to sit in front of her for her turn. "Don't you think we should try some different distractions... something that would please them. A tidbit of good news, perhaps? "

Tess paused from her task of making the bed and

put her hands on her hips. "That's a grand idea, I don't know why we didn't think of it in the first place."

"It was the best the boys could come up with," Anne said, nodding.

"I wasn't sure about you joining us, Nancy." Tess plumped the pillows and folded up her nightgown. "Us three were used to being the only girls here, but I reckon you'll fit right in."

Nancy felt her cheeks turning pink and turned to the dressing room table to get a ribbon for Anne, not quite knowing where to look. Tess's words meant more than she probably realised. "That's nice of you to say, so," she murmured. "I know you're all from different backgrounds, but I was worried you might not like me being here, especially as I'm a little bit older than you." She quickly finished tying Anne's hair up and patted her on the shoulder. "That's you done. How about we all go downstairs and help Moira with the breakfast? I reckon the poor woman is run ragged, looking after us lot, so I expect Miss Kingsley would be grateful for us to take on some of the chores."

As they all trooped downstairs, Mr Popinjay eyed them all from his perch in the middle of the entrance hall. Nancy had got used to the fact that the parrot seemed to be allowed free run of the house, and she was growing rather fond of him already. He had a small repertoire of words, which he liked to surprise them with, which always made the younger ones giggle.

"Good morning...good morning...good morning..." Mr Popinjay bobbed up and down on his perch with each word and tilted his head to one side, clicking his beak.

"Good morning, Mr Popinjay," the girls all chorused back at him. Nancy smiled to herself and felt a surge of gratitude towards Arthur, that fate had inspired their paths to cross and that she was now living at Kingsley House. Being separate from her family was hard, but her new friends made everything bearable, she was coming to realise.

Nancy was surprised that Moira was nowhere to be seen as they went into the cavernous kitchen at the back of the house. The range had been stoked, and the empty saucepan was waiting next to the earthenware pot of oats to make porridge, but there was no sign of the housemaid, who usually did most of the cooking.

"Moira must be busy with something else, but we can make breakfast, girls," Nancy said. She bustled around the large wooden table, marvelling at the fact that the kitchen was larger than the entire wooden hut she had lived in at the railway camp. There was an enormous mahogany dresser against one wall, with the everyday crockery they used, and a clothes airer on a pulley above the range with all the teatowels drying on it from the previous day's laundering. Beyond the kitchen was a scullery with a boiling copper and sinks for washing vegetables, a large pantry for all the dry goods, and a larder with marble shelves to keep the meat and dairy products cold. The large wooden table at the heart of the room was surrounded by mismatched chairs. The children ate breakfast in the kitchen, but lunch and the evening meal were either taken in the kitchen or the dining room, depending on how Miss Kingsley felt on any particular day it seemed.

"Are you sure Moira won't be cross if we start doing the porridge?" Sophie plugged her thumb back in her mouth, and her eyes rounded with worry.

"I used to make it all the time for my family," Nancy reassured her. Since she had arrived, Nancy had an overwhelming urge to show Miss Kingsley that inviting her to join the other children hadn't been a mistake. Throwing herself into as many tasks as she could was the only way she knew how. She had become so used to the future feeling uncertain because of Papa Ezra's nerves that she still half expected that Miss Kingsley would draw her to one side and explain that it had all been a terrible mistake and that Nancy was no longer welcome.

"Nancy is right," Tess said. "Moira is run off her feet looking after us." She dragged a chair over to the dresser and climbed up on it to start getting bowls down for their breakfast. "We used to have a full-time cook called Miss Harcourt," she explained to Nancy.

Just at that moment, the younger boys clattered into the kitchen. Blake, who was eight years old and the same age as Tess, made a retching sound as he heard the conversation. "Thank goodness old Harcourt went and got herself in the family way and left. I know she called herself a cook, but what that woman did with a meat stew was an affront to my digestion."

The two cousins, Robert and Rick, doubled over and clutched their bellies in a parody of being sick. "Her bread rolls were hard enough to break your toe if you happened to drop one of them," Robert added.

"And remember her custard? You could slice the skin off the top and turn it into elastic to hold up a pair of bloomers." Rick pranced around the table, pretending to be wearing voluminous cotton under-garments.

Nancy bit her lip to hide her amusement, but it was no good, and she joined in with all the others as they roared with laughter.

"Miss Harcourt used to work for the family in India, which was why Miss Kingsley kept her on. She was a housemaid, really, and never really liked cook-ing, so when she started courting and left to get married to the butcher's brother, it was a bit of a relief to have Moira instead." Blake lifted the lid of the pan on the range and sniffed the leftover ham and pea soup appreciatively.

"I love Moira," Tess said stoutly. "Her cooking might be plain, but we've never gone hungry, which is more than I can say about when I worked at the mill. Many's the night I used to lie awake in the dormitory, wishing for some bread and a scrape of butter to stop my stomach rumbling."

"How long will breakfast be, Nancy?" Blake prowled around the table and dipped his finger in the jug of milk, scooping some of the thick cream off the top and smacking his lips as he licked it off his finger.

"Get off that. You know Moira doesn't like you pinching food." Sophie tried to slap his hand away, but Blake ducked out of her reach with ease.

"It won't be long. Ten or fifteen minutes." Nancy stirred the oats, which were starting to thicken. "Hopefully, Arthur will be back by then."

"Plenty long enough for you boys to go and fetch some wood in for Miss Kingsley's parlour," Anne said.

Nancy had the feeling that, given the chance, the boys would happily have sat at the table and waited for the porridge to be ready, but Blake shrugged and prodded Robert and Rick back out of the kitchen. "Don't start breakfast without us," he called over his shoulder. "It looks like you know what you're doing on them oats, Nancy, and I don't want those greedy girls taking more than their fair share."

"He's always hungry," Sophie said, rolling her eyes. It reminded Nancy of Luke, and she smiled to herself. Perhaps things weren't so different here after all.

CHAPTER 11

*J*ust as they were finishing their porridge, Moira came rushing into the kitchen clutching a piece of paper. Her mob cap was askew, and her cheeks were flushed. "Lawks, I had a terrible thought for a minute you'd be all sitting here, wondering where your breakfast was."

"I hope you don't mind that I went ahead and cooked the porridge and served the younger ones." Nancy pulled a chair out and offered it to Moira. "Would you like some too?"

Moira shook her head sharply, making her mob cap tilt even more perilously. "I'd love to, Nancy, but I ain't got no time to sit down and eat today." She looked at the list on the paper and pulled out the tattered recipe book she kept propped on the dresser.

"Chicken terrine," she mumbled. "They could have given us a bit more warning..." Pushing a strand of hair away with the back of her hand, she started thumbing through the pages, looking flustered.

"What's going on, Moira?" Arthur asked.

"Haven't you heard?"

Arthur gave her a good-natured smile and patted her hand. "Take a deep breath, and tell us, Moira. You look like you're about to have an attack of the vapours, and I'm sure Miss Kingsley wouldn't want that. Whatever it is, you know we will help out in between our lessons today."

"I do feel a bit faint from not eating." Moira sank gratefully into the chair and fanned herself with her apron. "The post boy delivered a letter to Miss Kingsley before sunrise this morning. Marigold and her new husband, Mr Holt, are arriving at Kingsley House later today."

"Today?"

"Did something bad happen?"

"I wonder what he's like."

There was a chorus of questions as everyone's mouths dropped open in surprise, and they leaned forward for more information.

"I thought they were staying in France for at least another month?" Arthur jabbed Blake with his elbow to stop him from eating the last slice of toast and pushed the plate towards Moira instead. Nancy noticed that even though the housemaid was in her early twenties, the children treated her more like an older sister.

"Exactly, so did Miss Kingsley and I," Moira explained. She spread butter on the toast and added a dollop of her homemade bramble preserve while Blake looked on longingly. "It's caught us proper by surprise, it has." She munched her food absentmindedly while Nancy poured her a large cup of tea to go with it. "They were meant to be staying in France for another month, you're quite right, Arthur, but for some reason, they've changed their minds, and they'll be arriving later today. I haven't even aired the bedroom in readiness, and apparently, Miss Marigold's new husband is very particular. He likes everything just so, which is why I've got to prepare a special meal for this evening as well as everything else."

"Are they going to be living at Kingsley House with us?" Sophie's face lit up. "It's not the same here without Miss Marigold, but I thought once she was married, they would have a house in the village."

Moira popped the last crust of toast into her mouth and hastily washed it down with some tea. "That remains to be seen, Miss Sophie." She adjusted her mop cap, and a frown furrowed her brow. "It's only ever been Miss Cressida and Miss Marigold living here...I don't know what it will be like having a new master about the place." Her words were quiet, talking more to herself than them.

Nancy stood up and started clearing the table. "I'm sure he will understand that the charitable home is Miss Kingsley's pride and joy."

"He probably won't even want to be involved," Arthur said, nodding with agreement as he sliced Blake another piece of bread, much to his delight. "Do you remember when Miss Kingsley was speaking to your parents, Nancy? She said that Mr Holt had some sort of jewellery business in Bath, which is how Miss Marigold met him, didn't she? Maybe he'll do something similar in Lower Amberley."

"You don't think he'll mind Miss Marigold looking after all us little 'uns, do you, Moira?" Anne looked worried. "Our parents didn't even like having just two of us, which is why they left us behind when they went to America." She said it very matter-of-factly and patted Sophie's hand, but her sister was more concerned with eating the last crust of bread that was left before Blake grabbed it.

"Yes, what if Miss Marigold's new husband doesn't like the idea of having the eight of us living at Kingsley House?" Rick said. He thrust his chin out mutinously.

Moira pushed herself up from the table and gave them all a bright smile. "There's nothing to be worried about, children. I was only feeling a bit over-whelmed at how much work there is to do today to prepare for their arrival. I shouldn't have spoken out of turn."

"But what if things change for the worse?" Rick muttered.

"Now, now, Rick, that's no way to talk. We all know that Miss Marigold would never have married a gentleman who didn't agree with having all you lot here. That would be ridiculous." Moira reached for the copper terrine mould and her large mixing bowl. "Good thing the butcher delivered more chicken and streaky bacon than we needed yesterday." Her thoughts were already turning to the long list of chores she had to get done.

"Yes, Rick, don't be so silly," Robert said, rolling his eyes with a kindhearted smile that showed he meant no malice. "Miss Kingsley has always told us that our welfare is her priority, and Miss Marigold ain't no different." He picked at a scab on his elbow and suddenly looked thoughtful. "It'll be like having a new pa," he said. "My old man was a drunken layabout, at least, that's what my mam used to call him. Miss Marigold's husband must be a decent sort of fellow if he has his own jewellery business."

"Anyway, that's enough speculation about Mr Dorian Holt," Moira said firmly. She glanced at the clock on the top shelf of the dresser. "You'd better look lively. Your lessons start in fifteen minutes, and you boys don't look like you've washed behind your ears this morning. You'll have taters growing out of them if you're not careful."

"I'm going to ask Miss Kingsley if I can help you with your jobs," Nancy said. She could tell that Moira was still feeling flustered about how much she had to do.

"I am, as well," Arthur chimed in. "The little 'uns need to do their book learning, but it won't harm for Nancy and me to miss a few hours in the classroom if it helps make your life easier."

A wash of relief crossed Moira's face. "Mind, you don't tell her it was my idea, though," she said hastily as she shooed the younger children out of the kitchen. "You know Miss Kingsley doesn't like you skiving her lessons."

"It's for a good cause," Arthur chuckled. "Nancy and I will be back in a minute once we've spoken to her. You'd better write a list of what you want us to do."

* * *

THE REST of the morning passed in a whirlwind of activity. As Nancy bustled up and down the stairs to dust and air rooms for the new arrivals, she could hear the younger children reciting their times tables and reading poetry to each other under Miss Kingsley's firm but gentle guidance. She made a good teacher and had an uncanny knack for getting everyone to learn without it ever feeling too difficult.

Every now and then, she would hear the tinkling of the piano from the front parlour as each child was let out of their lessons, in turn, to go and do their music practice. The latest one was Blake with a haltering rendition of three blind mice, and Nancy hummed it as she worked. Sophie and Anne had sweet voices, and it was always a pleasure to listen to them singing together. She wondered if they might do a few songs to welcome the new arrivals later that day.

Miss Kingsley had decided to give Marigold and Mr Holt the best rooms in the house: Miss Marigold's bedroom, the generous-sized dressing room next to it, plus the room which had been used as a nursery when the children were younger. The cots and old wooden rocking horse were covered with dust sheets now, and she thought Dorian might like to use it as a study or quiet reading room if he wished. Together, they made a generous suite of rooms that were at the end of the upstairs hallway, as far away from the children's bedrooms as possible, which Nancy thought was probably a wise move.

She threw the windows open and dusted with

speedy efficiency before laying a fire in the bedroom grate. She would light it later to banish any lingering dampness and take the chill off the room from it being unused for a while.

"That's better." Moira stood in the doorway with her arms full of sheets and pillowcases. They stood on either side of the bed, and it was soon made with neatly tucked-in corners and extra blankets folded up and stored in the blanket chest at the end of the bed. The sheets still smelt faintly of spring sunshine and the lavender water that Moira liked to use when she ironed.

Nancy glanced around at the floral wallpaper, the mahogany dressing table, which gleamed from being polished, and the elegant chintz chaise longue under the window. "Imagine having a bedroom like this, Moira. We never had anything so lovely at the railway camp. I still have to pinch myself about living here."

The housemaid chuckled. "I didn't come from a well-to-do background either, but you'll soon get used to it. Miss Kingsley saw me traipsing around town one day looking for employment after my pa died and took a chance on me. I used to cook for the children in the workhouse before Pa took ill. I thank my lucky stars, I tell you."

"We're all fortunate she took us on. What would you like me to do now?"

"You're a good girl, Nancy. I don't know what I would've done without you and Arthur helping me today." Moira straightened the feather eiderdown so it was precisely centred. "I reckon that's everything done for up here, other than perhaps a vase of flowers. What do you think?"

Nancy could see Arthur trundling across the lawn with a wheelbarrow full of logs and nodded eagerly. It looked as though he still had several loads to go, and there were some early flowering lupins and wild roses near the wood store, which would look perfect with the pale green fern fronds which were so abundant under the trees. Plus, she always enjoyed being in Arthur's company, and it was a glorious day outside.

"You mean I can cut and arrange the flowers? Doesn't Miss Kingsley usually do that?"

"Ordinarily, yes, but she already has the vicar coming round for tea and cake to discuss fundraising, so I'm sure she would be happy for you to do it today. Do you know one flower from another? You're not going to end up picking a bunch of weeds by accident?"

"Of course not." Nancy laughed and shook her head. "We've always lived in the countryside. My pa used to like teaching me about wildlife and flowers, so you don't need to worry about that. Shall I pick some to go on the dining table as well?"

"Might as well while you're at it." Moira rested her hands on her hips and surveyed the room carefully, only nodding once she decided everything had been done to her satisfaction. "Don't be too long, mind. I'm just doing that leftover soup with bread and cheese for lunch. Something easy for all of you before I start cooking the roast beef for later. I don't want the little 'uns under my feet this afternoon, neither," she added in her soft west country burr.

"I can't wait to meet them. Miss Cressida speaks so fondly of her sister."

"You'll like Miss Marigold," Moira said, walking to the window to look out across the driveway. "It was such a surprise when we found out she was courting. And a gentleman with his own business, no less." She turned and winked. "It was all very mysterious. I always had her marked as a spinster, but before we knew it, this gentleman we'd never even met swept her off her feet and whisked her away to get married." Her expression softened, and she sighed wistfully. "Chance would be a fine thing that might ever happen to me. But as long as Miss Marigold is happy, we're all pleased for her."

CHAPTER 12

y the time the shadows started to lengthen on the lawn, everyone was in a state of high excitement. Nancy had helped the girls get changed into their best dresses, which were usually only kept for going to church on a Sunday, and they had all redone their hair to make sure it looked tidy. Meanwhile, at Miss Kingsley's suggestion, Arthur had set Blake, Robert, and Rick to work, raking the gravel drive and weeding for a couple of hours to use up some of the energy, which threatened to spill over into naughty behaviour.

Tantalising smells of delicious food wafted from the kitchen, and Nancy was still glowing from Miss Kingsley's enthusiastic praise for her flower arrangements, telling her that the wild, unstructured look was perfectly charming, if a little unusual.

"I can hear something," Anne cried, leaping up from her chair like a jack-in-a-box and scattering bobbins of cotton in every direction. They were all sitting in the library, which was used as their school-room. Miss Kingsley had told them they could amuse themselves with genteel pastimes until Marigold and Dorian arrived, so the girls were sewing, and the boys were whittling wooden soldiers.

"Look out, will you," Tess grumbled, chasing after the bobbins to put them tidily away back into the sewing box. "Don't spoil everything by being too overexcited. Mr Holt will expect us to be well-behaved, not like squealing children with no manners."

"Good morning...good evening...good night." Mr Popinjay bobbed on the top shelf of the bookcase, sensing their excitement, which made Rick giggle.

As one, they all packed their things away and ran down the hallway and into the front parlour to press their noses to the window.

"Don't smudge the glass," Sophie said. "Anne and I cleaned the windows after lunch."

"Goodness me! Look how grand their carriage is." Even Moira had rushed from the kitchen to join them, and her eyes widened with surprise as a matching pair of dappled grey horses pranced in front of the gleaming landau carriage, rolling up the drive.

"Blimey," Blake breathed, "he must be worth a pretty penny. Miss Kingsley will be delighted. She'll never have to worry about money again for this old house."

"Are you ready to come and say hello, children?" Cressida Kingsley bustled into the parlour behind them, smoothing her hands over her ruffled silk gown. She looked slightly self-conscious as everyone stared at her. The children were used to seeing her in plainer dresses, but tonight, she looked as though she was dressed for a high society ball, and a diamanté necklace added the finishing touch.

"Oh, Miss, you look beautiful," Nancy blurted out before clapping her hand to her mouth.

Miss Kingsley inclined her head graciously and smiled, but the way she patted her hair gave away her nervousness. "Why thank you, dear. It's not too much?"

"No," the girls all cried. They crowded around her and stroked the elegant silk ruffles before returning to look out of the window.

"I have to confess, I'm as excited as you to meet Mr Holt. Marigold's courtship was something of a whirlwind romance, and the only time he visited Kingsley House was when I happened to be out, so this is the first time I've met him. We must all remember not to overwhelm the poor fellow with too many questions about their honeymoon in

France." She patted her wispy bun again and straightened her shawl. It was made of shot silk in shimmering oranges and yellows that reminded Nancy of an eye-catching sunset.

"I'm going to say 'Bonjour Monsieur Holt.'" Robert grinned. It was the only French he knew. "Perhaps he'll tell us all about it in one of our geography lessons?" he suggested hopefully. It was no secret that Robert wanted to join the Royal Navy when he was older, and even the thought of crossing the English Channel by boat was something he was eager to hear about.

"I suppose I should return to the kitchen?" Moira could hardly tear her gaze away from the carriage, which was just pulling to a stop outside the front of the house, and she sounded slightly envious that the children could stay.

"Certainly not," Miss Kingsley said, patting her shoulder. "I wouldn't be able to run Kingsley House without all your hard work, Moira. You must come and greet Mr Holt with the rest of us as long as nothing is burning or needs your attention."

"I can?" The maid beamed and straightened her shoulders. Most servants were treated as though they were invisible, but her employer wasn't like that. "Everything in the kitchen is in hand. I even put my best apron on because I know how Miss Marigold would like me to make a good impression with the new master."

Miss Kingsley led them all out of the parlour and threw open the large front door so they could all stand at the top of the steps. A liveried coachman jumped down from his seat and opened the carriage door. Nancy exchanged a smile with Arthur and brushed a piece of lint from his shoulder.

"Shoulders back, boys," Arthur muttered under his breath. They stood in a line from the tallest to the smallest.

"My tummy feels funny," Sophie whispered, tugging at Anne's sleeve.

"It's just because we're excited, that's all," Anne hissed, glaring at her younger sister. "You better hadn't tell me you feel sick. I'm not missing this for the world."

"Hush, now, everyone." Miss Kingsley's smile was strained. "It's not as if it's Queen Victoria arriving to inspect us...let's all remind ourselves that it's just Miss Marigold and her new husband. We are family, after all."

Nancy held her breath. She imagined Mr Holt to be tall and slim with an aquiline nose and dark hair swept back from a high forehead. But instead, as he emerged from the carriage, she was surprised to see he was thickset, with broad shoulders and a barrel chest, which his waistcoat could barely contain. His nose was slightly flattened and crooked. He didn't look like someone who owned a jewellery shop in the elegant streets of Bath. In fact, he looked more like a prizefighter, even though his suit was finely cut.

"Home sweet home," he boomed, throwing his arms wide. As he handed Miss Marigold down from the carriage, what surprised Nancy more than anything was that he did so rather carelessly. She had expected to see tender smiles passing between them, but Dorian Holt seemed more interested in looking over his shoulder at Kingsley House. His gaze roamed over the building, and his smile seemed rather distracted as his new wife shook the creases out of her gown after their long journey.

"Oh, Cressida, it's so good to be back in the West Country," Marigold cried happily. She ran lightly up the steps and hugged her sister, blinking back tears. "Dorian and I had the most wonderful time on our honeymoon, but all that strange food and the heat became rather trying for us."

Cressida Kingsley hugged her sister in return and then stepped back slightly. "I was very surprised to receive your letter, saying that you were coming back already, but it's wonderful to see you again. I do hope nothing went wrong to make you return so soon?"

Dorian Holt strode up the steps with his arm outstretched to shake hands. "I'm to blame, Miss Kingsley," he said cheerfully. "Dear Marigold would happily have stayed for longer, and I feel dreadful that I'd promised her several months away. The thing is, I had business matters to attend to, which couldn't be put off any longer. We stayed in Bath for a couple of nights before returning here. I have assured your dear sister that I will make it up to her in the future. Perhaps a grand tour of Europe next year."

"A grand tour?" Cressida tried not to look surprised as she smiled at her sister. "Well, you're certainly going up in the world, Marigold, if that is your carriage."

Marigold looked embarrassed and shook her head. "Oh, no, Cressida, you've got the wrong idea. Dorian doesn't own the horses and carriage, but he wanted us to start married life back at Kingsley House in a grand way because he says that's what I deserve."

Nancy sensed Tess starting to giggle next to her, and she nudged her to be quiet.

"Nothing but the best for my new wife." Dorian put his arm possessively around Marigold's shoulder. "It's true, my dear, you do deserve to arrive home in luxury, and you must admit, it was enjoyable seeing the yokels staring as we came through the village."

Cressida winced. "Well…quite…but we don't call them that, Mr Holt. The farmers are our friends and neighbours."

"Call me Dorian. We're family now." He chuckled

expansively and surveyed the house and grounds. "Very nice…very nice indeed."

"I'm so glad to be home," Marigold said again.

Nancy thought the way he was eyeing up Kingsley House looked rather proprietorial, as though he already owned the place. "I would buy a nice landau once the money comes through from selling my business in Bath, Cressida, but you know how slow some of these business deals can be to be finalised. I hired the coachman and carriage just for the journey."

"Charming, if you felt it necessary," Cressida said. She pressed her lips together before she could be tempted to say more.

Dorian nodded. "We really are very tired from our travels, so if you could take care of paying the coachman for his troubles, Marigold and I will go upstairs to rest before dinner."

"I should introduce you to all the children, Dorian," Marigold said hastily. "Look how much effort they've gone to, waiting politely to meet us." She didn't quite meet his eye as she said it, and Nancy saw the shock on Miss Kingsley's face at the brazen way that he had just assumed that she would pay for the hire of the coach and horses.

"Can't it wait until later, my dear?" He stifled a yawn, and his gaze was disinterested as it raked over them until it came to rest on Arthur and Nancy last. "You two look fairly strong. The coachman will unload our trunks, so if you could bring them upstairs immediately, that would be most helpful."

"Yes, Mr Holt," they chorused.

He turned to smile at Moira. "You must be the housemaid? Bring a bottle of your finest wine and two glasses up to our room. I like to take aperitif before dinner, and Marigold has become accustomed to doing the same as well."

With that, he tucked Marigold's hand into the crook of his arm and swept into the entrance hall with a spring in his step, clearly looking forward to making Kingsley House his new home.

"Mr Holt didn't even ask our names." Sophie's chin trembled, and tears pooled in her eyes. "Doesn't he like us?" She scrubbed her hand across her face. "And why is he living in such a fancy way if he hasn't got enough money to pay for the carriage."

"Sophie, stop behaving like a baby. They're just tired from the journey." Tess looked worried as well but was putting on a brave face about the brush-off.

Moira was still too stunned to speak for a moment. "Should I...do we even have enough wine to take upstairs for him, Miss Kingsley?" she stammered. She wasn't used to being ordered about in such a way, let alone in such an extravagant fashion. Wine was reserved for special occasions and taken only in the dining room, not upstairs.

Miss Kingsley tightened her shawl and gave them

all a reassuring smile. "We must remember, everyone, that this is my sister's special day. I wasn't able to attend the wedding because they held it in Paris, so we shall do our very best to make Mr Holt feel right at home. I'm sure he'll soon realise that we like to live a little more frugally, but for today, we'll do what he suggested. Arthur, you and the boys can take the luggage upstairs; Nancy, you can help Moira get dinner ready and fetch a nice bottle of wine from the cellar."

She bustled away to fetch some money to pay the coachman, but not before Nancy saw her brow furrow with concern when she thought nobody was looking.

"Well, I ain't sure about this..." Moira muttered under her breath.

"What do you think of him, Arthur?" Nancy said quietly as the other boys started picking up the hatboxes and bags next to the carriage to carry upstairs.

Arthur scratched his head and gave her a rueful look. "I'm not sure yet, but I can tell you things are certainly going to be very different here at Kingsley House. He seems like the sort of fellow who likes to get his own way and expects others to jump when he clicks his fingers."

"The cheek of expecting Miss Kingsley to pay for his extravagant carriage."

"There's going to be interesting times ahead, Nancy. I reckon it's up to you and me to keep an eye on him and make sure the little 'uns and Miss Kingsley don't get taken advantage of. You can see that Miss Marigold is too smitten to question his strange ways."

"I agree. And the good thing is that he won't suspect a thing because you can see he's not really interested in us children."

With Arthur's dire warning ringing in her ears, Nancy hurried after Moira and tried to ignore the sense of alarm that gripped her. Just as she had started to get used to her new life at Kingsley House, it seemed that Dorian Holt's arrival heralded the winds of change again. And not necessarily for the better, she thought glumly.

CHAPTER 13

*N*ancy pulled a wet sheet from the wicker wash basket and shook the creases out before draping it over the washing line. She pegged it in place and pushed a strand of her long hair back from her face. A warm breeze was blowing, tugging at her skirts and lifting her hair on the back of her neck, where it had escaped from the bun she had hastily pinned earlier that morning.

"Remember how short your hair was when you first arrived five years ago?" Arthur's comment from across the lawn was accompanied by a wry chuckle of amusement.

"How could I forget? I felt like a freshly shorn sheep. It's a wonder Miss Kingsley ever let me stay here looking like that."

Arthur picked up the axe and placed a new log on

the chopping block. His broad, muscular shoulders were clearly defined underneath his shirt as he swung the axe in an arc and the log split. Nancy felt the heat rise to her cheeks as she watched him surreptitiously between the sheets, which were flapping on the washing line. Now that she was fifteen and Arthur was almost seventeen, occasional thoughts about how handsome he had become floated into her mind, although she pushed them hastily away. He was certainly her best friend, but that was all. If anything, she regarded him as a big brother, occasionally rather annoying, but a confidante and the person she knew she could trust with her life and her innermost secrets.

Moira had washed all the linen napkins earlier that morning, and Nancy rummaged in the peg basket to make sure she would have enough pegs. She took her time at the task, enjoying the early summer day and the sun on her cheeks. She knew it would bring her freckles out, but she didn't care about that. Maintaining a delicate peaches-and-cream complexion was only something well-to-do ladies needed to worry about, and it wasn't as if she ventured out from Kingsley House often.

Her thoughts drifted back over the last few years as she got into a rhythm of shaking the creases out of each napkin and pegging them in a tidy line to dry.

The thing which astonished her most was how

quickly the years had passed. She could still remember the week she first arrived when it seemed unimaginable that she might spend the rest of her childhood separated from Ma, Pa, and her siblings. But now, if she was being honest with herself, Miss Cressida and the other residents at Kingsley House felt more like her family.

Her ma and pa had managed a few visits during her first year in Lower Amberley, but each time felt more awkward than the last. Their lives had taken different paths, and it felt as though they had little in common anymore. Of course, she still loved them dearly, but she had to get used to not seeing them to stop feeling overcome by homesickness. She dutifully wrote a letter once a month, on a Sunday morning after church, and hoped that they felt proud of how she was progressing with her book learning.

Not long after her eleventh birthday, her ma had visited just with Primrose and the new baby, Josiah. He was a bonny little thing, and Nancy felt a pang of regret that he would barely know her. Her ma had explained that, true to his word, Mr Harrington had offered Ezra a promotion because he was so impressed with his work as a clerk. The only problem was it would entail another move to a different railway camp, further away. They were moving to Oxford, Margaret informed her.

"But when will I see you again?" Nancy could still

recall her sense of panic. But, much to her surprise, her ma had unclipped the old silver locket she always wore and placed it in Nancy's hand.

"I know it was hard being left behind, Nancy, but we had no choice. And this promotion has done Ezra's confidence the world of good. I hope you understand that we have to accept otherwise, Mr Harrington's support will have all been for nothing." She handed Primrose a handkerchief as she sniffed while she turned the pages of one of the picture books from Miss Kingsley's collection. "It's better for all of us, but that's why I want to give you this necklace as a little keepsake." They both knew it wasn't worth much, and the silver plate was tarnished on the back, but it meant the world to Nancy.

She had put it on immediately, tucking it inside her gown to keep it safe. "I did miss you all to start with, but Miss Kingsley and the others have always been kind to me."

Her ma had nodded briskly as though to stop herself from becoming maudlin. "We are very proud of how you've settled in. The thing is, now that Ezra's job is taking him further away, we will have to stay in touch by letter instead of being able to visit you."

Nancy had nodded mutely, not daring to speak in case she started crying. Once she had got control of her emotions again, she bounced Josiah on her knee, making him giggle, and realised that she had been half expecting this anyway. *I should count myself lucky compared to the other girls.* She thought about the fact that Anne and Sophie had never heard from their parents again after they'd sailed to America, and Tess was all alone in the world, much like Arthur.

"I'll keep writing my letters too, Ma," she said, putting a brave face on things. "Who knows, if I get a job as a governess when I'm older, I might be able to live closer to wherever you and Pa are living by then."

A PAIR of collared doves cooed in the oak tree, then flapped down onto the lawn in front of her, snapping her back to the present. Now, five years after arriving, thinking about her family didn't make her feel homesick anymore. She was pleased that Pa had recovered from his bad nerves and that Luke was happy working with the other navvies. Her last letter from Ma had explained that Luke was doing well, and if he carried on that way, he might be made a supervisor as soon as he was old enough.

Sometimes, she wondered whether her parents would summon her back if they needed her to go out to work to contribute to the family finances, but as much as she loved them, she hoped they wouldn't. The thought of leaving Arthur and the other children felt almost as bad as how she had felt when she had first left her own family.

Fancy me thinking like that now. It only goes to show how we can all manage to adapt to new situations. She smiled to herself at the unexpected insight.

"Penny for your thoughts?" Arthur grunted. The axe arced again, and shards of wood splintered around the chopping block. "You look miles away... either that or you're daydreaming about what's for lunch."

She roused herself. She didn't have time to stand around, pondering such things when there were plenty of jobs that needed doing before she went to help Moira prepare lunch. She had rushed through her lessons that morning, and all she had left to do for her schooling was piano practice, but that could come later. Now that she and Arthur were older, Miss Kingsley had slowly allowed them to do more than just study. It didn't feel as though they were servants, though, more that they were part of the fabric of Kingsley House, helping with its smooth running. Miss Kingsley had recently arrived home from an outing with two more toddlers in her care. They had, by turns, howled with hunger and then shivered silently with fear, clinging to each other for comfort for the first few days. It had fair broken Nancy's heart to see them looking so forlorn, but now they were settling in and being as rambunctious as little ones were at that age, into everything, and causing mischief wherever they went. Nancy figured

Miss Kingsley was probably grateful for any help she and Arthur could provide in taking care of some of the other chores that needed doing.

"I don't have to go inside straight away," she said, strolling across the lawn. "Do you want me to pick up the kindling that you've chopped?"

Arthur's face lit up at her suggestion, and he smiled in that lopsided way of his, which lately had made her heart skip peculiarly in her chest. "I thought you were never going to offer." He wiped the sweat from his brow with the back of his hand. "Miss Kingsley has asked me to repair some of the cupboards in the new nursery she's using for the babies. The backs have got a few woodworm holes, but nothing a drop of vinegar won't solve, and then I'll make some new doors for the front. I can make a start on it before lunch if you help me with this."

They worked together in companionable silence for a few minutes. Arthur had an easy way about him that Nancy admired. When the younger children were being mischievous or struggling with something new, he invariably stepped in to help them with patience and good humour.

Just as Nancy had filled a box with kindling, the scraping sound of a window being opened caught their attention. It was the sash window of Dorian's study, and she caught a glimpse of his angry expression as he turned back to speak to Marigold. They were shielded from his view by the woodshed, and as his voice rose, Nancy knew he hadn't realised they were close enough to hear every word.

"I don't know why your sister insisted on taking in those new children, Marigold. Goodness knows, haven't we already got enough with the other eight?"

Nancy caught Arthur's eye and put her finger to her lips, telling him to be quiet. He nodded, and they both edged a little closer. They had long suspected that Dorian didn't agree with how Cressida ran Kingsley House, and sure enough, here was their proof.

"She couldn't leave them behind," Marigold said plaintively. "The poor things were blue with cold and looked like they hadn't eaten for days. Little Ernest had just been orphaned, and Jane's mama was in the clutches of a terrible opium addiction. It was just sheer luck that Cressida happened to be near the orphanage when the matron said they had no room for any more children."

"Sheer luck?" Dorian's tone was disparaging. "I wouldn't call two wailing toddlers rampaging about the place and constantly hungry luck, Marigold," he snapped. "All of these wretched children are nothing more than a drain on our finances, which are already in a perilous situation, I'll have you know. Why should we bother feeding and clothing and educating them when their own parents don't even care."

Nancy gasped at his cruel words and shrank back as he suddenly appeared at the window again. He stood with his hands behind his back, looking out at the garden with a mutinous set to his jaw. "If it was down to me, I'd throw them all out onto the street again instead of mollycoddling them. I'll wager they're not even grateful for everything you and Cressida do for them."

"Oh, Dorian, don't say such a dreadful thing," Marigold cried. She came to stand next to him in the window, her slim hands fluttering to her chest as she timidly tried to get him to understand. "Running a charitable home for poor urchins and the waifs that society doesn't want was Cressida's dream, and I always promised I would support her. It's what we wanted to do with Mama and Papa's inheritance money."

Dorian scowled, and Nancy shook her head as she looked at Arthur. "Look at Dorian's face. It's the money that seems to be the sore point," she whispered.

"I think you're right," Arthur whispered back. "He talks a good talk, but since he supposedly sold that business of his in Bath, I don't reckon Miss Kingsley and her sister have seen a penny of it."

Nancy nudged him to be quiet as they started talking again.

"Please tell me you'll never let Cressida or the

children hear you say anything like that again, Dorian?" Marigold had a pleading expression, and she pulled a lace handkerchief from her sleeve, dabbing it to catch the tears rolling down her cheeks.

Dorian sighed extravagantly and then relented. "I'm sorry, my dear." He patted her shoulder in a half-hearted fashion. "I've been looking around the house, and you have to admit it's starting to look rather dilapidated. A place like this requires a lot of money for its upkeep. It could be worth a lot when we sell it one day."

Marigold's mouth dropped open with shock. "Sell it?" she said faintly. "Cressida will never sell this place while she still has a breath left in her body, and I wouldn't want her to. Whatever made you suggest such a thing?"

Dorian grimaced to himself but then gave a hearty chuckle and patted Marigold's hand again. "Silly old me. I was only talking hypothetically, my dear. Of course, Kingsley House must never be sold. It's Cressida's pride and joy. I was just worrying about the cost of upkeep."

"He's changed his tune," Arthur muttered. "He's as slippery as an eel, I reckon."

"I know, but Marigold can't see it." Nancy pursed her lips, her thoughts racing. The fact that Dorian had even mentioned selling Kingsley House filled her with alarm, but it wasn't as if they could tell Miss Kingsley that they had been eavesdropping.

"I think it's high time for a few things to change around here, Marigold," Dorian continued in his bossy way. He smoothed his moustache and squared his shoulders as though he was preparing to be the saviour of the hour.

"I know you'll have the answer to our money worries." Marigold hated confrontation, and she looked relieved that a full-blown argument had been averted.

Dorian nodded decisively. "I think it's time for me to take over the reins a little more. I want to support Cressida's endeavours, and she's so busy teaching the children and caring for the new toddlers, it's the least I can do."

"What are you thinking of Dorian? You're already doing the books. I tried my best in the past, but Papa always said I never had a head for numbers, and everything was so hard to tally."

Nancy and Arthur both tiptoed forward, but before they could hear any more, Dorian closed the window again with a clatter, cutting off the rest of their conversation.

"Blimey, what do you think he has in mind?" Nancy picked up the box of kindling and rested it on her hip.

"No idea." Arthur raked a hand through his hair

and frowned. "I don't know what it is about him, Nancy, but I just don't trust him. He disappears for hours, claiming he's away on business matters, but as far as I can tell, there's never anything to show for it."

"Perhaps he's finally realised he needs to pull his weight a bit more? If he had a jewellery shop, he must have good business sense, surely?"

"It's nice that you see the good in people, but I think we should stay alert until we know what he's got planned. All we can do is hope that he has our best interests at heart. Miss Kingsley would be devastated if anything bad ever happened to the place."

ARTHUR FILLED his wheelbarrow with bigger logs and followed Nancy across the lawn. "I may as well put these in the parlour, ready for this evening," he said, shooting her a grin.

As they walked into the entrance hall, Nancy could hear Ernest and Jane crying. Tess came charging down the stairs, brandishing a book. "Don't worry, Sophie is looking after them. I ran upstairs to get the book of fairytales to read them a story."

"Good idea," Nancy said. "I always used to tell our Primrose a story when she was tired and grizzly, and it always soothed her."

Mr Popinjay flapped down from the upstairs

landing bannister and settled himself on top of the stuffed head of a gazelle in the hallway. "Stop, thief," he squawked.

"Have you been teaching him more words, Arthur?" Tess jumped as the parrot squawked loudly again and then casually lifted one of his wings to groom himself.

"Me? Certainly not." Arthur pretended to look innocent but then dissolved into laughter. "Oh, alright, I might have done. The little 'uns egged me on."

"You could have thought of something more appropriate," Nancy said, giving him a look of mock despair.

Dorian suddenly appeared in the doorway of his study. "That bird's been saying 'stop, thief' all morning."

Nancy expected him to be cross about it, but instead, Dorian smiled, joining in the joke. "I don't suppose there's any harm if the younger children know about what you used to do in your past, Arthur."

Arthur shrugged as he picked up some of the logs from the wheelbarrow and stacked them in the crook of his arm. "I've never made any secret of it, and I'm not ashamed of what I had to do to survive," he said briskly. A gleam of amusement came into his eyes. "You should have seen Bernard Doyle's face when Miss Kingsley said she wanted me to come and live here. Hopping mad, he was. I was his best pickpocket, and I reckon he had plans for me to go up in the world and start stealing more valuable stuff." He looked awkward for a moment. "Hark at me boasting about something so trivial. That's all in the past."

"Well, it's a good thing Cressida did invite you here, Arthur. Otherwise, who knows where you might have ended up." Dorian cleared his throat and glanced up at the parrot, who was regarding him with a beady look that bordered on insolence. "It's funny you should say you were his best pickpocket. Didn't he have any girls in the gang?"

"Girls?" Arthur sounded surprised.

"Yes. When I had my shop in Bath, I used to see a few pickpockets. I could recognise them a mile off, but it was surprising how many of the well-to-do ladies and gentlemen had no idea. I always noticed that the girls seemed to be better at it than the boys," he mused as though it was of no real interest. "I suppose it's just because they were less likely to be suspected. It was always the young lads the constables were chasing, and half the time, they hadn't even realised the girls were robbing someone blind at the same time while they were distracted."

"I don't know about that," Arthur shrugged. He reached for another log, but as he did so, the one he had just picked up fell out of his arm and landed at Dorian's feet.

"Let me get that for you."

"No, it's fine, I've got it." Arthur picked it up quickly and smiled his thanks before reaching for one more from the wheelbarrow and wedging it under his chin.

It was unusual for Dorian to be so chatty, and Nancy wondered whether they had misjudged him wrongly in the past. She supposed it must be rather strange living with so many children who weren't his own.

"Now that you say it," Arthur mused, "I always used to think Nancy would make a good pickpocket."

"What do you mean?" She rolled her eyes. "You do say the strangest things sometimes, Arthur."

"All I'm talking about is the first day we met. Do you remember...I happened to be watching when I saw you picking up Mrs Harrington's brooch."

"I've never heard this story." Dorian leaned against the hearth and looked at her with a curious expression.

"A well-to-do lady dropped her expensive brooch in the lane without realising, and Nancy picked it up without anyone even noticing. She could easily have pocketed it, but she's not that sort of girl."

"I returned it to Mr and Mrs Harrington," Nancy explained, taking up the story. "It was worth a lot of

money, and like Arthur said, I could have kept it."
Something about Dorian's unexpectedly friendly
demeanour made her drop her guard. "I have to
confess, I was tempted to keep it. I considered taking
it to a pawnbroker to sell. My family could have done
with the money, but I overheard Mrs Harrington say
something about her daughter, Rosie, and she looked
sad, so I returned it to them."

"That's a very noble thing to do." Dorian nodded
approvingly.

"Mr Harrington helped find my pa a different job,
and now his health is much better. It was a nice
reward for doing the right thing."

Nancy suddenly caught sight of Moira bustling
back and forth in the kitchen and remembered she
was meant to be taking the kindling into the parlour
before helping her cook lunch.

"Well, don't let me keep you from your chores,"
Dorian said. "I have an appointment in the village at
noon…what time is it?" He frowned in puzzlement as
he looked down at his waistcoat and realised his gold
pocket watch was missing. "That's odd…I'm sure I
put it on this morning." He looked down again and
fingered the buttonhole where the chain should have
been.

Nancy couldn't keep a straight face any longer,
and she burst out laughing.

"This one, you mean?" Arthur chuckled as he

pulled the fob watch on its chain out of his shirt pocket and dangled it in front of Dorian like a magician.

"Stop, thief!" Mr Popinjay squawked.

"Well, I'll be..." Dorian shook his head, lost for words. "Did you take that from me just now? Without me even noticing?"

"Actually, it was me," Nancy said, with another splutter of laughter. "Arthur has been teaching me some of his old...skills." She suddenly remembered herself. "Don't tell Miss Kingsley, will you. We only do it for fun."

"I told you she's a natural, didn't I," Arthur added with a grin as he handed the watch back. "We'd make a great team...not that I would ever go back to that sort of life," he said hastily.

"Very amusing. You got me good and proper." Dorian shook his head with a rueful expression, but there was also a newfound look of respect in his dark eyes. He threaded the chain through his waistcoat buttonhole and slipped the watch back into his pocket, tapping it again as though to make doubly sure it was still there. He started to walk away but turned around again, having just remembered something. "I'm in the process of opening another shop for my jewellery business. I've noticed how hard you two work, and I was thinking about asking Miss Kingsley whether you might both like to help me in the shop some days. It might be a good experience for you."

"Us?" Arthur looked shocked.

"Good afternoon…good evening!" Mr Popinjay bobbed his head up and down again and flapped his wings.

Dorian sighed and held up his hands in resignation. "I think we should continue this conversation tomorrow without that parrot interrupting us. I'll speak to Miss Kingsley and see what she thinks."

Once he had returned to his study, Nancy followed Dorian into the parlour to put the kindling next to the log basket. "I didn't see that coming. It looks like he was doing business matters on all those outings after all."

"Maybe we've been too quick to judge him," Arthur agreed. "It would be fun, don't you think, Nancy? The two of us working together."

Her heart did a strange flip in her chest as he straightened up and gave her his lopsided smile.

"I'd like that very much, but we'd better not get our hopes up until Miss Kingsley agrees."

CHAPTER 14

$\mathcal{N}$ancy spooned a dollop of strawberry jam into each bowl of porridge and swirled it through before handing them around to all the other children. Ernest and Jane were sitting in their highchairs at the end of the table, babbling happily, as Tess fed them fingers of buttered toast and chopped boiled egg.

"No news?" Arthur asked Nancy quietly as he walked behind her to go and wash his hands in the scullery. He had two rabbits hanging from his belt, which would go into the game pie Moira was making later.

She shook her head. "Nothing yet. Perhaps he didn't mean anything by it, or Miss Kingsley didn't agree."

"Didn't agree to what?" Blake asked. He gave them

a suspicious glance, his spoon hovering midway to his mouth. "You two aren't leaving Kingsley House, are you?"

"Of course not, silly," Nancy said hastily. "It's nothing. Do you want this last spoonful of porridge?" She knew the question would distract him, and he nodded eagerly. She didn't want to tell the others what Dorian had discussed with them the other day. Many other orphanages would have thrown her and Arthur out by now, given that they were plenty old enough to go to work, and even though Miss Kingsley had always assured them all that she operated differently, it was a natural worry for all of them. They had heard rumours aplenty about young girls and boys being sent into service, or worse, to work in the harsh conditions of the factories and mills when the orphanages were too overcrowded to keep them.

Moira bustled into the kitchen, carrying the breakfast tray she had taken up to Cressida earlier. Nancy noticed that her coddled eggs were uneaten, and she had scarcely taken a bite from her toast and marmalade. "Isn't Miss Kingsley feeling well?"

Moira put the uneaten food in the centre of the kitchen table, and the boys fell upon it like hungry gannets. Her brows drew together in a frown. "She's not ill as such, but I reckon she's working too hard. This is the third morning in a row she's barely touched her breakfast. She was already up, poring over one of those ledgers that Mr Holt keeps on his desk."

"She was going through the accounts?" Arthur sounded surprised, and Nancy felt a ripple of concern as well. Everyone knew that Dorian had taken over the bookkeeping not long after arriving. If Miss Kingsley was going through the ledgers as well as not eating, perhaps his remarks about the dwindling finances of Kingsley House they had overheard between him and Marigold were true.

"She told me she was just keeping abreast of things," Moira said. She rolled up her sleeves and set to scrubbing the porridge pan with gusto. "I'm sure she'll be as right as rain by tomorrow. I got the feeling she has something on her mind, but I'm sure she would tell us what it was if we needed to know."

After Moira's comments, Nancy was surprised when Miss Kingsley glided into the kitchen half an hour later. She paused from her task of kneading a mound of dough to bake bread. Arthur was busy skinning the two rabbits he had caught, and the rest of the children were already in the library, making a start on their arithmetic lessons.

"I'm glad you're both here," Cressida said as she walked across the flagstone floor and gazed out of the window for a moment, lost in her thoughts. "I couldn't bear to leave Kingsley House," she murmured quietly to herself. "It would feel as though we let you down, not to mention made poor use of Papa's inheritance." She turned back to face them, and Nancy noticed the paleness of her cheeks and dark circles under her eyes.

"Is everything alright, Miss Kingsley? Arthur and I don't mind taking on more chores; you only have to say the word."

She shook her head and straightened her shoulders. "Don't mind me, my dear. Papa raised me to be made of stern stuff, and Marigold and I will keep this place going until the day we die."

"Perhaps you're tired because of the extra work, taking in Ernest and Jane," Arthur ventured. "Don't forget, that nasty cough you had all winter fair knocked the stuffing out of you as well."

Miss Kingsley walked around the kitchen table and poured herself a cup of coffee from the pot that was sitting on the side of the range. She added a dash of milk and one lump of sugar with the silver tongs and stirred it with a thoughtful expression on her face.

"Dorian came to see me in my parlour the other day."

Nancy and Arthur exchanged a glance. Would she agree to his plan?

"He gave me a suggestion which was rather unexpected, so I've needed a few days to mull it over. You know I pride myself on only doing what I think is best for you and the other children."

Nancy slipped away to the pantry and returned with two sugared shortbread biscuits on a plate. Miss Kingsley was looking almost gaunt, and she knew they were her favourites. *Should we tell her he spoke to us already?* She decided there was nothing to lose by doing so. "Mr Holt did mention something to us, but we didn't think he was serious."

Cressida didn't look surprised as she sat down. "Neither did I, to start with." She took a sip of coffee and a dainty bite of one of the biscuits, and some colour returned to her cheeks, making her look more like her old self. "When Mr Holt first came here, he always sounded rather vague when he talked about his shop in Bath. Between you and me, I wondered whether he had embellished a few details to make himself more appealing to my dear sister, but I was wrong. You may have noticed he's had a fair few days away from Kingsley House in recent months. It turns out he has been setting up a new jewellery shop. In Woodchester town of all places."

Arthur gave a low whistle. "Woodchester, between here and Thruppley? That's a shrewd move. When I was pickpocketing for Bernard Doyle, Bernie always said that Woodchester was where all the most affluent toffs live. If anyone can afford fine jewellery, it will be them. Bernard knew a thing or two about well-to-do gentlemen and ladies," he added with a wink.

"I've never been there, even though it's only a couple of miles away." Nancy sprinkled some flour on the table and carried on kneading the dough, enjoying the yeasty smell that filled the room.

"Now that you're both getting older, I was starting to wonder about whether it was time to help you find paid work beyond what we have here." She gave Nancy a warm smile. "It's not that I don't value everything you have done here. Both of you have been exemplary in your studies and helping Moira. It's children like you who I dreamt about helping when I first set Kingsley House up, but you are the first ones to fly the nest, so to speak."

"You don't mean you're sending us away?" Nancy couldn't stop herself from asking as her old insecurities surfaced.

"Certainly not," Miss Kingsley said quickly. "You're part of the family, both of you. Besides, the other children would miss you dreadfully. No, what Dorian suggested was that you could work for him at his new jewellery shop. I was very surprised, I have to say, but now that I've given it some thought, I think it would be good for you. You'll have a chance to work with an established businessman and interact with some of the more well-to-do families in the area. I'm hopeful some other employment opportunities might come of it once people get to see how charming and well-behaved you are."

"What about our chores? We don't want things falling behind." Arthur had a glint of excitement in his eyes, but he was too polite to agree to the suggestion straightaway.

"I THINK Blake and Tess are ready to take on a few extra chores, don't you?" Cressida drained her coffee and dabbed her handkerchief at the corners of her mouth, looking revived by the refreshments.

"Will it help ease the house's financial pressures?" Nancy knew it was a direct question, but for once, Miss Kingsley didn't immediately change the subject at the mention of money.

"That was part of the reason why Dorian suggested this," she admitted. "I never like to worry you children, but you're old enough to understand that this is an expensive house to run. Some of the charitable donations have dried up in the last couple of years as two of our generous benefactors moved away from the area."

"You've done so much for us. We'll always be grateful."

She stood up and patted her hair. "It's nothing to worry about, but Dorian has kindly agreed that if you two can work for him, he will be able to contribute more. It might even give us a chance to have a few more children here. I've been disappointed for a while that there are only ten of you. I know we recently welcomed Ernest and Jane, but I'd envisaged helping more children." She sighed. "Finances haven't permitted it, sadly."

"I think Arthur and I would like it very much." Nancy deftly gathered the pile of dough in front of her and dropped it into an earthenware bowl before covering it with a tea towel so it could prove before baking. "When is the shop opening? Will we start next month?"

"Oh, it's already open." Miss Kingsley said, giving them a wry smile. "My brother-in-law is rather a dark horse. Marigold and I knew nothing about it. I suggest you start tomorrow morning, bright and early. Dorian sounded very keen not to delay matters."

Nancy couldn't keep the surprise from her face but nodded eagerly. "I'd better make sure our best clothes are in good repair. What do you say, Arthur?"

He grinned and also nodded, bubbling with his usual irrepressible enthusiasm. "It will certainly be a change for us, Miss Kingsley, but if it's what you and Mr Holt think is for the best, we'll happily start work tomorrow."

"I thought you would say that." Cressida nodded to herself. "Dorian was right. You're both old enough to work for him and represent Kingsley House in the wider community. I think this will be a wonderful new chapter for you both, and I'll always be very grateful for the good-natured way you tackle everything. You're a marvellous example of being able to overcome the challenges of your past."

"With a bit of help and guidance from you and Mrs Holt," Nancy said stoutly.

DORIAN'S STURDY COB MARE, Queenie, clopped along the lane the following morning, and Nancy couldn't help but smile as the first sight of the small market town of Woodchester came into sight. It was the first time she had been in the brougham carriage or even left Lower Amberley since arriving at Kingsley House, and her first impressions of the town made her smile even more. There were winding lanes lined with small cottages made from the traditional honey-coloured stone of the area, as well as larger, grander houses dotted between the cottages. As they progressed a little further, the lanes opened up into a large market square, at the heart of which was a long stone building on pillars. The underneath part was open, full of costermongers shouting their wares. Slate steps led up one side to a wooden door with an enormous iron knocker, and diamond-leaded windows looked over the square on every side.

"Corn Square, this is called," Dorian explained, "and that's Market House. It used to be for the wool sales, but now the magistrate has his office there. I've been lucky enough to secure premises for the shop just on the yonder side of the square over there." He pointed towards a two-storey building. It had a pleasing symmetry, with the door set in the centre and generous-sized bow windows on either side. The three windows above were tucked under a mossy tile-stone roof. There was a small half-circle flower bed next to the door, and a rambling trailed charmingly over the portico roof, which jutted out above the door.

"It's in the perfect position for people to see it easily." Nancy admired the smartly painted sign over one of the windows. *Woodchester Jewellers*, it said, in gold lettering against a midnight blue background.

"It looks very quaint," Arthur said. He straightened his jacket, looking slightly self-conscious. He wasn't used to wearing his best clothes very often or having to stay clean and tidy all day.

There was a wide pathway between the road and the shop front, with ample room for the well-to-do ladies and gentlemen to stroll past the shops and stop to look in the windows without fear of being in the way of passing wagons and carts. She looked at some of them and could already tell by their clothes that many of them were wealthy.

"It's market day today, which means it's busier than usual." Dorian steered their horse and carriage through an archway between the shop and the tavern next door. "The stables belong to The Golden Fleece Tavern, but Stanley Morris, the landlord, is more than happy for us to put Queenie here because he knows we don't live in Woodchester. His stable lad feeds and waters the horse, so we don't even have to contend with that."

"I suppose, if the weather was bad, we could walk here." Nancy was surprised at how quickly they had arrived. She had expected it to be further from Lower Amberley, with the palaver of hitching up the horse and carriage, but then she remembered that people like Mr Holt weren't used to having to walk to most places like those who were less well-off.

"Indeed," Dorian said. "I also have living quarters over the shop, so if we were ever snowed in, it wouldn't be the end of the world."

Dorian led them through the cobbled back pathway from the stables to the shop a few minutes later and withdrew a large ornate key from his waistcoat pocket to unlock the back door.

"Do the customers ever come in this way?" Arthur asked, keen to start learning immediately.

Nancy glanced around, noticing how private it

was. Other than one small attic window on the side of the tavern, the rear approach wasn't overlooked at all, and the stone walls were shrouded in ivy and honeysuckle. She couldn't even hear the rumble of carts passing through the town square. It felt almost like being in the countryside, and the musical trill of birdsong filled the air as a robin flitted from one side of the path to the other, hoping for some crumbs.

"No, this pathway only leads to the back of my shop. It's nice and private, and I'd like to keep it that way, so don't go telling anyone about it." Dorian gave them a wink, which Nancy thought was rather strange.

The wooden door had warped slightly, and Dorian leaned his shoulder against it to lever it open.

"I'll plane that wood back a bit. Have it fixed in no time," Arthur said.

Nancy was surprised by how tidy the backroom was. On one side, there was a long workbench with several oil lamps, and a wooden shelf held an array of rasps and sets of pliers. "I didn't realise you made jewellery," she said.

"It's mainly for repairs, plus I like to repurpose some of the less attractive pieces and add a bit of my own flair." Dorian breezed onwards through the heavy velvet curtains which led to the front of the building where the shop was. As she followed him, Nancy had a glimpse of a range in the corner of the backroom behind piles of wooden crates, the contents of which were wrapped in cloth.

"Ta-dah! Welcome to my latest endeavour: Woodchester Jewellers, for all discerning customers looking for quality jewellery." There was a hint of self-satisfaction in Dorian's deep voice as he gestured around the shop.

"Lawks, I've never seen so many beautiful things in one place," Nancy gasped, her mouth gaping as she looked between Arthur and Dorian. "We were expecting the place to be empty. Miss Kingsley said you had opened the shop already, but we never imagined it would look like this."

If Dorian was surprised by Nancy's startled comment, he was too polite to show it. "It's quite something, isn't it?" He puffed his chest out, clearly very proud of what he had created. "Go on," he nodded, "you can have a good look around, but don't touch anything. Some of these pieces are very rare and worth more money than you've probably ever dreamt of."

He hurried away to shut the back door, and Nancy clung to Arthur's arm, still in shock as they slowly walked around the displays.

"I've never seen anything like it," Arthur whispered in reverence. "I mean, I've pickpocketed a few bits and pieces of jewellery in my time from the toffs, but this is in another league."

The shop was full of ornate mahogany cabinets with glass-fronted doors, and there were plump velvet cushions in the window to display his wares. Precious and semi-precious stones winking in the sunlight...necklaces, bracelets, brooches, and more, not to mention silver trinkets.

"It must have cost hundreds of pounds to come by all of these. Do you think he brought them from his shop in Bath, and Cressida and Marigold never knew about it all this time?"

Arthur glanced towards the backroom, looking puzzled. "I can't understand it," he said in a low voice. "It feels as though we don't know Dorian at all. I've never heard Cressida or Marigold mention any of this. Or that he makes jewellery."

Dorian strode back into the shop and walked straight to the front door, shooting back the bolts. "I heard what you just said, young Arthur." He gave them both another grin, but it didn't quite reach his eyes. With his back to the windows, his face was cast in shadow, and Nancy shivered slightly at the way his dark eyes hardened for a second. In all the recent excitement, she had forgotten that her original impression of Dorian had always been that he was not a man to be crossed. He tapped the side of his nose and smirked. "It's all perfectly above board, but I find it's best not to trouble Marigold and Cressida with too many details about my business. They already have more than enough to think about taking care of the children. And it's not as if either of them has much of a head for business."

Nancy cleared her throat and smoothed the front of her gown, wanting to look neat and presentable. "What work would you like us to do, Mr Holt?"

He gave her a shrewd look for a moment as though weighing her up and then nodded curtly. "I'll give you a list of jobs in a minute, but for now, I just want to impress upon you that what happens here at the jewellery shop is not to be discussed back at Kingsley House. A man in my position, in possession of so many valuables, needs discretion. The last thing I want is some of the younger children blabbing to all and sundry about what we have here." He pressed his lips together in a thin line. "Cressida and Marigold have an unfortunate habit of thinking the best of people and being blind to how they might be taken advantage of. As far as we're concerned, we will go about our day-to-day business in a professional manner, but we won't talk about it with the others. Is that clear?"

Nancy could sense Arthur's concern at Dorian's mercurial change of mood, so she nudged him slightly with her elbow.

"Perfectly clear, Mr Holt," Arthur said hastily.

"Miss Cressida said how important this job was to your shop and for the future of Kingsley House, so you can put your trust in us, Mr Holt," Nancy lifted her chin and smiled politely as two ladies came through the door, setting the bell tinkling to announce their arrival.

"The souls of discretion," Dorian murmured again, giving them a firm stare before he turned to greet the new arrivals. He gave the women an ingratiating smile, and yet again, Nancy was surprised at how his moods could change in a flash, depending on who he was talking to.

"Welcome…welcome," he said jovially. He took one of the ladies' hands and gave a small bow over the top of it, making her blush and laugh delightedly. "I'm charmed to make your acquaintance. Mr Dorian Holt at your service, and I assure you that once you have availed yourself of our delightful pieces of jewellery here, you'll never want to shop anywhere else."

"Good morning." Nancy bobbed a curtsey.

"What a wonderful shop you have." The ladies exchanged happy smiles.

"Thank you." Dorian bowed again with a flourish. "Now, please, tell me how I may help you while Arthur makes a start on his backroom chores and Nancy makes a cup of tea or coffee for you to enjoy while you browse." He jerked his head slightly to indicate he wanted them to leave, and Nancy edged away behind Arthur.

"Really? A cup of Earl Grey tea while we look at your charming necklaces...what a delightful idea, Hermione, don't you think?"

The two ladies twittered and blushed even more as Dorian gently guided them around the display cabinets, pointing out which jewels would be most becoming and would match their silk gowns best.

"What a performance," Arthur muttered once they were safely out of earshot. "Those toffs certainly seemed to fall for his charm." He picked up a broom to start sweeping the storeroom floor.

"I've never heard him talk like that to Marigold." Nancy hurried over to the range and saw that Dorian had already put the kettle on the hotplate. "And what about those ladies," she whispered, "they already had more expensive-looking jewellery than I've seen anyone wear just for strolling around town."

"He's not daft. That's why he chose Woodchester." Arthur paused and leaned on his broom. "I still don't know why he needs us here, Nancy. Something doesn't sit right with me about this."

"It might not be what we expected, but this won't be a bad way to spend our days, and if it helps Kingsley House, we just have to do as he says."

As the kettle started to whistle, Nancy added a scoop of Earl Grey tea leaves to the teapot and gathered two dainty bone china cups and saucers to put on the tray. Part of her was longing to tell Tess,

Sophie and Anne all about the shop when they got home, but they had promised Mr Holt they wouldn't. At least she had Arthur to share the experience with, and as he was her favourite person in the whole world, that was all that mattered.

CHAPTER 15

The early morning sun was already hot as Nancy and Arthur walked through the lanes, and Woodchester came into sight. They had been working at the shop for a month, and Dorian had taken to staying in the rooms above the shop several nights a week.

"Do you think Marigold misses him when he doesn't come home?" Nancy picked a pink campion flower from the hedgerow and tucked it into her dress.

"Honestly? I think Kingsley House always feels more peaceful when he's not around. I know he can turn on the charm for his customers, but he doesn't really seem very fond of Marigold. I overheard him grumbling about how much money she had given the greengrocer's boy the other day and complaining that she had bought a new lace collar for her dress. She looked upset when she left his study."

Nancy nodded. "I sometimes wonder why they ever got married, but I suppose she must have seen something in him."

"More like he saw something in her. A grand country house that he hopes to get his hands on one day."

"He shouldn't need to, with his own business doing so well."

Arthur kicked a pebble, and a look of concern crossed his face. "We only have his word to say that the business is doing well, Nancy, don't forget that. I'm still not sure about his motivation for having us working for him. It's not as if we've been run off our feet; half the time, we're just tidying the storeroom or running small errands."

"I'm rather surprised he needs us, too," Nancy agreed. A sticky strand of cleavers clung to Arthur's jacket, and she brushed it off absentmindedly, then blushed slightly as their eyes met, and he gave her a warm smile. "I mean, I suppose it's useful, having me out the back to make cups of tea and coffee for the customers, but the shop isn't as busy as I thought it would be."

"I suppose there are only so many jewels and

baubles well-to-do ladies can wear," Arthur chuckled. He shook his head in disbelief. "Did you see how much those two old ladies spent last week on those brooches? Each one would've been enough to pay for Miss Kingsley's bill at the butchers for six months, I reckon."

"It's funny, you should mention those brooches," Nancy said slowly. "I saw them on Dorian's work-bench. I think the opals were part of a necklace origi-nally, so I wonder why he turned them into brooches instead."

They stepped aside as a horse and cart rumbled past, and the farmer lifted his hand in greeting. Three Cotswold ewes bleated in the back, and a wooden crate filled with freshly picked vegetables was balanced on the seat next to him. Clearly, he was heading to market.

"Search me. Maybe he can earn more by selling two items instead of one. All I know is that I've never seen so many wealthy people as seem to live in Woodchester and the surrounding villages. Old Bernard Doyle and his gang of pickpockets would have a field day if they started working those streets." He grimaced slightly as if the thought had stirred up bad memories.

"Don't worry," Nancy said, patting his arm. Arthur rarely looked upset, but when he did, it always cast a shadow over her day as well. She couldn't imagine life without him in it, and although he never spoke of it much anymore, she knew it was only through Miss Kingsley's timely intervention that Arthur hadn't ended up thrown into prison or worse. "There's no reason to ever think you'll cross paths with Doyle and his gang again."

"I hope so," Arthur said, cheering up again. "He never forgave me for leaving the gang, and if he ever had an opportunity to get his own back, I'm sure he would take it." He linked arms with Nancy companionably and started whistling a jaunty tune.

"Not if I had anything to do with it." She wondered whether he realised that she had started to hope that one day, they might be more than friends. Her heart pitter-pattered, and she glanced away to cover the confusing emotions which swirled through her.

"What would I ever do without you, Nancy? You're always there to cheer me up, and we work well together. Let's hope Miss Kingsley allows us to carry on with the arrangement and doesn't send me away to work somewhere else."

"We'd better make ourselves indispensable to Dorian. That way, we'll always be able to work together." Nancy started untying the ribbons of her bonnet as they reached Corn Square and hoped that

Arthur would think her rosy cheeks were from the warmth of the sun and not because of her budding feelings of love for him.

AFTER WALKING through the archway and along the back path to the shop, Arthur shouldered the back door open. They were both shocked to see Dorian slumped over his workbench.

"Dorian! Are you alright?" Nancy ran forward and shook his shoulders, thinking the worst, and was relieved when he jerked upright on his stool and blinked blearily at her. The smell of stale brandy hung in the air, and he rubbed his eyes before hastily shaking out a cloth and draping it over whatever he had been working on.

"Is it morning already?" He yawned and flexed his shoulders, wincing as a bone in his neck creaked. "Stanley invited me to the Golden Fleece for a couple of drinks, and I've been working most of the night. I must have drifted off just before daybreak."

Arthur had already been out to get water from the pump, and he placed the bucket near the range so that Nancy could make a pot of strong coffee. "You should come back to Kingsley House and have a proper night's sleep. Miss Marigold must be concerned that you're overdoing it, although she probably won't say anything. You know how she doesn't like to worry anyone."

Dorian stood up and yawned extravagantly again. "Don't open the shop yet. I'm going to have a wash under the pump, and when I get back, we need to have a little chat."

Nancy put an extra spoonful of ground coffee in the pot and darted a worried glance towards Arthur as Dorian hurried away. "That sounds ominous. Perhaps you're right, and the shop isn't doing as well as we thought. What if he's going to tell us he doesn't want us working for him anymore?" Her heart sank. She knew Miss Kingsley couldn't keep her and Arthur living there for much longer without them working, and she couldn't imagine anywhere else that would take them on together.

Arthur knelt down to scoop the ash out of the bottom of the range, taking care not to get any soot on himself. "Let's not worry unduly. We've barely been coming for a month. I wonder what he's been working on all night," he said in a low voice. He stood up again and edged closer to the workbench, glancing through the open doorway to make sure Dorian wasn't returning already. "He certainly covered it up quickly enough."

"Don't be nosy," Nancy exclaimed. "It must be something he doesn't want us to know about."

A mischievous glint came into Arthur's eye. "All the more reason why we need to see what it is." He lifted the corner of the cloth and gave a low whistle. A gold bracelet studded with rubies and emeralds was lying on the bench. It had been prised apart into smaller sections, and there was also a silver platter with what looked like a family crest engraved at the centre.

"Where does he get these pieces from?" Arthur pondered out loud. "We never see him having any dealings with anyone—"

"He's back," Nancy whispered urgently, cutting Arthur off.

"That's better." Dorian used his shirt sleeve to wipe the water from his face and ran a hand through his greying hair.

Arthur hastily replaced the cloth and picked up the ash bucket, whistling nonchalantly.

"Is that coffee ready yet? I'm parched." Dorian had dark circles under his eyes, and, combined with his crumpled shirt, he looked unusually scruffy. He would certainly need to smarten up before opening the shop.

"I made it extra strong for you," Nancy said. She poured the thick brew into his favourite cup and handed it to him. Even the aroma seemed to banish his tiredness, and he sniffed appreciatively and took a gulp before sinking wearily back onto the stool at his workbench.

"I'm going to come right out and tell you a few things," he began. His tone was serious enough for Arthur to put the bucket down again.

Nancy drifted closer to him, all thoughts of getting on with her chores forgotten. Standing next to Arthur would give her strength in the face of whatever bad news Dorian was about to break.

"We really like working here for you," Arthur interjected, hoping to plead their case to stay.

"I can tell. I wouldn't have asked you if I didn't think you were suitable." Dorian took another gulp of the bitter dark coffee. It was still so hot it brought tears to his eyes, but it also hardened his resolve. "The finances of Kingsley House are in a parlous state. The chimneys need repairing, the floorboards in the dining room need replacing and feeding everyone costs more than you might think. What's worse is that Marigold has decided that they need to take on a governess to teach the younger children. Cressida's health is ailing, and it's all becoming too much for her, but she's far too stubborn to let the place go." He pinched his lips together with a pained expression.

"Perhaps I could teach the little ones to save you the cost of hiring a governess?"

Dorian shook his head sharply at Nancy's suggestion, not caring if it offended her. "No. I need you here in Woodchester helping me."

Arthur glanced at Nancy. "Are you sure you need both of us? It's just..." he chose his words carefully, "you don't seem that busy with customers. Although I'm sure as word gets out about your jewellery, it might get busier."

"I've come to a decision, and it's one I haven't made lightly, but before I share it with you, I need your word that you will never speak of this with anyone." Dorian's words were measured, but there was no mistaking the steely expression on his face, and Nancy shivered. *Does he intend to make us work in the factories? Or perhaps he wants to send Arthur away, and I'll never see him again?*

"We promised we would give you our discretion when we started here, Mr Holt," Arthur said, folding his arms across his chest. "We might be what some folk might think of as charitable cases, but we're true to our word, aren't we, Nancy."

She nodded. This time, it was his turn to edge slightly closer to her. She could feel the heat from his arm where it brushed against hers, and she found his solid presence at her side comforting.

"There are some very wealthy people who stroll through these streets of Woodchester town and also Thruppley village further down the valley every day of the week." Dorian finished his coffee with a faraway look in his eyes. "They browse at the shop windows and share the latest high society gossip, with barely a thought about what or who is around them."

Nancy shuffled her feet and caught Arthur's puzzled expression out of the corner of her eye. She was equally as confused by Dorian's sudden, seeming change of topic. "There certainly are plenty of well-to-do ladies and gentlemen here, but surely that's a good thing for the business?"

A sly look flitted across Dorian's face. It came and went so fast that if she had blinked, she would have missed it. But it had been there, and it sent a chill of foreboding down her back.

"Most of these well-to-do ladies and gentlemen, as you put it, Nancy, have more money than they know what to do with. They treat themselves to trinkets and jewels with not a care for those less fortunate than themselves," Dorian stood up from his stool and started pacing back and forth next to his workbench, with his hands clasped behind his back. There was a pugnacious set to his jaw, and his brows were drawn down into a sharp frown above his crooked nose, making him look more like a prize fighter than ever. "I need you to do more to help Kingsley House. Are you willing to do so?"

Nancy and Arthur nodded as one. "Of course,"

they both said in unison. "We all owe Miss Kingsley a debt of gratitude," Arthur added.

"Quite," he said crisply. "I want you to return to your previous occupation, Arthur. With Nancy's help, this time. A few days a week, you will wander through the streets of Woodchester and occasionally further afield in Thruppley. And you will take some of the items that these wealthy folk have so little regard for."

Arthur's mouth gaped open, and the silence stretched between them. "Do you mean...are you telling me...you want me to become a pickpocket again?" His voice rose with shocked disbelief, and he shook his head. "Never! I put that world behind me the day Miss Kingsley offered me a way out."

Hysterical laughter bubbled inappropriately in Nancy's chest, and she pressed her hand to her mouth, not knowing how to stop it. "Is it April Fools' Day? Has Miss Kingsley told you to say this as some sort of test for Arthur? The only pickpocketing I've ever done was what Arthur taught me, and that was just for fun. Surely you're saying this as a joke?"

Dorian stopped abruptly from his pacing and glowered at them. "You say that Miss Kingsley saved you, yet you have the temerity to question my authority."

"But...you're asking us to break the law." Tears pricked the back of her eyes

"You have no idea how perilously close we are to having to close Kingsley House once and for all. What do you think would happen to the little ones then? Ernest and Jane would be thrown into the orphanage, where they would suffer a wretched, loveless childhood. And as for the rest of them...they would probably be sent to work in the cotton mills or labouring from dawn till dusk in the iron foundries of the Midlands. Is that what you want for them?" He thrust his head bullishly forward. "Would you be happy to have that on your conscience, Nancy? And haven't you always bragged that you were Mr Doyle's best pickpocket, Arthur?"

Arthur straightened his shoulders and shot a defiant look back at Dorian, which made Nancy reach out and put a restraining hand on his arm. It signalled what they both knew: that they owed Cressida Kingsley for rescuing them in their time of need, which meant that, by extension, they were under Dorian's thumb as well. To defy him could bring Cressida and Marigold's dream crashing down and send the rest of the children to miserable futures.

"Did you plan this all along?" Arthur muttered. "I've been wondering if there was something not quite right about this shop and where you get your jewels from that you make into other pieces. Is everything stolen? Are you a crook?"

Nancy gasped. "Hush, Arthur," she whispered. To

her surprise, Dorian threw back his head and roared with laughter.

"That's more like it, Arthur." He slapped him on his back. "I always suspected you had more fire in your belly than you let on, running around doing chores for Cressida like a meek little lapdog." He chuckled again and rubbed his hands together. "It's good to see that flash of anger. It will help keep you on your toes while you get back into your old ways. Except this time, you'll be answering to me instead of Bernard Doyle."

"But I still don't understand," Nancy said slowly. "Why do you want us to steal things? Won't it risk bringing your shop into disrepute?"

Dorian shook his head. "That's the beauty of my plan, Nancy. I'm an established jeweller and a well-respected businessman. Who would ever suspect me of having anything to do with such dreadful crimes? And as for you two, the good people of Woodchester are used to seeing you running errands."

"People will soon realise there's something going on." Arthur sounded stubborn.

"Pah, you give them too much credit. Besides, it won't be every day, and you'll be working together so that one of you provides the distraction while the other one steals whatever you can. As you know, I repurpose items to make new pieces of jewellery. If anyone comes looking, they won't find what you stole. It's a foolproof plan, and you'll be playing your part to save Kingsley House."

Nancy marvelled at how he made it sound as though it was the most natural thing in the world, even as her stomach clenched with fear.

"It goes without saying that only the three of us will know about this. Cressida and Marigold will continue in blissful ignorance, doing good works for needy children." He poured himself another cup of coffee and started to head towards the stairs to go and get changed into something more presentable. "I heard Bernard Doyle has been sniffing around the area as well," he said calmly. "The local constabulary are a hapless bunch, but if they do get an idea into their heads that there are crimes going on, I'll be able to point the finger at him."

Arthur's shoulders sagged. He knew when he was beaten. "You do realise that if the constable ever catches me, I'll be sent straight to prison. They'll know I used to be a pickpocket in the past, and I doubt Miss Kingsley would be able to save me twice."

Dorian shrugged as though the conversation was already over. "You'd better make sure you don't get caught, then, Arthur," he said with a tight smile. "You can both start tomorrow. It's the day that the well-to-do ladies of the choral society are going to the Lavender Tearoom to discuss their summer concert. I doubt they'll be paying much attention as they wander through town, talking about which operettas they'll be singing. It will be the perfect opportunity for you to start practising."

Nancy's mouth had gone dry, and her legs trembled. She felt Arthur's fingers grasp hers to give her courage. "If you really think we must," she croaked.

"I do," Dorian said firmly. "I most certainly do."

CHAPTER 16

"Should I wear my bonnet? What about this dress, do you think it's too smart? Too scruffy?" Nancy peered at her reflection in one of the shop mirrors that Dorian encouraged customers to look at themselves in, to admire what he hoped they would purchase from him as they tried things on. It was still early in the morning, but Nancy had been too anxious to sleep, so she and Arthur had walked to Woodchester as soon as it got light.

"You look perfect, just as you are." Arthur gave her a sympathetic smile as he looked up from his task of polishing the silver dinner service displayed in one of the cabinets at the back of the room.

Nancy blushed, and he realised that his comment could be taken several ways.

"I mean, you look perfect for what we'll be doing

today." He shook his head and chuckled. "And you look perfect every day," he added. "You probably don't even realise how pretty you are, but I'm hardly going to tell my best friend that, am I? We don't want you getting a big head." He walked past her and gave her a playful thump on her arm, suddenly looking slightly bashful.

If Nancy's heart hadn't been thudding loud enough that she was convinced everyone would hear it before, it definitely was after that. A combination of being flattered by the first hint of romantic interest from Arthur and sheer terror at what lay ahead for them during the day.

"What if we make a mess of the pickpocketing today? I know you taught me everything you know, but I've never done it for real. Not like you."

"All you have to do is provide the distraction and leave everything else up to me." Arthur wiped his hands clean on a rag and slipped his waistcoat back on. He fiddled with the buttons, and Nancy gave him a quizzical look. "I've sewn an extra pocket in the lining," he explained, opening the waistcoat again to show her.

"Will you be wearing a jacket as well?"

Arthur nodded. "Yes, and it has a secret pocket as well. It's not just about stealing something; it's getting away without anyone knowing and having somewhere to hide it." He placed his hands on her shoulders and looked steadily into her eyes. "We won't do this forever, Nancy, I promise. I swore to myself that I would never steal again, but Dorian has given us no choice. As sickening as it is, the only way we'll get through this is if we work together."

"It's not how I was brought up." Nancy's mind raced, and her thoughts about what lay ahead felt jumbled, but she could tell that he understood. "I suppose we have to remind ourselves that we'll only target the really wealthy ladies and gentlemen, who can easily afford to replace what we steal."

"That's what Bernard Doyle used to tell me." Arthur stuck his belly out and waddled around the room, mimicking the portly man who had made him work in his gang all those years ago. "'Tis stealing from the rich to help the poor, Laddie...if every poor soul had enough money to put a hot meal on the table every day, we wouldn't have to do this." Arthur grinned. "He used to say that and give me a wallop round the back of my head any time I said I didn't feel like stealing. I soon managed to ignore any feelings of guilt because Bernard could send me reeling and make my ears ring for days with one of those reminders. He used to say a good smack sharpened my mind." He rubbed the back of his head as though he could still feel the sting of the man's fist.

"But what if it's something of sentimental value, and we don't realise," Nancy countered. She chewed her lip and clasped her hands together to stop them trembling.

"Sentimental value? Rubbish! There's no room for any thoughts like that," Dorian said sternly as he strode into the shop. "If you start fretting about such mawkish things, you'll get caught by the constable before the month is out, as sure as night follows day. You're to put everything like that out of your mind and remember that you're doing this for those poor little children at Kingsley House." His lip curled scornfully. "Those wealthy folk don't know how lucky they are. But we have to keep the wolf from the door for the likes of Ernest and Jane so they don't end up being carted off to the orphanage."

"Yes, Mr Holt," Nancy said hastily. If she was going to have doubts, it was clear she would have to keep them to herself or risk angering Dorian, and they couldn't afford to do that.

* * *

"What should I do to distract them?" Nancy asked Arthur a couple of hours later as they started to walk through the town. It was busier than usual, with maids hurrying past doing errands for their mistresses and horses pulling carts rumbling over the cobbles. The fine weather had brought everyone out, and she could hear the distant strains of the brass band playing in the park.

"The secret of a good distraction is making it something very ordinary." Arthur had his hands in his pockets and sauntered alongside her, looking as though he didn't have a care in the world. Nancy tried to take a leaf out of his book to quell her nerves, knowing that if she looked agitated or anxious, it was more likely to attract attention.

"I used to see it with the other children who were just starting to become pickpockets," Arthur continued. "They would create such a palaver that people would gather and stare. Invariably, the constable would come over to see what was going on, and their plan would be doomed from the start." He scratched his chin, looking thoughtful. "Something as simple as dropping your handkerchief, but doing it so that it's in their way, works well. They will probably just walk around you, still talking. But while they're busy watching you, I'll wander past at the same time, doing what I need to do."

Nancy felt encouraged by his reply. "I think I can manage that," she chuckled. Another ripple of concern coursed through her. "Promise me you'll be careful, Arthur. I couldn't bear it if you were thrown into prison."

He nudged her with his elbow and gave her a warm smile, which banished her nerves and instantly made everything feel better. "I have no intention of ever going to prison, Nancy. How would I manage without seeing you every day? Besides, you wouldn't want to marry someone who's felt the long arm of the law," he added with an upward twitch of his eyebrows. "Just joking," he added, giving her a bashful grin.

Before Nancy had a chance to digest his off-the-cuff comment, Arthur suddenly nodded his head surreptitiously in the direction of the opposite side of Corn Square, where it led into Admiral Street. "That's the ladies over there," he said casually. "We'll cut through the back lanes and walk past them first so that I can get an idea of what jewellery they're wearing. Remember, as far as anyone else is concerned, we're just running a couple of errands for Dorian, just like we do on any other day."

Nancy's heart started to beat faster, but she realised it wasn't only from fear. If she was being honest with herself, there was also a tingle of excitement mixed in with it. She knew it was only because Arthur was by her side. If she were acting alone, she would have been absolutely terrified, but she loved Arthur enough to trust him implicitly.

"Don't let me make any mistakes."

"You're working with the best."

Nancy took a deep breath. He would look after her, and from what he had just said, it sounded as though he wanted them to have a future together as well. They quickened their pace and ducked into Water Lane, which would bring them out just in front of the Choral Society ladies. It was now or never.

* * *

"OH, I'M SO SORRY." Nancy bobbed her head apologetically at the three ladies as she jumped forward to rescue her handkerchief, which had blown out of her hand and landed at their feet.

"Goodness me, girl, you should be more careful." The tallest of the ladies gave her a haughty glare while the other two stepped around her.

"... I'm not sure the Vicar really appreciates how much time we've put into practising those songs." Their conversation continued as Nancy bent over. She saw Arthur's feet nearby out of the corner of her eye.

"I know it's rather an unchristian thing to say, but you're right, Patricia. When I think how much money my dear Hubert has donated to the church over the years, you'd think the Vicar would be falling over himself to accommodate our polite request."

Nancy stood up, shook the handkerchief and blew her nose loudly. She saw that Arthur was already walking away. He was whistling quietly under his breath and then strolled across the cobbles, seemingly intent on looking at the cakes in the bakery window.

The tall lady recoiled and pressed her gloved hand to her mouth as Nancy blew her nose again. "I shall be most annoyed if I catch a cold from that wretched girl," she said, turning to her two friends, sounding exceedingly irritated.

"Never mind that Olivia, let's go to the tea room and discuss the concert. There's still a lot to prepare, and perhaps we can come up with some ideas on how to make the Vicar understand how important we are in this town."

Nancy was overcome with the urge to run after Arthur and get away as quickly as possible but then slowed down again as she remembered she needed to look natural.

"What did Dorian say he wanted us to get?" she said as she reached his side in front of the bakery. The question was just for show, and she strained to listen to the ladies. She half expected one of them to shriek with outrage and raise the alarm at the realisation that they had been robbed, but they were already deep in conversation again. *I bet they don't even notice us ordinary folk and the poor of society.* The realisation gave her comfort. If they were going to be pickpocketing for Dorian, she suddenly understood how useful it was to be so invisible. Wealthy people only viewed the likes of her and Arthur for what they could do for them, but in every other respect, they might as well be non-existent. It would come in rather useful as a thief.

"A couple of currant buns," Arthur said. He winked and patted his pocket. "We could afford enough cakes for a month," he said quietly, "but Dorian probably has other plans for the silver compact and opal earring I just took from two of those ladies."

"You robbed two of them?" Nancy's eyes widened with surprise at his boldness.

"Only because you did such a grand job of distracting them. Blowing your nose like that...you should've seen the look on their faces." His face creased into a grin as he started laughing.

"What made you choose those items?"

"Eager to learn more, are you?" He stuck his hands in his pockets and glanced around to make sure they couldn't be overheard. "If you only take one earring, they're more likely to think it was lost rather than stolen. And the woman whose compact I took had her reticule gaping open. She'll think it slipped out, and none of them will suspect us." He shrugged, looking slightly embarrassed. "I'm not proud of knowing this, but it's important. Most dippers only get caught by being careless and greedy."

"I hope Dorian knows that too." Nancy's stomach

rumbled because she had been too worried earlier to eat any breakfast.

"A currant bun, my dear?" Arthur gallantly offered his arm, and they wandered into the bakery to buy the treats, buoyed up by their first success.

As they started heading back to the jewellery shop a few minutes later, through the quieter back lanes, Nancy pushed her sense of guilt away. From what she had overheard of the ladies' conversation, they wouldn't miss the small items Arthur had taken, just as Dorian had assured them. Although she hated the fact that he was forcing them into doing something that felt so wrong, she thought she might be able to bear it as long as they only targeted those types of well-to-do gentry.

"I only hope Miss Kingsley never finds out what we're doing," she blurted out. "Her and Marigold would be so disappointed in us."

"We're doing it to keep Kingsley House going."

"And repaying them for helping us and my family." Nancy almost managed to convince herself that she believed Dorian only had their best interests at heart. She held up the buns the baker had wrapped in paper. "We'd better take these straight back to the shop, hadn't we?"

Arthur smacked his forehead. "You go on ahead. I'll catch you up shortly. I just remembered Dorian asked me to go to the coal merchant to order some more coal. He has a new firing oven arriving for his workshop so that he can start melting down silver and gold."

"It sounds like this is going to turn into more than just stealing the occasional item if that's what he has planned."

Arthur nodded, and his eyes clouded with worry for a second. "Remember what I said, Nancy. I know it doesn't seem like it now, but we won't always have to do Dorian's bidding. I'll try and find a way out of this for us when we're a bit older, I promise."

As Nancy walked away, she turned to look over her shoulder. She wanted to believe Arthur, but her fear was that now they had started down this path, it might end up being impossible to turn away from it again. With a troubled sigh, she carried on her way. She needed to pick up some more needles and thread for Marigold from the haberdashery and dried fruit for Moira from the grocer, but after that, she would head back and tell Dorian the deed had been done. *The first of many.* The thought made her grimace. She only hoped he would be pleased with the silver compact and earring hidden in Arthur's waistcoat pocket.

CHAPTER 17

"*M*r Holt said he will pay you for the coal upon delivery if that is acceptable to you?"

Mr Romley, the coal merchant, nodded and flashed Arthur a broad smile. His teeth looked strikingly white against his skin, which was dark and ingrained with coal dust from so many years of manhandling the heavy sacks on and off his wagon. "Perfectly fine with me, lad. Mr Holt is a good customer and has a sound business head. Tell him I'll come by with his coal first thing tomorrow morning. Don't want to keep him waiting."

Arthur started walking away, but the man hurried after him. "How is Miss Kingsley and that fine sister of hers?" He pressed a shilling into Arthur's hand, his eyes misting with emotion. "It's not much, but give this to Cressida. She was so kind to me when my wife passed away, and I know how hard she works providing for all the children in her care."

"They're both keeping well, and that's very generous of you, Mr Romley. I'll pass your message on, and please don't apologise. Miss Kingsley is grateful for every penny that the good people of Woodchester donate."

The coalman shook hands with Arthur and doffed his cap. "You're the eldest of her charges, aren't you?"

Arthur nodded. "I am. There are ten of us at the moment, but she hopes to help more children in the future."

"Well, if you're anything to go by, Cressida and Marigold are doing a marvellous job of raising fine, upstanding folk who could so easily have lost their way in life or turned to crime."

Arthur nodded hastily, not quite able to meet the kind-hearted man's eyes. "I'd better get back. Mr Holt is expecting me." As he walked away, he felt the familiar sense of guilt and wretchedness that he had always disliked when he'd been working in Bernard Doyle's gang of pickpockets.

"I can't believe Dorian has got me back into doing this," he muttered as a surge of anger rose in his chest. "This isn't the person I want to be." He sighed, irritated at the way that Dorian had played on their heartstrings and manipulated him and Nancy. She was still too young and innocent to see it because she liked to think the best of people, but he recognised his ploy for what it was. Dorian had that same gleam of greed in his eyes that he knew so well from seeing it in Bernard Doyle's eyes, too. But what was worse was how Dorian liked to portray himself as a respectable gentleman and an important businessman in the local area. At least Bernard Doyle had never pretended to be something he wasn't. Everyone knew Bernie was a crook. In fact, he'd made sure of it to further his reputation as someone not to be crossed. But Dorian was like a wolf in sheep's clothing and liked people to think well of him.

Should I have told Nancy all of this? Is it better for her to truly believe that we're doing this for Kingsley House? The questions and suspicions swirled through his mind, but there were no easy answers. If he told her what he really thought of Dorian Holt, she might be more likely to lose her nerve when they were stealing from folk. He couldn't afford for her to make any mistakes because if she ended up in prison, he would never forgive himself.

He spoke under his breath, trying to sort his muddled thoughts out. Maybe Dorian was being honest with them? It was impossible to tell. "It's better that she believes we're doing this to help Miss Kingsley. We might be doing something wrong, but

we're doing it to protect something good and right."
*We won't be the first people to fall into crime to help the
less fortunate folk of society, and that's what I'll have to
help Nancy believe.* He nodded decisively. It was as
much to convince himself as to practice convincing
Nancy.

The coal merchant was a little way out of Woodchester, and Arthur picked a piece of grass from the
hedgerow and stuck it in the corner of his mouth,
trying to banish the feeling that he was letting everybody down by returning to his criminal ways. An
image of Nancy's sparkling green eyes and the way
tendrils of her brown curls often brushed her rosy
cheeks floated into his thoughts, making him smile.

*Nancy Burton...or maybe one day long in the future...
Mrs Nancy Pittman.*

He smiled to himself, liking how the name
sounded. His feelings towards her had changed
recently, although he hadn't plucked up the courage
to say anything. She had gone from feeling like a
younger sister to someone who engendered a sense
of protectiveness deep in his heart. And a more
confusing emotion, which he had never experienced
before and which he wasn't ready to pronounce as
love quite yet. All he knew was that the thought of
Nancy getting into trouble because of what Dorian
was expecting of them was too painful to consider.
She didn't deserve to be tainted by turning to crime,

and his stomach lurched as he thought about what might happen if Miss Kingsley ever discovered what they were doing.

Cressida Kingsley was like a ma and a pa to him, and she had trusted him when many others hadn't. It made him feel sick to think how he was breaking that trust, but also angry that Dorian was heartless enough to think so little of the Kingsley sisters and everything they had done to create a happy home for him and the other children. Dorian was jeopardising everything with careless disregard for who might get hurt.

"It's up to me to make sure this works," he muttered under his breath, throwing the piece of grass away. "I'm the only one who can pull this off to appease Dorian's greed but also to keep Nancy safe,"

It was a heavy load to bear, but now that he had come to that conclusion, Arthur was surprised to realise that he felt better about everything. He'd had to learn to rely on himself and get by on his wits from a very young age. Some folk might call it being cunning, but he liked to think of it as being street-smart and wise to the ways of the less salubrious side of society and the criminal fraternity. He started whistling again, and there was a spring in his step as he turned into Appletree Lane. He had a sneaking suspicion that Dorian underestimated him, and that's just the way he wanted to keep it. Bernard Doyle had taught him that it was far better to be underestimated. That way, you could always be one step ahead of the folk who fancied they knew best and who thought they were in charge."

As Arthur hurried along Appletree Lane, the sun was directly in his eyes, and he was looking forward to a nice cool drink of water from the pump when he got back.

"Look where you're going, young man." The stooped woman hobbling towards him with the aid of a walking stick sounded querulous.

"Sorry, Mrs Blanchard." Arthur neatly sidestepped her and gave her a polite smile. She was one of the widows who did the flowers at church and was known for having a rather brusque manner. "Would you like me to carry that basket of shopping for you?"

She shook her head, and her lips pursed into a thin line. "Don't write me off yet, Arthur Pittman. I might be old, but I'm more than capable of carrying a couple of apples and a parcel of bacon home, thank you very much."

"Just offering," Arthur muttered. No sooner were the words out of his mouth than he saw Nancy up ahead of him. Except, rather strangely, she was wearing a different dress. She glanced over her shoulder, but there was no smile of recognition or friendly wave, which was even more curious. *Is she cross about something?*

He quickened his pace to catch up with her. "Nancy!" he yelled, "wait for me. What have you been doing? I've never seen you in that gown before." He lowered his voice as he reached out to tap her on the shoulder. "Don't tell me you've got a taste for taking things and stole this dress?"

She spun round to face him, looking outraged. "Get off me." She frowned. "And I haven't stolen this dress, I'll have you know."

His mouth gaped open in surprise. He had been so convinced it was Nancy...she had the same tumbling brown curls and green eyes, but her clothes looked completely different, and she was treating him like a stranger. What was going on?

"Don't be silly, Nancy. What's got into you?" He peered into the basket she was holding, but instead of groceries, it was full of freshly cut flowers. He shook his head, puzzled by what he saw. "How did you afford to buy those? Don't tell me you stole them as well. We have to be careful."

The girl took several steps away from him as though he was deranged. "It's none of your business. I don't know who you think I am, but I wish you would stop speaking to me as though you know me." She tossed her head and gave him a hard stare. "I suggest you leave me alone. Otherwise, I'll scream for help."

Arthur backed away, holding his hands up. The last thing he wanted was for the constable to come running and fingering his collar under the mistaken belief that he was pestering this girl. "I...I'm sorry," he said apologetically. "You look exactly like a very good friend of mine, but I can see now I was mistaken. Please don't be upset, miss. I'll get on my way and bid you a good day."

He hastily doubled back on himself and cut through into Wilton Terrace, his mind whirling. He felt annoyed with himself that he hadn't thought to ask what the girl's name was, but knew that if he followed her again, it would be too risky and that she would shout for help. But he couldn't believe how similar she had looked to Nancy. *Are they related? What will she say when she finds out?*

Nancy had never made any secret of the fact that she had been adopted, but she had always said that her ma told her she had been left behind by travelling folk. He couldn't wait to tell her, but he would need to choose the time carefully. It wasn't a conversation he wanted Dorian to overhear or anyone else. It was a private matter for Nancy, so he hugged the secret tightly to himself.

* * *

Nancy tucked the packs of dried fruit into her basket and stepped back out of the grocery shop. She glanced up and down the street, hoping to see Arthur, but there was no sign of him. As Dorian had said that there was no need for them to rush back to the shop, she decided on a whim to take the long route and go via the ornamental gardens. It was rare for her to have a moment to herself, and she savoured the sense of freedom.

By the time she got to the park, the brass band had packed up and left, but there were still a few people picnicking on blankets near the pond. Children played, rolling their wooden hoops and darting in and out of the trailing willows, and several courting couples were walking arm in arm. She sighed wistfully, wondering whether that might be her and Arthur one day in the future.

She was so lost in her thoughts that it was only as a well-dressed gentleman stepped right in front of her that she realised someone was talking to her.

"What are you doing in Woodchester?" he asked, looking her up and down curiously. "I wasn't expecting to see you here. Are you running an errand for your mama?"

Nancy felt a prickle of alarm and hastily looked around. Was this some sort of trap? The man was tall, with light brown hair, and he wore a finely cut suit, which looked as if it had been tailored in London. He sounded well-spoken and was most definitely not the sort of gentleman who would normally pass the time of day with someone of her social standing.

Did he see me helping Arthur pickpocket the ladies, and now he's just stalling for time until the constable arrives?

"I'm not sure what you mean," she said cautiously, backing away slightly in case she needed to start running. "I've never met you before."

The man lifted his top hat and gave her a small bow with a polite smile on his face. His brown eyes twinkled with amusement. "Another one of your funny jokes. Wait until I tell Lillian. Speaking of which, we're looking forward to seeing you and your family at the summer fete."

Even though every instinct was telling Nancy she should run away, her curiosity was piqued. Why was this well-to-do gentleman talking to her as though they were acquaintances or even friends? It made no sense.

"Who are you?" she blurted out.

The gentleman's smile faltered, and a frown furrowed his brow. "Are you feeling unwell, my dear? Have you had a blow to the head? You know perfectly well who I am…Horace Smallwood, of course—"

A sudden shout across the park interrupted them. "Nancy! Are you coming? We need to get back." It was Arthur, and he was gesturing urgently.

Nancy looked at the gentleman again, and the whisper of a memory came back to her of sitting in the front of the cart next to Ezra on a spring day, looking across the valley towards a grand house in Thruppley village. *Horace Smallwood?* She knew that name. He was the gentleman who owned the Rodborough Hotel. The man Ezra had discussed on their journey to the railway camp all those years ago when he had pointed out the hotel and Chavenhope House where he lived.

"Hurry up!" Arthur shouted again and kept looking over his shoulder as though he was worried about being followed.

"Sorry, mister, I think you must be mistaken. We've never met, and I have to go." With that, she walked briskly away. When she reached the park entrance, she glanced back over her shoulder again. Mr Smallwood was still standing in the same place, watching her with a puzzled expression. She was half-tempted to run back and ask why he thought he knew her, but Arthur grabbed her arm and hurried her away.

"Who's that toff you were talking to?" he asked. He sounded slightly breathless, as though he had been running.

"You won't believe it. It's Horace Smallwood, the gentleman who owns that grand hotel in Thruppely.

My pa told me about him on the day we were in the horse and cart heading to the railway camp."

Arthur looked shocked. "No offence, Nancy, but why was he hobnobbing with you?"

"We weren't hobnobbing, as you put it," she said, pretending to be offended. "It's very odd. He was talking to me as though he knew me. Said something about looking forward to seeing me at the summer fete. I told him I didn't know him."

Arthur stopped abruptly and turned to face her. "Well, isn't that just the strangest thing? Not ten minutes ago, I thought I saw you walking along Appletree Lane."

"I wasn't there. I only went to do the errands for Moira and Marigold."

"I know now. It turned out to be a complete stranger, but she looked so much like you. I made a proper fool of myself, Nancy. She was wearing a smart gown, and because I thought it was you, I asked if it was stolen. She was so offended she threatened to scream for help, so I scarpered pretty quick."

"So, who was it? What's her name?"

Arthur shrugged, his mind already turning towards getting back to the shop to give Dorian the stolen items. "Maybe it's a distant relation who you knew nothing about. Didn't you say your ma reckoned you'd been left at that foundling's home by travelling folk?"

Nancy's thoughts were a jumble of conflicting scenarios as they hurried back towards Corn Square. Was it really a coincidence? Did she have a distant relation from her real family living nearby? *I can hardly go and ask a gentleman like Horace Smallwood.* She thought about how wealthy he was. One of the wealthiest men in the West Country by all accounts. He would never want to speak to someone as lowly as her. It must just have been a strange coincidence, she told herself.

But what if it's someone who's related to me? Who might like me? She felt a sense of yearning. She had always wondered about her true family but had put it to the back of her mind since moving to Lower Amberley. Now her curiosity was piqued again. Perhaps one day, she would bump into Mr Smallwood again and have an opportunity to ask him. A small flicker of hope flared in her chest. She had never imagined that she might actually meet anyone from her real family, but sometimes the impossible happened, didn't it? She liked to think so.

CHAPTER 18

"Are you all ready to go?" Arthur asked. He glanced across the shop at Nancy and was suddenly struck by a strange sense of déjà vu. She was looking in the mirror, adjusting her bonnet, just as she had done three years ago on the first day they had ventured into town to pickpocket from the choral society ladies. Instead of worrying about whether she should wear her bonnet or not, this time, she was just making sure that it was on straight.

"I've been ready for half an hour. It's you who's been dawdling out the back." She gave him a mischievous smile, and her green eyes sparkled, which made his breath hitch in his chest.

"I wasn't dawdling," he said, giving her a wry smile. "I was helping roll in the barrels of beer for the landlord at the tavern and then chopping wood for him. Dorian asked me to do it as repayment for keeping Queenie in their stables so often."

Now that he was twenty years old and Nancy was eighteen, he knew without a shadow of a doubt that he loved her and wanted to marry her one day. The only thing holding him back from mentioning it was that he wanted to be free of Dorian's demands. He didn't want to propose to Nancy until he could look at his own reflection in the mirror and know that he was no longer part of Dorian's criminal activities. He wanted to offer Nancy a better life, free from worrying about whether they might get caught by the constables, and until that day arrived, he would have to keep his feelings for her secret.

"What's the plan for today?" Nancy bustled around the back room, tidying up the tools on the workbench.

"More of the same, I suppose."

Arthur was surprised when Dorian suddenly appeared in the doorway from the back path. He had been shut away in his study at Kingsley House when they left bright and early that morning, and judging by the scowl on his face, he was in a bad mood.

"More of the same isn't going to be good enough anymore," Dorian stated baldly. "Have you made me a coffee, Nancy, or do I have to do everything myself?"

Nancy hastily put the old tin kettle back on the range to boil again. "I'll do it right away." She scooped coffee beans into the grinder, making sure there were more than usual and turned the handle quickly before adding the freshly ground coffee to the pot. When Dorian was like this, it was best not to question anything he said.

"What do you mean by that? Is there something else you would rather we were doing?" Arthur asked cautiously. He braced himself, ready for a reply that he didn't really want to hear.

Dorian gave a long sigh and slumped onto his stool at the workbench, folding his arms. "I'm worried that folk are getting a little suspicious about how many petty thefts there are in Woodchester."

"We've been pickpocketing for nigh on three years. I suppose it was bound to happen, although Nancy and I are always careful to only take bits and pieces that people are likely not to miss until they get home. Or better still, just assume they were careless and lost them."

"I've heard rumours. A few tongues wagging in The Golden Fleece when I want to enjoy a quiet pint of ale."

"It's probably nothing to bother about. What people talk about when they're drinking is mostly forgotten by the morning."

Dorian folded his arms and glanced around the back room and shop beyond with a sour expression. "In spite of everything I'm trying to do to balance the books at Kingsley House, Cressida spends money as though it's going out of fashion. She seems determined to keep taking on more children, and the fact that she refuses to send the older ones out to work isn't helping." He took the cup of coffee from Nancy without bothering to say thank you. "In my opinion, it's high time Tess and Blake were making themselves useful by doing proper paid work instead of just the chores at Kingsley House."

"I suppose Miss Kingsley thinks it's better than spending money on extra maids," Nancy ventured. She always liked to stay loyal to the woman who had given her a new start in life. "There's only so much Moira can do, even with Anne and Sophie helping in the kitchen."

"If I wanted your opinion on how to run a charitable home for children, I would have asked for it," Dorian snapped.

Arthur gave Nancy's arm a brief squeeze of reassurance as he walked behind her with a new bucket of coal for the firing oven. He could see she looked hurt, and he bit back what he would have liked to say to Dorian, telling him he should be grateful everyone worked so hard.

"There's only one thing for it. I need you both to start stealing more valuable items."

The bucket clattered as Arthur put it down, and he spun around to give Dorian his full attention. "I don't think it's safe to do that. If you think there are rumours floating around about things being stolen, the constables are probably already on the lookout." He could feel his temper rising, but a look from Nancy held it in check. "What you have to remember," he added mildly, "is that if something goes wrong when we're stealing, it will be me and Nancy who have to pay the price, not you."

"Can't you just charge more for the pieces that you make from what we steal?" Nancy suggested. She resorted to flattery, which usually worked. "The customers speak so highly of your jewellery, I'm sure they wouldn't mind paying a little more for it."

"I'm already staying over the shop several nights a week and working my fingers to the bone." Dorian sounded like a petulant child, and Nancy deliberately avoided looking at Arthur. Dorian might have thought he was working hard, but compared to most people, he barely knew the meaning of the words hard work. He was a grifter, getting by doing what he enjoyed while they took all the risks.

Nancy wracked her brains. "What about selling some of your pieces back in Bath again? You must have contacts there, and you always said there are plenty of well-to-do gentry eager to buy."

"No." Dorian's lips pinched. "I've already decided I'm going to raise my prices, but it still won't be enough. My mind is made up. I want you to start taking the horse and cart to some of the other local towns and villages. We need to spread the net wider, and you need to make sure you're stealing more valuable items."

Arthur opened his mouth again to say that it was a bad idea, but Dorian held his hand up to stop him.

"I want Nancy to stay in the shop today. Arthur, you're to go to Dartminster village this morning. It's close enough to Gloucester that there are a few wealthy merchants' wives there who are bound to be out shopping. Don't come back until you've got something worthwhile."

"Surely I should go with him?" Nancy sounded worried. They always worked together, and this suggestion was an unwelcome departure from the careful routine they had honed over the last three years.

"I have a couple of well-to-do gentlemen coming into the shop today to buy gifts for their wives. They will respond better to you serving them than me, Nancy."

"Maybe we should go to Dartminster tomorrow together instead?" Arthur scooped a shovel of coal into the firing oven and pumped the bellows to get it going.

"No," Dorian snapped mulishly. "You'd be wise to remember who's in charge here, Arthur, and do what I've asked. Imagine what Cressida would say if she found out what Nancy's been doing these last few years." The threat behind his words was plain and made Arthur's blood boil. But Dorian didn't care. He drained his coffee and stood up, businesslike again. "And mind you don't get caught," he added. "The last thing we need is to have the constables sniffing around and bringing trouble to my door."

BY THE TIME Arthur had ridden Queenie to Dartminster and paid a few coins to leave her at one of the inns, the village market was in full swing. He was pleased that it was so busy because it would make his job easier. The hustle and bustle of the costermongers shouting their wares and people hurrying past to get home or standing in groups to gossip with their friends would provide better cover for him to slip into the throng and steal something. Also, he would be less likely to stand out as a stranger, which was something of a relief.

"A twist of mint humbugs?" a man in a garish checked coat called.

"Ignore 'im. What you'm wanting is a posey of flowers to give to your sweetheart." A wizened flower seller pushed in front of Arthur and grinned up at him from under her black straw bonnet. "Or how about a lucky sprig of heather? Just what a handsome young man like you needs to get himself a wife."

"Maybe later," Arthur murmured. He didn't want to start haggling with the market sellers, but it was a useful interlude to give him time to watch everyone else and decide who to rob.

"Don't forget to come back to me, ducky," the old woman said. "Steer clear of her at the other end of the street. Her flowers ain't never as fresh as mine."

Out of the corner of his eye, Arthur noticed two matronly ladies. They were better dressed than most and weren't carrying baskets of shopping. No doubt they had servants to do all that for them. They were deep in conversation, and with a polite nod at the flower seller to say he would be back later, Arthur walked briskly away and started following the two women. He had already seen the flash of jewellery glittering at one of the women's throats as it caught the sun. It would be risky to take a brooch from under her chin, but it looked valuable, and he hoped it would keep Dorian off their back for a few weeks. He fell into step behind them, sizing up the opportunity, and they were so busy chattering they didn't even notice him.

"Are you all ready for your daughter's wedding, Rosemary?"

"Almost, Marjorie," the woman replied. "We have the dress fitting next week, then I'll decide on the menu." A horse and cart rumbled past, and they stopped talking as they ducked into a shop doorway to get out of the way. "Goodness me, I swear the village is busier than ever. Remember when we could enjoy a pleasant walk to the tea room without fear of being run over by some oafish farmer rushing past, not looking where he's going."

"Nobody seems to care about good manners anymore," her friend replied. They looked at the retreating farmer with annoyance as he continued on his way, blithely unaware that he had upset the two women.

Arthur waited for the next horse and cart to pass, then crossed the street and sped up so he could get ahead of them. He wanted to be walking towards the women, not behind them. He was pleased to see that they were deep in conversation about wedding preparations again as he approached them a moment later. He felt strangely unsettled by not having Nancy with him; he had never worked alone like this, and Dorian had no appreciation of how much harder it would be. He would have to provide the distraction and steal the item, which was no easy feat.

If only Nancy were here...it's so much easier when we work together. He walked slowly, wanting to look relaxed and unconcerned. The women were approaching a dressmaking shop, and he hoped that they might pause to look in the window at all the lace and ribbons.

"Whoah there, Fester!" The drayman's shout was loud and urgent, and Arthur was as startled as everyone else at the sight of the muscular cart horse prancing in its harness, scattering everyone in its path. The barrels on the back of the wagon swayed dangerously, straining the ropes keeping them in place. "Settle down, Fester!" the driver yelled again. He was standing in his wagon seat, trying to wrestle the horse into submission as he hauled on the reins. Two young children had darted out into the road, spooking the horse, and the drayman was not best pleased. "Get out of the way, you wretched brats. Ain't your parents taught you any common sense?"

This is my chance! Arthur realised that in the commotion, one of the ladies had stumbled and fallen over. He sprang forward and spread his arms wide to protect them. "Stay still, and the horse will pass without endangering you."

"Oh...how terrifying...I lost my balance," the woman stammered.

"Marjorie, have you hurt yourself?"

Arthur quickly helped the woman to her feet again and steadied her as the horse thundered past, its mighty hooves making the ground shudder.

Now that she was upright again, the woman shook Arthur off. "I don't know what the world is coming to," she cried, shaking her fist at the drayman. "What a rude man, not even bothering to check if we were hurt."

"We're surrounded by uncouth fools," Rosemary said. The two women clutched each other, looking outraged, their hats askew and their silk gowns covered in dust.

"The danger is over now," Arthur said quietly as he surreptitiously pocketed the brooch. Neither of the women had noticed, but instead of thanking him for stepping in to protect them, they both turned to glare.

"It's low-class types like you who are ruining our lovely village," one of them snapped. She sniffed disapprovingly and squared her shoulders. "Come along, Marjorie. I need to sit down with a cup of tea and a slice of poppy cake to get over the shock. Out of our way, young man."

Arthur shook his head with a rueful smile as the two women marched away. It seemed they were the types to be permanently offended and annoyed.

That won't be anything compared to when they discover what they've lost. In all the commotion, he had also managed to steal a gold hatpin and a few coins, as well as the brooch. He felt a pang of guilt but then remembered Dorian's veiled threats about Nancy. It had been too good an opportunity to miss, and he lengthened his stride, glancing over his shoulder to make sure the women hadn't realised. They were still talking loudly about their narrow escape as they turned into the tea room, and he heaved a sigh of relief. He was determined to tell Dorian that he and Nancy needed to work together. It was far too dangerous working without his side-kick, and Dorian would just have to take his word for it.

Arthur whistled jauntily, and his spirits started to rise. He wondered about having a small glass of porter at the inn before riding back to Woodchester. It was always good to listen to village gossip at one of the pubs. He could learn a lot about Dartminster and whether it would be worth his while coming here regularly.

Thinking about it afterwards, Arthur realised he had let his guard down. He was relieved the robbery had gone smoothly and was looking forward to telling Nancy about it later. That was why he didn't notice the two men who had been following him until a strong hand snaked out from the shadows, and he was roughly yanked into a dark alleyway between two tall buildings and slammed face-first against the bricks.

"Do as you're told, and you won't get hurt." The voice behind him was hard and uncompromising, and Arthur winced as his hand was twisted up behind his back. He yelped as pain shot through his shoulder, but it only made the man twist his arm higher. "Keep the noise down."

"What the...who are you?" he groaned, demanding to know.

He yelped again as a fist was driven into his back, right where his kidneys were.

"Stop squawking like a baby," a second voice growled. "Someone wants to speak to you, that's all. But if you keep complaining, we'll drag you there half-conscious if that's what you'd prefer."

Arthur's mind raced as they marched him unceremoniously through the dark, twisting back alleys of the village. Clearly, it wasn't anything to do with the police. This was something different and more sinister altogether.

A moment later, they stopped in front of a heavy wooden door. The paint was peeling, and a rat scuttled along the gutter in fetid pools of rotting rubbish as the door swung open.

"Well, well, well, if it isn't young Arthur Pittman, all grown up and running his own little racket now."

Arthur gasped with shock at the portly man standing in front of him. He had lost a couple more teeth, and his jowls sagged now, but there was no mistaking who it was. "Bernard Doyle. I should have guessed this was something to do with you."

The two men released Arthur, and he rubbed his shoulder, wondering if he would be able to sprint away if need be. Bernard had never liked to take part in anything violent himself, but it seemed he still had a few lackeys on hand to do his bidding.

"It's been a while, Arthur, hasn't it?" Bernard rubbed his plump hands together, looking for all the world like some sort of jovial friend enjoying a warm-hearted reunion instead of the man who had first led Arthur into a life of crime.

"A good few years," Arthur agreed. "What's this about, and was it really necessary to have these two fools rough me up?" This was no time for niceties, and he glanced back at the two thugs who grinned. He could tell they were eager to inflict more pain if Bernard gave them the nod.

Bernard tilted his head to one side and sighed as though he regretted the whole conversation. "I've been keeping an eye on you these last few years." He rocked on his toes and winked. "I consider you some-thing of a protégé."

"It's a long time since we parted company. Are you still holding a grudge about Miss Kingsley offering me a better life?"

"Of course not. I don't hold grudges. The thing is, Arthur, I don't mind you pickpocketing a few trin-kets with that lovely young lady of yours. But coming over Gloucester way today is a bit rich, don't you think?"

Arthur decided to call his bluff. "I don't know

what you're talking about. It's a free country, isn't it? I was just running a couple of errands, that's all."

Bernard's belly quivered as he chuckled and shook his head. "Arthur...laddie...I taught you everything you know, remember. Those two old dears will be hopping mad when they realise what you stole from them today. Well done for picking two of the wealthiest women in the village, by the way. You've still got a good eye."

He shrugged. "I've got to make a living, one way or another, Bernard, you know how it is."

"The thing is, this is my patch. I can let it slide just this once if you stay working in Woodchester and over that way, but I can't accept you working the same patch as my own gang again if it's going to become a regular occurrence. You know how it is," he added, echoing what Arthur had just said. His eyes narrowed, and a cunning look came over his face. "I might be willing to overlook it if you tell me who you're working for. There are too many robberies happening for this to be down to you alone."

A prickle of apprehension ran down Arthur's back. He realised he had underestimated Bernard Doyle by assuming that he was part of his past. It seemed Bernard had been watching him all along. But he couldn't afford to give up Dorian's name; there was no way that would end well. "You're wrong this time, Bernie," he said casually. "Like you said, I've just been stealing a few trinkets here and there. I just sell them on for a few bob to help look after the children at Kingsley House."

"Very charitable of you," Bernard said dryly. He suddenly leaned forward and jabbed a finger in Arthur's chest to underline his point. "You'd better watch your back, laddie. I don't take kindly to people working on my patch and stirring up trouble. You stick to Woodchester and over that way; otherwise, this won't be our last meeting." He smirked and gave a humourless chuckle. "We certainly wouldn't like your lovely lady friend to come to any harm, would we? Nancy…what a lovely name."

Arthur's heart sank. *Of course, he's made it his business to keep an eye on me. How could I forget that's the way Bernie operates?*

He knew he couldn't afford to show his fear of the threat about Nancy because Bernard would think him weak. It was a fine line to tread. "Very well. You leave Nancy out of this, and I'll make sure I don't come back to Dartminster. Agreed?" He reached out and shook hands with Bernard before waiting for an answer.

This time, Bernard's smile held a grudging hint of respect. "If you change your mind and tell me who you're working for, there's always space for a good pickpocket in my gang again."

"I don't intend to be doing this for much longer," Arthur shot back.

"That's what everyone says," Bernard chuckled. "I'll see you around, laddie. You know where to find me."

The two thugs stepped back and gestured for Arthur to leave, and he hurried away, his heart hammering in his chest. The encounter had only served to make him more determined than ever to get Nancy away from Dorian and his criminal ways. Bernard's interest was an unwelcome reminder that even though Arthur liked to think he had escaped his past, he had never really shaken it off.

CHAPTER 19

*N*ancy took a deep breath to steady her nerves as she stood in the shadows. It was the first time she had visited Thruppley village, and the honey-coloured cottages and cheerful chatter of the villagers going about their business made her feel both comforted and guilty at the same time. Comforted by the cosy rural scene and friendly villagers but guilty that she would be spoiling some-body's day very shortly.

It's so unfair of Dorian to keep expecting us to steal. The familiar thought buzzed in her mind. She felt trapped and knew Arthur did, too. They often talked about how they might be able to break free from his demands, but the truth was Dorian held all the cards in this situation they had become ensnared in. If they stopped stealing, she suspected he wouldn't hesitate to get them sent away from Kingsley House in disgrace. Or worse, arrested and thrown into jail. He had a cold and ruthless heart beneath his genial exterior.

It had been a week since Dorian had sent Arthur to Dartminster. Even though Arthur had told her and Dorian all about being dragged in front of Bernard Doyle by the two thugs and being warned away from their patch, Dorian was still insisting they should steal more valuable items and work separately now and again.

"Good afternoon, maid. Are you'm lost?" A farmer with ruddy cheeks looked at her with a kind smile, and he spoke with the slow West Country burr of a man who rarely hurried. Straw clung to his jacket, and his hands were ingrained with mud. "I noticed you standing here while I was delivering potatoes to the greengrocer over the road. Perhaps I can point out where you need to go."

"Oh no, thank you. I'm just waiting for a friend, that's all." Nancy fiddled with her shawl, willing the man to go and hoping that he hadn't managed to get a good look at her.

A sharp wind swirled through the village, blowing his hat off and sending it tumbling over the cobbles. "Beggar me, 'tis a playful wind today." He glanced up and down the street, and his eyes alighted on a young man walking towards them. "Well, he'm be a lucky fellow to be walking out with a beauty like you if that's yer sweetheart." He grinned and limped after his hat, jamming it on his head and giving her a cheery wave goodbye.

Nancy decided it would be better if she strolled through the lanes rather than lurking in the shadows. It would be less likely to draw attention to herself, so she set off at a brisk pace. Turning the corner, she gasped as she ran slap-bang into an old woman with milky eyes, practically knocking her over. She walked with a stick and had a colourful collection of feathers stuck jauntily in her hat.

"I'm so sorry," Nancy said, reaching out to steady her. "I wasn't looking where I was going."

"That's alright, dear. It's this wind." The woman tilted her head to one side, reminding Nancy of a small bird. "I know you..."

Not again. Why are these villagers so friendly?

"No...this is the first time I've been to Thruppley," she said hastily.

The woman reached up and traced her hand over Nancy's cheeks. "I don't see very well, but I'm sure..." Emotions chased over her face. Confusion, then a soft smile of happiness.

"No, I don't know you." Nancy knew she sounded rude, but she was here to steal, not make friends with strangers.

"I'm Ava Piper."

The name sounded familiar. And suddenly Nancy remembered where she had heard it. This woman was the fortune teller who had given Miss Kingsley the feather and told her she would have many children. Nancy felt torn. She wanted to linger and talk to the old crone, but the more people she spoke to, the more likely it would be that they would remember her. And when news came out about people being robbed, it would make it another village she and Arthur would have to avoid. Resentment and anger towards Dorian roiled in her stomach. *Why should we have to avoid people and constantly be looking over our shoulders because of him?*

"I…I'm sorry, but I have errands to run."

Before Nancy could walk away, Ava plucked a feather from her hat and handed it to her. "Take this. There are people very dear to you who will help you when the time is right." A shadow crossed her face. "But you must beware of the man with two faces. He will betray you."

"What do you mean?" A shiver of foreboding ran down Nancy's back.

"You'll understand. What's your name, my dear?"

"Nancy. Nancy Burton," she blurted out without thinking.

"Perfect. It was a pleasure to meet you, Nancy. And now, if you'll excuse me, I must share some good news with a very good friend of mine." With another soft smile, the woman turned and walked away surprisingly quickly for someone who looked so ancient and frail. A horse and wagon rumbled over the cobbles, and by the time it had passed, she had disappeared from view.

How strange. What is it about this place that is making it feel as though people know me?

Nancy tucked the feather into her shawl, trying to refocus on the task at hand and continued walking, looking out all the while for a suitable person to pickpocket. There was a pleasing selection of shops in the village. She felt a pang of hunger at the tempting smell of meat pies wafting out of the bakery, but she was too nervous to eat. A little further along, she paused at the dressmaker's, admiring a display of pretty buttons and lace trims in the window. Inside, she could see a dark-haired woman expertly measuring and pinning the folds of a bustle on a half-finished velvet gown, which was draped on a mannequin. As if sensing her presence, the woman turned around and stared at her before waving and breaking into a broad smile of recognition.

Not another one!

Nancy was reminded of the time Horace Small-wood had greeted her as though he knew her. The woman laid down her tape measure and looked as though she was about to come and speak to her.

Without waiting a moment longer, Nancy hurried away and darted into a narrow alleyway that she thought would take her through to the next street. She couldn't afford to get into conversation again and return to Lower Amberley empty-handed. Dorian was becoming ever more demanding these days, and she and Arthur suspected that he had fallen in with bad company. The thin veneer of civility and respectability was starting to crack, and Nancy was afraid of what he might do if they failed him.

A moment later, she emerged from the alleyway into a different street. It was wider than the one she had just been in, and the wind funnelled down it stronger than ever. Nancy noticed a well-dressed couple. Even though it was windy, the sun was bright, and the woman was struggling with her parasol.

"Just fold it up for a while, Zoe," the man said, looking alarmed as it nearly smacked him in the face.

"We'll be out of the wind as soon as we get to the end of the street, Brian," the woman replied, sounding frustrated. "Without my parasol, I'll either get dreadful freckles from the sun, or my bonnet will blow away, and I'm not prepared to take my chances on either of those."

Nancy walked along the side of the road towards them, her skirts whipping around her legs. She had already spotted a gleam of gold across the man's waistcoat. If she could get close enough, she could take the pocket watch in a flash, and she knew Dorian would be pleased with that.

"Brian!" the woman shrieked. Another gust of wind had turned her expensive parasol completely inside out. "It's ruined." Tears filled her eyes, and the sight of the beautiful silk being ripped to tatters made her shriek again. The man went to grab the parasol to try and right it, and Nancy walked faster, reaching them just as they were most distracted.

"What did I tell you, Zoe," he said, wrestling the parasol back under control. "It's not salvageable, I'm afraid, but don't worry, my love. It's my own fault for suggesting we come outside on such a blustery day. I'll buy you another one the next time we go to Bristol. You know how much I like to treat my lovely wife."

Nancy hurried away and rounded the corner into the village square, slipping the gentleman's gold pocket watch into a hidden pocket sewn into her gown. She didn't feel quite so bad, hearing the man's promise to buy another parasol. It showed that they were a wealthy couple and would probably be able to replace the pocket watch with just as much ease.

"Nicely done." Arthur's voice behind her made Nancy spin around in surprise.

"What are you doing here?"

He gave her a lopsided grin, and his blue eyes

crinkled with amusement in a way that made her stomach flip. "I told Dorian I would run a few errands for him. He thinks I'm in Nailsbridge, so let's keep this between ourselves. I know how nervous you must have felt doing this by yourself, and I wanted to make sure everything went smoothly for you."

They fell into step together, and she instantly felt protected, as though nothing could ever go wrong with Arthur by her side. "I really don't like the way things are changing," she said with a long sigh. "It's starting to feel as though we'll never be able to do enough to satisfy Dorian."

Arthur nodded, looking thoughtful. "I know what you mean. I overheard Cressida and Marigold talking about paying the butcher's bill the other day."

"You mean they didn't have enough money to pay it?"

"Quite the opposite," Arthur sidestepped an urchin who was offering to polish his boots, throwing the boy a penny, which he pocketed before wiping his nose on his sleeve and mumbling a thank you. "Marigold was telling Cressida that their accounts are in good order. They've even managed to save some money this year for unexpected costs and making another nursery so they can take on more little 'uns."

"That doesn't make sense. Dorian is always drumming it into us that it's such an expensive house to maintain and how we're only one disaster away from having to sell up and put all the children in orphanages."

"Maybe he's not being honest with us."

Nancy stopped abruptly and put her hands on her hips. "Do you think we're doing all this pickpocketing for his own benefit? Are we risking being thrown into jail just so that Dorian can feather his own nest?"

Before Arthur had the chance to answer, the sound of heavy footsteps behind them caught her attention, and she turned around to see who it was. They had been so deep in conversation that they had broken their own rule of always being alert to see who might be watching them.

"There she is!" The man raised his hand and pointed directly at her and Arthur. He had lank ginger hair, and his small eyes gleamed with spiteful satisfaction.

"Elmer Fernsby?" Nancy felt as though she needed to pinch herself to wake up from a bad dream.

"That's the girl, Constable Redfern," Elmer cried triumphantly. "I always knew she'd turn out to be a wrong'un when we lived at the railway camp. I just saw with my own two eyes that she stole a pocket watch from those toffs down the street. She should be thrown into jail."

"Do you know him?" Arthur asked out of the side of his mouth as the constable bore down on them.

"He's just a bully who bears a grudge towards me from many years ago," Nancy murmured. "I seem to recall I knocked you over and beat you up last time we met, Elmer," she added, loud enough for everyone to hear.

He bristled. "Only because you took me by surprise."

She lifted her chin defiantly, even though her heart was thudding under her ribs. "I'm not a frightened young girl anymore, Elmer, I'm a young woman now. I don't know what this scoundrel has been telling you, Constable, but he takes great delight in stirring up trouble. At least he used to when he was the camp bully."

"I'll be the judge of that, miss," the constable said. He looked her up and down and frowned, clearly puzzled. "I must say, you don't look like the typical sort of pickpockets we see around these parts. Most of them are dressed in rags without so much as two pennies to rub together."

"That's because we're not pickpockets," Arthur said firmly. He doffed his cap and leaned forward, shaking hands with the constable. "I'm Arthur Pittman, and this is Nancy Burton. We live at Kingsley House. Perhaps you've heard of it?"

Recognition dawned in Constable Redfern's eyes.

"Of course. I know Miss Kingsley and her sister Marigold in Lower Amberley. Fine, upstanding, charitable women they are too." He glared at Elmer, whose cheeks had turned a dull red. "Are you sure you weren't seeing things, young man? I don't take kindly to having my time wasted."

Elmer scowled. "She ain't the angel she'd have you believe, constable. I know what I saw. Her whole family were a bunch of crooks who fancied themselves better than everyone else, even though her pa was a snivelling wreck any time there was a loud noise working on the railways."

Nancy drew herself up to her full height. "My pa is very well respected in the railway company, I'll have you know, Elmer. He works as a senior clerk, and Ma's buttons are in great demand with all the wealthy ladies."

"I suggest you run along," Constable Redfern said, shooing Elmer away. Once they were alone again, he turned back to Nancy and Arthur. "I have to take complaints like this seriously. I can't just let you go. The senior constables at Gloucester already think we're too lax in the villages, so you'll have to come to the station with me so that I can write everything down for my records and keep them happy."

"Is that really necessary?" Arthur said, giving his most charming smile. "I'm sure you're a busy man."

"I'm afraid it is." The constable gripped them

firmly and propelled them ahead of him. "The station building is just up yonder. It won't take long. I'm sure none of Miss Kingsley's charges would do such a terrible thing as pickpocketing, but if I don't make a record of Elmer's complaint, he'll only stir up more trouble." He gave Nancy a sympathetic smile. "You know what he's like, it seems?"

"Only too well," Nancy sighed. She smiled back at the genial constable, praying that the hidden pocket in her dress would do what it was designed for and keep the stolen pocket watch concealed from prying eyes.

They had barely gone a few steps when a portly woman with pink cheeks and a large bonnet tied firmly under her chin bustled towards them, stopping them in their tracks.

"There you are, Harold. I came to bring you some lunch. You're looking too thin. Also, I've been meaning to call round to the station to ask how things are going with that new constable who's been foisted on you…Mr Peregrine Jenkins, is it? Sounds very lah-di-dah if you ask me." The woman lowered her voice and glanced furtively towards the police station. "I heard a few rumours that he's got more in common with the criminal fraternity than any gentleman of the law should have."

"Hush, Mrs Truelove, and you're to call him Constable Jenkins." He gestured for Nancy and

Arthur to wait next to the wall for a moment and edged closer to the woman.

"Don't hush me," she said, batting her fan against his arm. "And don't call me Mrs Truelove. It sounds ridiculous when I'm your aunt."

Nancy and Arthur exchanged a look, and she bit her lip to stop herself from giggling. It was clear Redfern was used to being chastised by the matriarchal woman as he bobbed his head apologetically. Out of the corner of her eye, Nancy saw Arthur waggle his fingers. She dropped her handkerchief on the ground, and as he bent to retrieve it, she slipped the pocket watch to Arthur, who hid it inside his boot in one easy movement.

"To be honest, Aunt Christine, I wish they'd never sent him here." The constable spoke in a low voice, but the wind had dropped, and Nancy and Arthur could hear every word.

"Why do you say that? Isn't he pulling his weight?"

"It's more that he seems to think I'm some sort of country bumpkin. He's forever telling me how dull it is around here and that the local crimes are barely worth investigating. Nothing more than a few turnips being stolen, he said this morning."

"The cheek of him. Doesn't he realise how much you do to keep the community safe? If he thinks it's dull and there are no exciting crimes, it's down to your hard work, Harold." The lady patted Constable

Redfern on the arm and gave him a twinkling smile. "Are the rumours about him true then?" she asked again, not caring whether anyone overheard.

After an awkward pause, Constable Redfern nodded. He leaned closer to his aunt. "A little bird told me that he got sent here from London because he was involved in some shady dealings with one of the gangs. Of course, you didn't hear that from me." He tapped the side of his nose, and his aunt beamed a smile at him.

"My lips are sealed. I've heard him out and about telling folk that it's because he had such a shining record of clearing up crimes that he's been sent here to show you a thing or two." She hooked her basket higher on her arm before slipping her nephew a freshly baked meat pasty wrapped in paper for his lunch. "Let's hope he soon gets bored of our country ways and takes himself back off to London again. We don't need his sort judging us and then trying to get all the glory for himself."

Constable Redfern suddenly remembered what he was meant to be doing and squared his shoulders. "Anyway, Mrs Truelove, I need to take these two to the station, so I'll bid you a good day."

As the old lady bustled past them, she rested her gloved hand on Nancy's arm for a moment. "That's my nephew. He's the best constable this village has ever had, I'll have you know." She walked a few more steps, then turned around again. "Don't forget you're coming for Sunday lunch after church, Harold. I'm making your favourite syrup sponge for pudding."

Constable Redfern blushed and waved her away before gruffly telling Arthur and Nancy to go into the police station and look lively about it.

CHAPTER 20

*C*onstable Redfern settled his wire-rimmed spectacles on his nose and dipped his fountain pen into the inkwell. "I'll need your full names and why you think Elmer Fernsby accused you of pickpocketing." He looked expectantly at Nancy, not noticing the splodge of ink which dripped onto the ledger open in front of him.

"Shouldn't you examine their clothes for any stolen items first?" The second constable hovered nearby with a steely glint in his eye.

"I think I know how to deal with this, thank you, Constable Jenkins," Redfern said. He gave his colleague a thin smile and rolled his eyes when he thought nobody was looking.

"That's not how we do things in London," Jenkins countered.

A muscle twitched in Constable Redfern's cheek. "Then it's a good thing we're not in London, isn't it." He nodded at Nancy. "Go ahead, please, miss."

Nancy shuffled her feet slightly and gave him a humble smile that she hoped would strike the right tone of deference. "My name is Nancy Burton, and this is my friend, Arthur Pittman."

"Oh yes, I remember you already told me that." Silence fell in the room, other than the scratching sound of his pen as he carefully wrote their names down at the top of the page.

"As I explained, constable, we both live at Kingsley House." Arthur glanced at Nancy. "I was the first child she took in. Nancy joined us a little while later, but it's like home to us."

"As you can imagine, times are hard for Miss Kingsley and her sister," Nancy continued. "There are fourteen children there altogether now. Arthur and I are the eldest, and we work for Mr Dorian Holt, Marigold's husband."

"Mr Holt, the jeweller?" Constable Jenkins gave them a sharp look.

"How do you know him?" Constable Redfern asked. "He has a jewellery shop in Woodchester. Not that I could afford anything that he sells."

"Oh, I don't know him personally," Jenkins said airily. "I used to walk some of the streets around Hatton Garden in London, where the jewellery shops were. It's just a name I heard…I doubt it's the same man. Holt is a very common surname, after all." He strolled past the desk and looked out of the window as though the matter was of no interest to him.

"And you're completely sure that you didn't happen to take anything that doesn't belong to you, Miss Burton?" Constable Redfern dipped his pen in the ink again.

"Elmer used to tell tales when I knew him at the railway camp," Nancy said hastily. "I think it's to make himself more popular." She couldn't quite bring herself to lie outright.

"I know the Fernsby family," Redfern harrumphed, nodding in agreement. "I always thought Cecil should have raised Elmer with a firmer hand, so we'll consider the matter closed." He laid his pen down and blotted his writing before pushing the ledger aside. "All this record-keeping they expect from us these days. It's as if local knowledge counts for nothing anymore. I've known Cressida Kingsley and Marigold for years, and the thought of any of their charges being involved in pickpocketing is ludicrous."

"I'm glad we won't need to take this any further," Arthur said. "Perhaps it would be best if this stayed between us. It would only upset Miss Kingsley, and she's not in the best of health."

"I think that's very sensible," Constable Redfern

agreed. "I suggest you steer clear of Elmer Fernsby from now on, Miss Burton. It wouldn't do to get embroiled in any sort of trouble and bring all of Cressida's good work into disrepute."

"THANK goodness he didn't search us," Nancy said a minute later once they were back outside and walking away from the police station. "I can't believe Elmer, of all people, was watching me. I haven't seen him for years, and isn't it just typical that he saw me at that precise moment."

Arthur lifted his cap and scratched his head, making his hair stick up in tufts. "I have a good mind to tell Dorian today that our time pickpocketing for him needs to come to an end. It's one thing doing it in a large city where folk don't know us, but too many people know everybody's business in the small villages around here."

"Do you really think we could stop?" Nancy felt a surge of hope as she rested a hand on his arm and looked into his blue eyes. "I'm still so scared that something will go wrong, Arthur. It's only through sheer luck that Constable Redfern knows Miss Kingsley and the fact that he admires her charitable work which made him think we could never be involved in criminal activities. If something like that happened again, we might not be so lucky."

He squeezed her hand reassuringly and squared his shoulders. "I'm going to speak to him this evening, Nancy. Even if it means we have to find different jobs in Lower Amberley, it's time for Dorian to accept that we're not going to do his bidding any longer."

Nancy nodded, feeling happier about things than she had for a while. She trusted Arthur to know the right things to say to Dorian, and she would back him up, whatever he suggested. "Shall we celebrate and share a pie from the pie shop? They smelt delicious earlier, and I didn't eat breakfast this morning because I was too nervous. I'm starving."

Before they had a chance to cross the lane, Nancy's heart sank as she saw Constable Jenkins walking briskly towards them with a serious look on his face.

"Let me do the talking," Arthur said quietly. "He's probably got a bee in his bonnet about Constable Redfern not searching us properly."

"Hold on a minute, you two," the burly constable called.

"Does Constable Redfern need us for something else?" Nancy asked innocently.

Panic surged in her chest when Jenkins didn't answer immediately but grasped their arms and steered them around the corner of the cobbler's shop into the shadows.

"I want to speak to you both without all the Thruppley busybodies watching," he said mysteriously. He leaned back out and looked left and right to make sure there was nobody nearby and then turned back to face them.

Nancy shivered with a sense of foreboding. It wouldn't take much for the man to discover the pocket watch and the fact that Elmer had been telling the truth. But the worst thing was it would be Arthur who would get the blame. She couldn't let that happen. "I can explain—"

Arthur nudged her with his elbow, cutting off her words. "Talking to us in this cloak-and-dagger way seems rather irregular, Constable Jenkins. What do you want?"

Much to her surprise, Jenkins folded his arms and leaned nonchalantly against the wall. He was the same height as Arthur but past his prime. His jowls were slack, and now that he was right in front of them, she could see broken veins in his cheeks. He was a man who enjoyed good food and too many glasses of port. She also noticed that his shoes looked as good a quality as those that Horace Smallwood wore. She wondered how a lowly constable could afford such things, and as she caught Arthur's eye, she could tell that he was thinking exactly the same thing.

"I've been watching you both for a little while," Jenkins said without preamble.

Nancy inwardly gasped. That was the last thing she had expected him to say. "I thought you only came to Thruppley recently?"

Jenkins raised one eyebrow. "I've been in the West Country for a couple of months. I've seen you both pickpocketing and taking the pieces back to Dorian Holt's shop."

Arthur's face paled, and Nancy's legs started to tremble. *This is it. The game's up.* She felt Arthur grasp her hand and wondered whether it was his signal for them to make a break for it and try to push past him to run away. But what would be the point? He knew they lived at Kingsley House. They would have to go on the run. Her mind whirled, and bile rose in her throat at the thought of being sent away from everyone she loved. *And never seeing dear Arthur again, for surely we would be in separate prisons.* Tears pricked the back of her eyes, and she blinked them back.

"Don't worry, Miss Burton," Jenkins said smoothly. "I'm not going to arrest you...at least I won't as long as you do what I ask."

"But...who are you...why..?" She could barely whisper as relief mixed with consternation swept over her.

"And what exactly is it that you want us to do?" Arthur's expression was grim.

Jenkins pushed away from the wall and took a couple of paces back and forth in front of them. "I want you to provide me with information, that's all."

"What sort of information?"

"I did a bit of digging, and I know all about your background before Kingsley House, Arthur. And it seems you've done a good job training Nancy in your devious ways as well."

"It's not what I wanted, but we were forced into the situation." Arthur didn't seem to be afraid of Constable Jenkins, Nancy realised. It was as though he was used to people in power not being quite who they appeared, almost as though he had expected it.

"Don't give me that. Everyone makes their choices," Jenkins said with a sharp glare. "I know you're giving the pieces to Dorian Holt and that he repurposes some of them. But I also believe that some of the most expensive items that you're stealing are being sold on."

"That's not true," Nancy said hotly. "He just makes them into other pieces so that they won't be recognised."

Jenkins shook his head and stepped closer, towering over her in a deliberate attempt to intimidate her. "I know I'm right, Miss Burton, and I don't expect you to challenge my authority. Is that clear?"

"Yes, Constable Jenkins." Her mouth felt dry, and she wondered whether the day could get any worse.

"From now on, I want to know exactly what Dorian's plans are, and I want you to keep your ear to the ground and your eyes peeled to find out who he is selling the jewellery on to."

"How are we meant to get this information to you?" Arthur lifted his chin defiantly. "Especially after all that business with Elmer and Constable Redfern today. If we're seen talking to you, Redfern will think it's rather strange, don't you think?"

"Don't you worry about that, Arthur. I'm sure, having worked for Bernard Doyle in the past, you'll know how to keep your wits about you. You both need to just carry on as though nothing has changed."

"How do you know Dorian?" Arthur shot back. "Have you had dealings with him in the past? There are rumours about you—"

"That's none of your business." In a lightning-fast change of mood, Jenkins suddenly threw Arthur against the wall, gripping him in a choke hold, and glowered angrily at him. "If I find out you've told Dorian or Constable Redfern about this conversation, you'll find yourself carted off to Gloucester jail faster than your feet can touch the ground. A quiet word in the right ear, and I reckon I could probably get you locked up for life. And I doubt young Nancy here would fare very well in jail either."

"Get off him," Nancy cried. Arthur's eyes were starting to bulge as Jenkins casually tightened his grip around his neck.

"I'm not a violent man, but I don't like having my polite request thwarted." Jenkins suddenly stepped back and released Arthur, who doubled over and wheezed as he tried to catch his breath. Jenkins jerked his head. "On your way then. And remember, you're to carry on doing exactly what Dorian asks of you, and I'll come and find you when I need more information. I need to get back now; otherwise, that bumbling fool, Redfern, will be wondering where I've got to."

With that, the constable sauntered away, whistling under his breath.

"Are you alright, Arthur?" Nancy put her arm around his shoulder, relieved to see that the colour had returned to his face, and his breathing sounded normal again.

"I will be." Arthur looked at her with a troubled expression. "There's nothing worse than a constable who's turned into a criminal, Nancy. I wanted to tell Dorian that we were stopping, but now we can't."

"We're completely trapped, aren't we." A leaden feeling of dread settled heavily in Nancy's stomach. "Do you know the strangest thing...I bumped into an old woman earlier today. It turned out she was Ava

Piper, the fortune teller, who told Miss Kingsley she would have lots of children."

"The woman who gave her the feather." Arthur nodded as he noticed the one tucked into Nancy's shawl. "That's a coincidence."

"She warned me about a man who would betray us. I thought she meant Dorian, but I think now it must be Constable Jenkins she was speaking about."

"He's got us backed into a corner, that's for sure." Arthur tucked Nancy's hand into the crook of his arm. He suddenly smiled, and his blue eyes twinkled. "Don't worry. I'll think of something to get us out of this. I don't know what it will be yet, but Bernard Doyle taught me well, and not just how to pick-pocket. He always used to say that greed was a man's downfall, and I know greed when I see it, Nancy. I reckon our Constable Jenkins is on the take. Why else would he not just arrest us?"

"He sounds like a dangerous man."

"Maybe he's met his match in us." He grinned again. "We just need to bide our time and look for an opportunity to expose him."

As they walked back out into the sunshine, Nancy hoped that Arthur's optimism was well-placed. It felt as though the net was closing in on them from all sides. Dorian's demands were becoming worse with every week that passed. He was becoming greedier than ever, and now they had Constable Jenkins breathing down their neck as well. Not to mention Bernard Doyle warning Arthur off.

"Perhaps I need to try and find that fortune teller again," she said with a rueful smile. "I always thought I never believed in such fanciful things, but I reckon we need all the help we can get right now."

"You might be right, but we can't tackle any of this on an empty stomach, so the first thing we're going to do is go and have a pie to eat." Arthur suddenly looked more serious and slightly bashful. "I do know one thing, Nancy: I wouldn't be able to do any of this without you by my side. It's nice not feeling alone."

In spite of their perilous situation, Nancy's heart swelled with happiness. "I only hope we can get through this unscathed," she murmured.

We need some sort of miracle, dear Arthur, and I'll do whatever is in my power to save us. The thought buoyed her up as they turned into Thruppley Village Square, but then she gasped with shock as she was confronted by a startling sight she would remember for the rest of her life.

CHAPTER 21

*N*ancy stopped in her tracks as she found herself face-to-face with another young woman. It was as though she was looking at her own reflection in a mirror, and she heard Arthur's sharp intake of breath next to her.

"Look…that's her…the girl I saw in Woodchester a few years ago, who I mistook for you, Nancy," he said.

The old woman, Ava Piper, was standing next to the girl, and she stepped forward. "Nancy, there's someone I want you to meet. This is Abigail, and I believe she's your long-lost sister."

"Or you are *my* long-lost sister," Abigail said, rushing forward to embrace Nancy.

Tears pooled in Nancy's eyes as she returned Abigail's hug and then stepped back to look at her properly. They had the same curly brown hair and green eyes. They were the same height. Other than the fact that they were dressed differently, they were identical.

"But…I don't understand," she said hoarsely, swinging between disbelief and elation. "I mean, I was adopted. I've always known that, but Ma never told me I had a sister."

"Or a twin sister at that," Arthur said. His face split into a wide grin, and he quickly took his cap off and shook hands with Abigail. "It was you I mistook for Nancy. I'm sorry if I scared you, but I was convinced you were her."

Nancy shook her head, still hardly daring to believe that it was true that she had a twin sister. "A gentleman called Horace Smallwood stopped me in the park one day and spoke to me as though we were friends. He must have thought I was you, and ever since then, I've wondered…" She trailed off, unable to put into words the deep ache of yearning she had always had to meet her true family. *My blood relation… my sister.* She couldn't believe it.

"I've always felt as though something in my life was missing, and I think you must have felt it too," Abigail said softly. She stepped forward and linked arms with Nancy as though she couldn't bear for them to be separated again. "Don't get me wrong, I've led a very blessed life; at least once we moved to

Thruppley. But I always longed for a sister and wished it would be one of my own age." She pressed her hand over her heart and blinked back tears. "It seems my wish has been answered." She turned to look at Ava and back at Nancy. "Did you know about this, Ava?"

Now, it was Nancy's turn to look at the fortune teller. Her milky eyes twinkled brightly, and she radiated happiness. "I never knew for sure, but many times, when I consulted the cards, they showed me that there was more to your family than met the eye. As for the full story, that's only something I can tell with someone else present...your real mama."

"But how do you know Abigail and her family?" Nancy wanted to learn everything about them.

"Aha, there lies a tale," Ava said, patting Nancy's hand.

Abigail jumped in. "My ma and pa live in a cottage in the grounds of the Rodborough Hotel where Pa is the head gardener. Horace Smallwood is my uncle. Jack Piper is my stepfather...and Ava is his ma. So Ava is like a grandmother to me, even though my real father is Dominic Smallwood, Horace's brother."

"Wait...what? This all sounds very confusing," Arthur chuckled, scratching his head.

"Let me try and explain it better," Abigail said, joining in with his laughter. "Dominic Smallwood, my real papa, was the black sheep of the Smallwood family. He took advantage of my ma...her name is Maisie. But when he discovered she was in the family way, he wanted nothing more to do with her. He ended up marrying a wealthy American heiress and running away to France with her. He was implicated in some rather unsavoury goings-on, which we don't talk about. He's never returned to England, and I don't know him. Jack, Ava's son, is my stepfather, but I love him as though he was my real pa."

Nancy nodded as everything became clearer. "I think I understand better now, but how can it be possible that you and I are twins, and we never knew?" She glanced at Ava, wondering whether the old woman was keeping the truth from her, but her expression was open and sympathetic. "My ma always told me that I was found abandoned on the steps of a home for foundling babies."

"Where exactly was it you were found, my dear?" Ava asked gently.

"Frampton Village is where we lived when I was adopted."

"That would make sense," Ava murmured.

"My pa, Bill Scott, was the gravedigger, but he died when I was still a baby, and Ma remarried. Papa Ezra took me on as though I was one of his own, and he and Ma have three other children: my brothers and sister, Luke, Primrose, and Josiah. I don't see much of them because when times were very hard for our family, and Papa Ezra had to move for his health to take up a different job with the railway company, they sent me to live at Kingsley House so that I would receive a better education."

"Kingsley House is a charitable home for children," Arthur explained. "Like an orphanage, but much nicer."

"I've heard of it," Ava said. "They do wonderful work, by all accounts." She smiled at them both. "If you two are anything to go by, you've both had a very good upbringing. I can always tell a kind-hearted person, even if they have been drawn into doing things they might not otherwise have chosen to do."

Nancy felt a ripple of alarm and glanced at Arthur. *Does Ava know we're pickpockets? Is this wonderful meeting with my twin sister about to be ruined by what Dorian has forced us to do?*

"I'm going to make a better future for Nancy," Arthur said stoutly.

Ava nodded serenely. "I know, my dear. I could tell as soon as I saw you that you two are destined to live together happily for many years, even though there might be troublesome times ahead."

"You must come and meet all of us," Abigail said excitedly. "It's not too far to walk to the Rodborough Hotel. Ma helps Gloria out at the dressmaking shop in the village some days, but she's at home today."

"Gloria? Is she another relation? That must be

why the woman in the dressmaker's looked at me as though she knew me," Nancy said with a wry smile.

"Gloria is a distant cousin of my ma's. It was only when we came to Thruppley when I was a little girl that we discovered we were part of a wonderful extended family who used to work on the narrow-boats." Abigail held up her fingers and ticked them off. "There's Verity and Bert...Dolly and Joe and their son Albert. They all live at the lockkeeper's cottage."

Nancy frowned, trying to keep up.

"Then there's Amy, who is Gloria and Dolly's younger sister. She's married to Billy, who is Joe's younger brother. They live at the blacksmith's cottage. And, Jonty, Dolly's brother, who works on the leisure boat, taking guests up and down the canal with Joe—"

"Wait...I think I've met Joe," Nancy said. "When I was a lot younger, and we were moving from Eaton Cottage to the railway camp, we stopped our horse and cart to look at the narrow boats on the canal. A very kind-hearted gentleman was showing all the well-to-do folks the daffodils in the field, and he spoke to us. His boy, Albert, was there as well."

"Yes, that's Ma's cousin, Joe, and his son."

"To think I had you and so many other members of my family, so close all this time, and I never even knew."

"We must put that right immediately. Will you

both come with us to where Ma and Pa live to meet them?"

Nancy suddenly felt shy and overwhelmed by everything, and Ava put a restraining hand on Abigail's arm.

"It's a lot for you to take in," the old woman said, giving her a sympathetic smile. "Perhaps we should let Nancy have a few days to come to terms with all this, Abigail." She chuckled. "You might not remember how overwhelmed you felt when you first met your extended family."

Abigail looked momentarily disappointed but then nodded. "I'm sorry, Nancy. It's just such a wonderful discovery that I want to share our good news with everyone. What about your ma and pa? You will surely want to tell them?"

Nancy sighed and felt her own excitement wane slightly. Would it be fair on Ma and Papa Ezra to rush headlong into this new family without them knowing? Even though she didn't see them very often anymore, they were the only family she had ever known, other than everyone at Kingsley House.

Arthur seemed to sense her conflicted emotions, and he squeezed her hand to reassure her. "Perhaps you should write to your ma before meeting everyone else?"

"We're not going anywhere, Nancy," Abigail said,

giving her another hug. "This is a shock for all of us, but you must do what you think is right."

Nancy nodded slowly. "I think what Arthur said is a good idea. I'll write to Ma this evening as soon as we get back to Kingsley House."

"Do you think she will be happy for us?" Abigail looked worried. "And my mama...I mean *our* mama... when should we tell her that we've met each other?" She looked at Ava for guidance.

"I think out of respect to Nancy's adoptive family, we should wait a few days so that Nancy has a chance to write to her mother."

The church clock struck the hour, and Arthur fidgeted restlessly. "We should get back to Kingsley House, Nancy," he said. "Dorian and Miss Kingsley might be wondering where we've got to, and we don't want to give them any cause for alarm."

"Can I come and visit you very soon, Abigail?" Now that Nancy had met her twin sister, she was suddenly afraid that something terrible might happen to stop them from seeing each other again. Also, she desperately wanted to speak to her real ma. *To find out why I was left behind and abandoned at birth...the forgotten child.* It was a sobering thought. Abigail's enthusiasm was all very well, but perhaps her real mother, Maisie, wouldn't want to meet her.

"I wouldn't have it any other way," Abigail said, tears welling in her eyes again. She brushed them away and quickly undid the silk flower, which was pinned to her dress, and pinned it onto Nancy's dress instead. "Take this so that you'll know that it wasn't just a dream, us meeting after all these years. And promise me that you will visit as soon as you have told your adoptive family."

Ava smiled at Nancy, sensing her misgivings. "Your real mother will be over the moon to meet you, Nancy. Maisie had many hardships to overcome when she was not much older than you. I think you'll grow to love each other very much."

"Maisie...and my twin sister, Abigail," she whispered. "What a miracle."

As THEY PARTED company and Nancy and Arthur headed back out of the village, she suddenly remembered they were meant to be getting something to eat.

"What about going to the bakery for that pie, Arthur? You must be ravenous."

He grinned and shook his head. "We don't have time to eat; there are far more important things to do. We need to find out more about the mystery of how you came to be separated from your twin sister at birth." A shadow crossed his face. "Not to mention thinking of a way to free ourselves from Dorian and Constable Jenkins' impossible demands."

"You're right. I've lost my appetite anyway, and there's so much on my mind, I can barely think straight."

They walked on, each mulling over the life-changing events which had just happened that day, both good and bad.

CHAPTER 22

*C*ressida bustled out of the parlour, her silver bangles jangling, and greeted Nancy with a beaming smile. "Guess what? We have visitors, my dear."

"We wondered who the horse and cart belong to out in the lane," Arthur said.

"It's your family, Nancy. All of them. Tess is entertaining all the children, and dear Ezra insisted on chopping up a load of wood outside while we waited for you to get home. Your mama has been entertaining me with stories of the navvies at the railway camps. It reminded me of some of the delightful gypsies and narrowboat travellers I've known in my lifetime."

"What a wonderful coincidence. I was going to write Ma a letter this evening, but now I won't have to." Nancy's smile faltered, and Cressida stepped forward.

"Is something wrong? Your cheeks are flushed. You're not coming down with a fever, are you?" She frowned. "I hope Dorian hasn't been working you too hard at the shop."

Nancy glanced at Arthur, and he answered for her.

"Nancy has just had rather a shocking revelation," he said in a low voice. "We've been to Thruppley today, and Nancy bumped into someone who looks just like her. It transpires it's her identical twin sister, Abigail, who just so happens to be the niece of Horace Smallwood."

Cressida Kingsley looked as shocked as they had a little earlier. "The Smallwoods of Rodborough Hotel and many of the large mills in the area?" She took Nancy's hand and gave her a searching look. "And a twin sister?" Her eyes misted with tears. "That's… that's wonderful, my dear." She glanced over her shoulder towards the parlour. "I suppose you will want to ask Margaret…your mama, many questions. Be kind to her, Nancy. I can tell that she still feels bad about sending you to live with us here at Kingsley House. She did it with good intentions, remember that."

Emotion thickened in Nancy's throat, and she nodded. "I know, Miss Kingsley. It's just—"

"You don't have to explain or worry about me being offended," Cressida said softly, squeezing her hand. "I like to think I've always done my best to make Kingsley House feel like a home for all of you, but I appreciate it's not the same as being raised by your own family, even if they were your adoptive family."

"I just have so many questions to ask her."

"Arthur, why don't you go to the kitchen and ask Moira to make a cup of tea for Margaret and Nancy?"

"Do you want me to be with you, Nancy?" Arthur was full of concern for her. Cressida's expression softened as she watched them both.

"No, I'll be fine, but thank you for offering. Finding out about Abigail doesn't change how I feel about Ma and Papa Ezra and my brothers and sisters."

There was a slight tremor in Nancy's voice, but it was of excitement, not regret. "If anything, I'm lucky. It will be like having two families, and I know how fortunate that makes me compared to many."

Arthur shot her a sympathetic smile before hurrying away. "I'll ask Moira for cake as well. We haven't eaten all day, and I don't want you fainting from hunger."

"He's a very thoughtful young man and thinks the world of you," Cressida said as she ushered Nancy towards the parlour. Her eyes twinkled. "I shouldn't be surprised if Marigold and I might need a new bonnet each to attend a wedding in the not-too-distant future. In you go now, and I'll be in the library if you need me."

Nancy was grateful for the lighthearted comment. It helped ease her nerves for the conversation she was about to have.

"Ma, this is a wonderful surprise!"

Margaret turned from the window in the parlour, where she had been standing, and hurried across the room to embrace Nancy. "I hope you don't mind us calling unannounced, our Nancy. Ezra's work is changing again, and it all happened so quickly there wasn't time to write you a letter. We're on our way to Gloucester to catch the train to Birmingham."

"Blimey, that's a change. I thought you were settled at the railway camp near Oxford."

A hint of pride came into Margaret's eyes. "Mr Harrington has been so pleased with Ezra's work that he's been promoted again. He's going to be a manager now, overseeing works in Birmingham where the railway is expanding apace. We're going to have our own house, and it's even got one of those new-fangled indoor privies, and I'll have a housemaid." She blushed. "Can you believe it? Us with a maid! Haven't we gone up in the world!"

"Oh, Ma, that's wonderful." Nancy felt genuinely

happy for them. "Papa Ezra deserves it, and so do you. And what about Luke? Will he change jobs?"

"Yes, he's had a promotion as well." Margaret's face clouded. "I'm sorry we left you here at Kingsley House. I've been thinking a lot about the past, and I hope you don't think that we abandoned you."

Nancy sighed and walked to the window. "Actually, Ma, there's something I need to talk to you about."

"Tea and cake for you both." Moira bustled in, humming a lively tune under her breath. "I'll just leave it here, shall I, Mrs Burton?" She sensed it was a private moment and hastily left the tray on the table, retreating after giving Margaret a small curtsey.

"What were you saying?" Margaret asked. "Has something bad happened?"

Nancy poured out two cups of tea and offered her one of the slices of rich fruitcake. "You always told me I was adopted, Ma, and I know you and Pa did your best for me." She took a sip of tea, wanting to choose her words carefully.

Margaret suddenly looked nervous. "We loved you so much, Nancy. That day when I first saw you in Bill's arms, under his coat...I'll never forget it."

"Is it really true that he found me abandoned on the steps of Hayton House? That I had been left there by travellers, who knew Mrs Lowell took in foundlings?" Nancy's heart thudded in her chest as

Margaret turned her head away, not quite meeting her eye.

"Why do you ask? Does it matter after all this time?"

"I met someone earlier today." The cup rattled slightly in the saucer as Nancy's hands trembled. "Her name is Abigail. She's my twin sister, Ma. And her ma...the woman who must have given me up is called Maisie. Did you know about that?"

Margaret put her cup of tea down with a clatter and jumped up. She started pacing in front of the hearth, and her face was pale. "It's not how it sounds, Nancy," she cried. "You have to understand that Bill never did anything wrong, and we were so desperate for a baby of our own after our little boy died in childbirth just a few days before Bill found you."

"So, is it true that Maisie didn't want me? She chose to keep Abigail, but not me?" Nancy blinked back her tears. When she said it like that, it made her feel bleakly wretched.

Margaret shook her head firmly. "No, it's not like that at all. Bill was the village gravedigger, as you know. He was walking through the village very early that morning, and Maisie's mother, Violet Griffin, came rushing out of their house. She was carrying you, wrapped up in a tatty old shawl. All she said was that Maisie had had twins but that you hadn't survived the birth. She was half deranged, talking no sense, Bill said. But she genuinely thought you had died during the birth, Nancy. Bill did as well. You were cold and blue…and such a tiny little mite." Her hand went to her throat as the memories carried her back to the past. "Bill was a decent man who believed in doing right for those who had passed away. He promised Violet, Maisie's mother, that he would bury you in consecrated ground in the churchyard rather than a pauper's burial."

A shiver ran down Nancy's back. How close she had come to not being in the world. "What happened then?" she whispered.

"Bill hugged you to his chest. The warmth must have revived you, and he realised almost immediately that you were still alive, thank the Lord. He knew that Violet and Maisie were practically destitute and didn't have the means to raise two children, and I had so much love to give but no baby of my own. He brought you back to our cottage, and from the moment he laid you in my arms, I knew my prayers for a baby had been answered."

The pendulum of the carriage clock over the mantle swung, and the sound of ticking filled the stunned silence. "Does Ezra know the truth?" Nancy asked eventually. She was practically lost for words.

"Yes, I never kept any secrets from him. Bill died, and when I remarried and we started moving around for Ezra's work, it seemed too complicated to tell you that you had a twin sister." Margaret's voice cracked with emotion. "I was afraid they might ask for you back, truth be told." She bowed her head, and tears rolled down her cheeks. "Can you ever forgive me, Nancy? I hope you believe that we did everything with the best of intentions. I always knew you were a bright girl, and that's why we wanted you to receive an education here at Kingsley House instead of working your fingers to the bone, making buttons like me. I never imagined that Ezra would recover from his illness or end up getting promoted."

Nancy took a deep breath and stood up, knowing that her next words had the power to make or break her relationship with her family. "When I first came here, I thought you wanted to send me away and forget all about me, but now I'm older, I can see that you wanted the best for me."

"We never forgot about you," Margaret cried, with a hint of relief in her eyes. "Luke and Primrose talk about you nonstop, and we miss you. In fact, our Primrose has been pestering me about whether she could come and work in the kitchen with Moira if Miss Kingsley will have her. She's a hard-working girl, but I said we would have to get settled in Birmingham first and then see about it."

Nancy felt a wave of compassion for her ma, all her old resentments forgotten. But she still had one more question she needed to ask. "Will you mind me getting to know Abigail? And Maisie?"

"Of course not." Margaret rushed to her side and brushed a lock of hair from her forehead, giving her a tender smile. "It's only natural you would want to. And I just hope that Maisie will understand what we did as well."

"You said you doubted she would have been able to raise two children?"

"It's true. They were as poor as church mice. Violet was very ill, and Maisie was a mudlark, barely scratching a living. And I wonder whether Violet even told her it was twins. There were rumours that Masie was taken advantage of because Violet pretended baby Abigail was her own. Nobody except Bill and I knew that it was Maisie who gave birth, but we left the village not long after because we couldn't risk anyone putting two and two together if they saw you. Maisie was rarely seen in the village because she suffered from amnesia, and her ma preferred to keep her at home."

Nancy's heart ached as she thought about the tragic events so long ago and all the secrets surrounding them. "You're still my family, Ma. But I would like to get to know Abigail. We look so similar; several people have mistaken us for each other."

"I'll write letters to Maisie explaining everything." Margaret dabbed away her tears and gave Nancy another hug. "You've grown into a fine young woman. I'm proud of you, Nancy."

The sound of Ezra's voice drifted in from the hallway. "Are you ready to leave Margaret? We don't want to miss the train." He strode into the parlour. "I hope you've caught up with all our news. I can't believe that you're grown up now, Nancy." He winked. "I fancy that Arthur has a soft spot for you. He's been helping me fetch the wood in and talked about nothing else but how wonderful you are."

"Nancy! How are you?" Luke and Primrose came running to the parlour, too, followed by Josiah, and everyone started talking over one another. "Anne and Sophie have been singing for us. We feel as if we've been to the theatre; they're so good."

"There's so much news. Nancy has discovered her real family," Margaret murmured to Ezra.

"And have you told her everything this time?" When Margaret nodded, he looked relieved. "We didn't like keeping the truth from you, and you'll always be my daughter."

Her heart lifted with happiness as they all discussed the move to Birmingham and the possibility that Primrose might come and work at Kingsley House, which Cressida seemed delighted by.

All too soon, it was time for them to leave, and

Arthur put his arm around Nancy's shoulder as they waved the horse and cart off.

"How did your ma take the news? Did you find out more?"

Nancy nodded and looked up into his kind blue eyes. "They thought I'd passed away when I was born. It was sheer luck that Bill realised I was still alive and Ma was desperate for a baby. She's given me her blessing to get to know Abigail and Maisie."

"And the rest of what sounds like an enormous family," Arthur chuckled. There was no envy in his voice, but Nancy knew he sometimes felt sad about having no family of his own.

"I want you to meet them all as well, Arthur. You're the most special person in the world to me, and I'll tell them so. I'm going to go and visit them tomorrow evening if you'd like to come with me."

He instantly looked happier. "Of course. And you're truly special to me as well."

"Is that a blush I see, Arthur Pittman," she teased.

"Certainly not! I was just trying to think about how we can outwit Dorian and Constable Jenkins and stop pickpocketing."

"It can't happen a moment too soon." They linked arms and walked back inside, where the whole household had gathered, clamouring to hear Nancy's amazing news.

CHAPTER 23

*D*orian looked up from his workbench when Nancy and Arthur came through the back door. He put his tools down and stood up, giving Nancy a smile, which surprised her. He barely stayed at Kingsley House anymore, and she couldn't help but feel sorry for Marigold. It seemed as though it was a marriage in name only, but she thought Marigold seemed happier when he stayed above the shop.

He rubbed his hands together. "I haven't had a chance to properly congratulate you about finding your long-lost sister, Nancy. It must have come as something of a surprise to discover that you are part of the Smallwood family. They are the wealthiest in the area." He pulled a face, attempting humour.

"Rather ironic that you came from such an impoverished background, but your black sheep father, Dominic Smallwood, could have given you a very different life."

Nancy didn't rise to the bait. "Dominic had nothing to do with Abigail's life either. But her uncle Horace is a kind-hearted, charitable man."

"So have you met all of your extended family now?"

Arthur started polishing the silver platters laid out on the workbench and cocked one eyebrow. It was unusual for Dorian to be so chatty and pleasant.

Nancy caught his look but figured that perhaps, for once, Dorian was genuinely interested. "Arthur and I went round to the lockkeeper's cottage the other evening where Dolly and Joe live with Verity and Bert. My twin sister, Abigail, was there, as well as my mama, Maisie."

"Oh my, it must have been a very heartwarming reunion," Dorian said. He actually looked moved, and Nancy eagerly told him about the meeting.

"Maisie never knew I was still alive when I was born. She can't even remember anything about her confinement because she had amnesia. In fact, she believed Abigail was her little sister for a while... something that Violet, Maisie's ma encouraged. That's why she never came looking for me. The best news is that all their distant cousins live locally in

Thruppley. Maisie and her husband, Jack Piper, live in the grounds of the Rodborough Hotel because Jack is the gardener, and Abigail said it's so beautiful there. She often goes into the hotel where Horace and Lillian Smallwood sometimes host grand gatherings." Her eyes shone at the thought of being invited there one day.

"So what about Horace Smallwood? Have you met him yet?" Dorian's question was casual as he started tidying away a few items of jewellery that he'd been working on. "He is your uncle, after all."

"No, not yet. Abigail told me that he's away on business at the moment, but as soon as he returns, they're going to introduce us." Nancy suddenly hoped it didn't sound as though she was getting above her station. "The rest of the family are just ordinary, hard-working folk like me. They work on the canal, in blacksmithing and dressmaking. I can't believe they've been so welcoming. Not just to me, but Arthur as well."

Arthur stood up and came to stand by Nancy's side. "While we're discussing this, I've come to a decision about our work with you."

"A decision?" The pleasant smile on Dorian's face slipped slightly, and his eyes hardened. "Since when have you started speaking on Nancy's behalf? Or thinking that you can tell me what to do?"

Nancy sensed the atmosphere change between

Dorian and Arthur as tension crackled between them. She knew exactly what Arthur was about to say and that Dorian wouldn't like it.

"I don't speak on Nancy's behalf, but I love her."

"Oh…" His words caught her off guard, and her heart flipped in her chest. It wasn't perhaps the most romantic setting she had dreamed of, but she didn't care. He was standing slightly behind her, and she entwined her fingers with his behind her back, where Dorian wouldn't see, to give him courage.

Dorian's lip curled in scorn. "I'm not quite sure why you're telling me that, Arthur. Romance is the fastest way to ruin a man, trust me." He sounded sour and resentful.

Arthur lifted his chin and gave Dorian a hard stare. "Just because you don't treat Marigold well doesn't mean I would ever behave the same way. Like I said, I love Nancy. Now that it has come to light that she's part of the Smallwood family, I'm sure you can appreciate that we can't continue pickpocketing and stealing for you, Dorian. I don't want anything to jeopardise Nancy's relationship with her new family, and frankly, this has gone on for far too long."

"How dare you say that." Dorian's face darkened with anger. "You know very well that the future of Kingsley House depends on you carrying on pick-pocketing. It will be on your conscience when all the children become homeless street urchins or sent to the orphanage—"

Arthur shook his head and held up his hand, stopping him mid-sentence. "Don't give us that, Dorian. We know it's not true. I overheard Cressida and Marigold saying that the finances of Kingsley House are in perfectly good order. You've been lying to us all this time. We know you want us to carry on pickpocketing just for your own greed. You must be sitting on a fortune by now."

Instead of looking defeated, Nancy shivered as Dorian casually shrugged as though he didn't even care about Arthur's accusations. "Fine," he snapped. "I'll agree to you stopping pickpocketing after you've done one last job for me. How about that?"

"You always have to have the last word, don't you," Arthur growled. "I'd rather we stopped here and now."

Dorian's lips pinched in a stubborn line. "If you don't agree to this one last job I'm asking of you, I'll tell the constables in Gloucester everything. I have several of them in the palm of my hand. All it will take is one word from me, and you'll both be thrown into jail. Wouldn't it be a shame for Nancy's new family to see her fall from grace when they've only just found each other," he sneered.

Nancy crossed her arms and couldn't stand

silently by. "If we agree to do this job, do you really promise it will be the last one? That this will be an end to it, and you'll never ask us to steal again?"

"Of course," Dorian said, brightening. He jerked his thumb towards her. "You could learn a thing or two from your sweetheart, Arthur. Nancy is a sensible young woman who understands that if you do what I want, you will have what you want."

Arthur looked at Nancy, and she gave him a small nod. It wasn't ideal, but they had no choice, really. "What is this job you want us to do?" he asked reluctantly.

Dorian rubbed his hands together, suddenly more businesslike. "I have it on good authority that Lady Ponsley-Mortimer is coming to the grand summer ball at the Rodborough Hotel next week. I know of her from when I used to live in London and Bath. She's extremely wealthy and wears only the finest jewellery." He grinned with a sly glint in his eyes. "She's a terrible show-off, but that works in our favour."

Nancy gasped. "Don't say you want us to rob her at the Rodborough Hotel? At my uncle's business of all places?" She wished they had never agreed.

Dorian gave a short bark of laughter. "It couldn't be more sublime, Nancy. You've already said that your twin sister visits the hotel often. All you'll need to do is pretend to be Abigail and go to the ball. Nobody will be any wiser."

"What if she's already going? We can't both be there."

"You'll have to think of some excuse to make her stay away. Pretend you want to meet her at Nailsbridge to look at the mill or to have a go in the narrowboat to find out more about your extended family. I'm sure you'll think of something to keep her out of the way for an hour or two. By the time she realises you're not there, the robbery will already be over. I'll make sure Arthur has a good suit, and he can pretend to be one of the servants, just long enough to create a diversion for you. You will steal Lady Ponsley-Mortimer's jewellery and bring it to me. It will be such a busy night, nobody will notice, and I'll be waiting nearby. It's the perfect crime and a fitting way for you to end your career as criminals working for me." He bowed with a flourish and another burst of laughter, and Nancy wondered whether he had finally tipped over into some sort of insanity.

"We can't agree to that," Arthur said bluntly but forcefully. "What sort of cruel joke are you playing by expecting Nancy to do this for you? If word got out that there was a robbery at the hotel, it would ruin her uncle's reputation."

Dorian shrugged nonchalantly again. "You might not realise that Dominic Smallwood, your papa, was a thief as well. That's why he had to run away to France." He gave Nancy a thin smile. "Criminality runs in your blood, my dear. I suggest you do what I've asked. Otherwise, you'll have to run away to France as well to escape the law. Is that really the life you want? With all your family, knowing that you are nothing but a common thief."

Anger rose in Nancy's chest, and she stepped closer to Dorian, determined not to show him that she was upset. "Very well. We'll do it, but after that… never again. I'm not afraid of you, Dorian. If you ever try to threaten us again in the future, I'll make sure that Cressida and Marigold know exactly what sort of man you are."

They locked eyes for a moment, and then Dorian waved in the direction of the shop. "You'd better open up. There will be customers coming in soon, and just think, in a week, everything will be over, and you can put all of this in the past.

"And what about you?"

"Me? I'll be long gone," he said airily. "A very wealthy man, and glad to see the back of Kingsley House, Cressida, and Marigold, not to mention all those wretched children." He hummed, full of self-satisfaction. "You probably know that Marigold and I are not really in love, so there's no point pretending otherwise. And that little fact remains between us for now, of course."

What a horrible man. Marigold will be better off without you. Nancy bit back the comment. They would have to come up with a plan fast, she realised. She and Arthur would go to visit Abigail after work. There was nobody else they could trust to help them bring Dorian down.

CHAPTER 24

$\mathcal{N}$ ancy still felt shy speaking to Jack Piper, Abigail's stepfather, but he was nothing but smiles when he saw her and Arthur walking up the path of the gardener's cottage at the edge of the grounds of the hotel.

"Evening, Nancy. Are you here to see Abigail? Or Maisie, perhaps?" He leaned on his spade, pausing from digging a new flower bed, and pushed his cap to the back of his head.

"Both of them, if that's possible?" She looked around appreciatively. "Your garden looks lovely, Mr Piper. And I've heard people in the village saying that hotel gardens alone are worth coming from London to visit."

"That's very kind of you, and you must call me Jack. There's no need for formality between family, is there?" He snipped off a cornflower and handed it to her. "Maisie is finishing making a dress with Gloria at the dressmaker's shop. Abigail has gone to Lock-keeper's cottage, and I expect Maisie will be there shortly, so if you head to the canal, you're bound to see them unless you'd rather wait and come back here later."

"It's a lovely evening, so we'll enjoy the walk and head to the cottage." Arthur and Nancy linked arms and continued on their way. It was a balmy summer evening, and birdsong filled the air as they followed the dusty lanes down to the canal so that they could walk along the towpath. Coots paddled in the reeds, and a heron flapped lazily up from the water meadows on the other side to sit in one of the oak trees next to the canal and watch for fish.

"Do you think we should just come clean and tell them everything?" Nancy asked him. "It feels risky because we've only just met them. But who else will help us?"

Arthur scratched his chin. "It's not something we can burden Cressida and Marigold with. They already have enough to worry about with all the children."

"I feel awful that Dorian is planning to leave Marigold, and she doesn't even know. What a humiliation for her to suffer."

"I think she'll be quietly relieved," Arthur said.

They stepped aside as a sturdy pony ambled towards them, pulling a narrowboat.

"Ta, mister," the lad called, walking next to the pony.

Arthur tipped his hat in greeting to the family on the narrowboat. "I heard Marigold talking to Cressida the other day," he continued. "Marry in haste, repent at leisure, was all I caught. Let's face it, he hasn't exactly been a kind and considerate husband to her, always making snide remarks about Kingsley House and the work they do for the children."

"I'm glad you're nothing like him," Nancy said without thinking. She blushed as he held her gaze for a beat. For a moment, she thought he wanted to say something, but he looked away again.

An avenue of willow trees lay ahead of them, and their fronds tugged on the surface of the water. There was dappled shade beneath them, and just as Nancy was thinking how romantic it looked, her heart sank when she saw Constable Jenkins appear from the shadows. "He's like a bloomin' jack-in-a-box popping up everywhere," she muttered to Arthur. "How does he always seem to know where we are? I hate the way he watches us."

"I was hoping to bump into you two," the constable said, striding towards them as though his behaviour was perfectly acceptable.

"I'd hardly call it bumping into us," Arthur shot

back sarcastically. "Obviously, you've been following us."

Constable Jenkins stood in front of them, blocking their path, and puffed his cheeks out, looking officious. "I make it my business to find out things which are important to me." He rocked forward on his toes and raised his eyebrows. "I gather something big is being planned?"

"What makes you think that?" Arthur wasn't going to make it easy for him.

Jenkins tapped the side of his nose and gave them a sly wink. "Like I said, I keep up with what's happening on my patch. So what exactly has Dorian asked you to do? And don't think about missing any of the important details," he added in a threatening tone.

"I'm to steal jewellery from Lady Ponsley-Mortimer at the summer ball next week," Nancy said quietly. She glanced over her shoulder to make sure that they were alone, still scarcely able to believe that she could talk about it as though it was the most natural thing in the world.

"Aha, the summer ball at the Rodborough Hotel?" Constable Jenkins nodded with a thoughtful expression. "I suppose it makes sense to make use of the fact that you have just discovered your long-lost twin sister. Dorian certainly wouldn't want to miss an opportunity like that."

Nancy opened her mouth to ask how he knew about her and Abigail discovering each other but then realised there was no point. It sounded as though Jenkins knew everything that was going on in the village.

"I'll be there as well to provide the diversion for Nancy." Arthur's words were clipped, and he made no secret of the fact that he disliked everything about the policeman.

"That sounds grand, and I have every faith in your abilities."

"Shouldn't you stop it from happening?" *Like a proper constable.* Nancy refrained from adding the last part out loud.

"No, this is the perfect opportunity to finally be able to put Dorian behind bars. I want you to go ahead with the theft, and then both come outside to give the jewels to Dorian. I will be waiting nearby with one of the constables from Gloucester so that we can arrest him in the act of receiving stolen goods."

"And what about us? Dorian has agreed that this is the last job we will be doing for him."

Jenkins lifted his hands, palms upwards, in a gesture of goodwill. "I shall tell the constable that you were merely acting on Dorian's instructions. We'll have to write a report for my superiors, but I'll explain that you were helping me catch a hardened criminal." He looked at them through narrowed eyes. "I expect you'll be let off without any further consequences because I'll put in a good word for you."

"Are you sure about that?" Nancy demanded. "It would be simple enough for us to refuse to do the job, and we only have your word that we won't get into trouble."

"I am an honourable man of the law," Constable Jenkins said, puffing out his chest and looking offended. "You might even receive some sort of reward, and I'm sure your uncle, Horace Smallwood, will be delighted at the part you're playing to bring down someone as odious as Dorian Holt."

"Where will we find you outside after the...after the theft?" Nancy stuttered, and her hands felt clammy at the thought of what they had to do. Jenkins was being rather vague about the details.

"Dorian said he would wait for us near the stables," Arthur explained. "It's easy for him to slip in and out of the grounds of the hotel and then walk across the common back to Woodchester or Lower Amberley."

"In that case, I'll wait near the stables as well." Jenkins was starting to look annoyed by their questions. "Don't worry. I deal with criminals day in and day out, and Dorian isn't as smart as he would have you believe. It will be a simple matter of you bringing the jewels outside, and then I will arrest him. Just make sure Mr Smallwood doesn't raise the alarm before I have a chance to bring everything to a satisfactory conclusion."

As Jenkins bade them a good evening and slipped away into the shadows again, Arthur frowned and shook his head. "I still don't trust him, Nancy. Bernard Doyle used to say to me that there's honour among thieves, but when someone who is meant to uphold the law turns to crime, that's when you need to watch yourself."

"We don't have any proof that he's a wrong 'un," Nancy pointed out. "We have to take him at his word. Otherwise, we're going to end up in prison."

As the lockkeeper's cottage came into view, Arthur turned to her. "I'd rather put my trust in your new family, Nancy. They're honest, hard-working folk, and they know more about Thruppley and the Rodborough Hotel than us. I think we should tell them everything. At least that way, someone will know that we haven't been given any choice about doing all of this. Maybe they will suggest that we have to tell your uncle before it happens? We have to ask for their help."

"You're right," Nancy said decisively. "The worst thing is for us to try and figure this all out alone. I might not have known Abigail for long, but I believe we've been brought together for a reason, and blood is thicker than water. Let's tell them everything and see what they say."

* * *

"I CAN'T TELL you how glad we are to welcome you into our family, isn't that right, Bert?" Verity Webster beamed with happiness and she brushed her grey curls off her face, which was pink from cooking. "You'll have more, won't you." Without waiting for an answer, she filled Arthur's plate with another helping of plum pudding. Nancy had soon learned that Verity liked the family to get together and eat their fill as often as she could persuade them.

Bert nodded, and then Dolly chimed in, too. "It's strange how all of us have discovered family that we never knew about, Nancy. When I was a child, my parents died, and that's when we went to live on the narrowboat with my Aunt Verity. We never even knew about her until after Pa died."

"And I never knew about all of you in Thruppley until I left Frampton to come and find Abigail when she was taken from me by Dominic," Maisie said.

"It's a coincidence for sure, but everything has worked out well." Nancy looked around the table at the people who were already so dear to her.

"I think we were all meant to find each other," Abigail declared. She nudged Nancy as Verity urged them both to have another one of her shortbread biscuits and another cup of hot chocolate. "I know you have your own family as well, Nancy, but I'm so happy I've met you and Arthur."

"It's going to be a tight squeeze when we all celebrate Christmas together," Bert chuckled. "Not that we'll let that small detail get in the way of a good knees-up. You should have seen what it was like when we all lived on *The River Maid*, our narrowboat, Nancy. All squeezed in together we were, but 'twas a jolly time, and I have many fond memories of Dolly and the others when they were little 'uns." He sighed happily.

"And you haven't even met Uncle Horace and Aunt Lillian yet," Abigail said. "You might be worried that they're terribly grand, but they're not, I promise. Uncle Horace taught me how to fish in the lake, and Lillian is so elegant, isn't she, Ma?"

Maisie smiled at both of her daughters. "They're not going to believe it when they see you both side-by-side, looking like two peas in a pod. I'm not exactly sure when Horace and Lillian get back to Thruppley from their business trip, but it must be any day, what with the summer ball coming up next week."

Nancy glanced at Arthur and felt all her pleasure in the warm embrace of her new family suddenly drain away. They had accepted her and Arthur so willingly and opened their hearts and homes to them. But now she was about to test their friendship with her shocking revelation.

Arthur squeezed her hand under the table and cleared his throat. "Now that you come to mention Horace Smallwood and the summer ball, there's something that Nancy and I need to tell you all. And we have a favour to ask."

"You want to come too? I should have thought of it myself," Abigail said excitedly. "We'll all be there, so I'm going to ask Uncle Horace if you can join us. It will be the most delightful night; I can hardly wait."

Nancy swallowed, her mouth suddenly dry, and she slowly rose to her feet. "No, it's not that." She took a sip of water. "I hardly know how to tell you this, so I'm just going to say it straight, but I want you to know that Arthur and I have been forced into this situation. I want to be honest with you all from the start so that there are no secrets between us." She licked her lips and took a shaky breath. "We need your help, you see."

"Go on, ducky," Verity said, seemingly unperturbed by Nancy's mysterious introduction. "There ain't much that we haven't had to deal with or that can shock us. And when one of our own needs help, you can rest assured that we won't turn our backs on you. Go ahead and tell us what's troubling you..."

"Thank you," Nancy said quietly. "It all started

when Dorian married Marigold Kingsley and came to live with us all at Kingsley House, the charitable home for children," she began.

By the time Nancy had explained their predicament and sat back down again with a thump, she fully expected everyone to look at her and Arthur with disgust and disappointment.

"So what you're saying is that Dorian Holt has been forcing you to steal for him these last few years, all for his own gain? While pretending that it was to benefit Kingsley House?" Dolly's lips pinched together in disapproval.

"Exactly," Arthur said. "He had us backed into a corner because every time we tried to stop, he just threatened to get us thrown into jail."

"But now Constable Jenkins wants you to go ahead with this audacious plan to steal Lady Ponsley-Mortimer's jewellery at the ball next week?" Verity's jowls wobbled with indignation, and she turned to Bert and jabbed him with her elbow. "Didn't I tell you I'd heard some rumours about that new constable swanning around as if he owns the place just because he came from London? Poor Harold...I mean, Constable Redfern has been run off his feet apologising to everyone for Jenkins' snooty manner with the villagers."

"You did, dear, and I know you're like a bloodhound for sniffing out folk who aren't who they appear to be." Bert gave his wife a fond smile and patted her plump hand.

"You've done the right thing by telling us," Dolly said firmly. She glanced at Joe. "It's almost like history is repeating itself."

"Dominic Smallwood forced Dolly to be a go-between with jewellery he stole, passing it on to a man at Frampton Basin, who was going to sell it on for him," Verity explained. She patted Joe on the shoulder. "You soon put a stop to that, thank goodness. And although I shouldn't speak ill of people, Maisie was well-shot of him when he high-tailed it off to France with that American woman. He's not the sort of pa who had any intention of doing right by ordinary folk like us."

"But what should we do about what's happening now?" Abigail's face was etched with worry as she looked between Maisie, Dolly, and Verity. "What if something dreadful happens to Nancy and Arthur when we've only just found each other?" She sniffed her tears back and shifted her seat a little bit closer to Nancy so that she could put her arm around her shoulders. "We're not going to let that horrible man put you in jail, Nancy. This family helped save me when I was abducted, and we're all going to pull together and save you as well."

"We desperately want to outwit Dorian, but we've never told Cressida and Marigold what's going on. They would be so disappointed." Arthur accepted another cup of tea from Verity with a nod of thanks.

"And we're worried that Constable Jenkins isn't genuine," Nancy said, wringing her hands with worry.

"He seems the type to double-cross you and put you in jail anyway," Verity muttered, "but we're not going to let that happen."

Abigail wriggled impatiently. "Do you think we should tell Uncle Horace and Aunt Lillian as soon as they get back?"

Joe, Dolly's husband, had been quiet until then, but he shook his head. "I think that's what Dorian and Constable Jenkins are expecting Nancy to do, Abigail." He stood up and walked to the window to close the curtains against the gathering darkness. "The only way to play this is to let the theft go ahead without Horace knowing about it beforehand."

"And then catch Dorian Holt and Constable Jenkins in the act," Verity said with relish and a broad grin. "They might think they can use our Nancy and Arthur for their own gain, but nobody gets one over us, do they, Bert?"

"No, dear," he agreed mildly. He steepled his

hands and leaned forward, looking around at everyone's worried faces. The lamplight flickered, and the corners of the kitchen were shadowy. "It's time for us to come up with a plan to save Nancy and Arthur. They'm our family, and we're not going to let them come to any harm."

Everyone nodded, and their voices rose and fell as they started to suggest ideas. Outside, a fox cried, and night creatures rustled in the undergrowth, but for the first time since Dorian had made them start stealing, Nancy felt safe.

CHAPTER 25

*N*ancy felt self-conscious as she came down the stairs into the back room of the shop. Her dark blue silk gown rustled, and she blushed as Arthur and Dorian both stared at her open-mouthed.

"Goodness me, Nancy," Arthur said with a smile that was suddenly shy. "If I didn't know better, I'd think you were one of the grandest ladies in the West Country dressed like that." He ran a finger around his shirt collar, which was a little too tight on his neck and tugged at his cuffs awkwardly.

Dorian walked slowly around Nancy and then smiled in approval. "Are you sure this is exactly the type of dress that Abigail would wear? If anyone sees you, we want them to think that you're her, remember."

Nancy gave him an innocent look. "Of course I'm sure. I want tonight to go well as much as you do, Dorian. It's not in my favour if they find out that I'm an impostor, is it."

Dorian nodded reluctantly. It seemed that, for once, he was feeling nervous about the upcoming theft because it would involve him as well. "How are you going to make sure that people don't see both of you there together? I wouldn't put it past Horace Smallwood to invite all of his extended family to the ball. He has that sort of annoyingly generous trait, I've heard."

Nancy shrugged, drawing upon all her self-control to not show any emotion. "She thinks I'm meeting her at Thruppley church to have a nice walk to Nailsbridge. Besides, I think you overestimate how close my family are to Mr Smallwood. Abigail has assured me that she never goes to any of those grand events."

"Her pa is the hotel's gardener, not a toff," Arthur reminded him.

"Horace Smallwood and his wife are putting on the ball as an opportunity to impress their wealthy guests from London." Nancy tugged on a pair of long white gloves and patted her hair. "And we agreed that I'm not spending the whole evening there. I'm just going to slip in for a few minutes when it's time to steal the jewellery."

Dorian harrumphed and crossed his arms. "We need to agree on a time. I think you should do the robbery just before ten o'clock so that when you come outside to meet me by the stables, it will be getting dark and nobody will notice us."

"We'll do our best to make it that time, but it's up to Arthur to judge exactly when to create the diversion."

Dorian crossed the shop and peered through the window. Dusk was already falling, and he drummed his fingers impatiently on the windowsill. "I suppose so, but don't keep me waiting. The longer I'm in the grounds of the hotel, the greater the risk of me being discovered."

Typical. Always worried only about yourself, Dorian. Nancy caught Arthur's grimace and knew he was thinking the same as her.

"You have to trust us to do the robbery in our own way," Arthur said firmly. "If we have to change the plan by five or ten minutes, so be it. We can't control everything that might be happening at the ball, and I have to pick the right moment. It's far more dangerous for me and Nancy than you."

Before Dorian could say any more, a horse and carriage stopped outside the front of the shop. "Right then, you'd better leave. Mind that you don't speak to anyone on the way. I'll see you at ten o'clock by the stables."

Arthur tucked Nancy's gloved hand into the crook of his arm. "Are you ready to go to the ball, my dear?" he asked, trying to lighten the mood.

The moment was ruined as Dorian glowered at them both from the doorway. "Don't mess this up, Arthur. There's a lot riding on this tonight, and I'm not about to have it spoiled by two of Cressida's waifs and strays. This is no time to be larking around trying to impress Nancy."

"We'll see you later," Nancy said, tossing her ringlets and sweeping past him to the awaiting carriage that he had arranged to take them to the outskirts of Thruppley. "And remember, Dorian, this is the last time we'll be stealing anything for you."

"Yes, yes," he grumbled, "I should be sailing from Bristol docks this time tomorrow anyway. The sooner I get out of this miserable backwater, the better, as far as I'm concerned."

By the time the carriage had dropped them in a quiet lane on the outskirts of Thruppley, Nancy's nerves were mounting.

"Try not to worry," Arthur said, sensing her anxiety. "If I don't think it's safe, we won't do it, and I'll suffer the consequences. I'll tell Mr Smallwood and the police that it was all down to me, nothing to do with you."

Nancy shook her head and turned to face Arthur, absentmindedly straightening his jacket across his broad shoulders. "You'll do nothing of the kind, Arthur Pittman. We've been in this together right from the start, and that's how we will continue."

He tucked a lock of her hair behind her ear and gave her a tender smile. "That's one of many reasons why I love you. I might not be good with poetry or fancy words, but it's important you know how much I care for you before whatever happens this evening."

Nancy's nerves were calmed immediately, replaced by a surge of affection for him. She stood on her tiptoes and brushed a kiss on his cheek. "I know you love me, but this isn't the time for romantic declarations. We have a job to do and a tricky one at that." They linked arms and walked briskly towards the hotel, then turned off to take the hidden pathway through the woods to Maisie and Jack's cottage, which Abigail had shown them a few days earlier. As the cottage came into sight, Arthur peeled away. Dolly had already discreetly arranged that Arthur would be working with one of the butlers, helping to serve drinks to the guests for the evening. He gave Nancy one final wave farewell and disappeared from her view just as Abigail came running out into the cottage garden.

"Come on inside, Nancy. Ma has a dress for you, and we need to make sure your hair is done just like mine would be." Her green eyes sparkled with intrigue, but there was a hint of seriousness there as well. "I don't know how you're being so brave," she said, hurrying Nancy into the cottage. "Promise me you won't do anything to endanger yourself."

"Of course she won't," Maisie said, bustling forward to welcome Nancy into their home. "I've spent all these years thinking you were lost to me, my dear, so we're going to make sure nothing goes wrong."

"I am nervous, but nowhere near as much as I would be if you weren't all looking after me. Arthur and I are very grateful for your help."

"I wish I was going to be there too, Ma." Abigail pulled a face. "Can't I just hide on the terrace, Pa?"

"Not this time, I'm afraid," Jack said with a wry smile. "We don't want everyone thinking they're seeing double...at least not until after that rogue, Dorian Holt, is safely behind bars." He tamped a plug of tobacco into his pipe and stood up from his armchair. "I think I'll wait outside while you ladies get ready for the evening."

His unflustered demeanour comforted Nancy. For a moment, she found herself wishing for her other family. Her ma, Ezra, and Luke, who would no doubt be teasing her. She hoped they would have a chance to come and meet Maisie and Abigail soon.

"This is the new dress Gloria and I have made for you," Maisie said, holding up a beautiful green silk gown that practically took Nancy's breath away. "It has the secret pocket sewn into the skirts, just as you asked us to do."

"It's beautiful. Arthur will hardly recognise me."

They had agreed that although Dorian had supplied a dress for Nancy to wear, she would change into a green one instead because it was Abigail's favourite colour.

"It's important for you to look just as Uncle Horace and Aunt Lillian would expect. They know that I would always choose green over any other colour because it matches my eyes."

"Did Dorian believe you when you told him that we wouldn't be going to the ball?" Maisie asked as they started to help Nancy get changed.

"Yes, he thinks Abigail and I are going for a walk. To be honest, he's too worried about everything going well to doubt what I said. We reminded him that Jack is a gardener and that the ball is only for the wealthiest guests of the hotel."

Maisie smiled with amusement. "It's a good thing Dorian is such a snob. That's probably how he would behave, and he would never understand that Horace is a humble man despite his success and wealthy connections. He has always included us in events like this ever since he first discovered how badly his brother treated us. Jack used to have a rag-and-bone round, but Horace respects him and often praises how he has transformed the hotel gardens. Jack's brother, Fred, does the round now."

"There are even more people in your family?" Nancy couldn't keep up.

"I can't wait for you to meet Fred. And then you'll have to get to know Uncle Horace properly as well," Abigail said as she whisked Nancy's blue dress away, and they helped her step into the green one. "He and Lillian are two of the kindest people you could ever wish to meet."

"And you'll meet their son, Chester. He's away in London studying with his tutor at the moment, but he prefers the West Country, so I'm sure he'll be home again soon. He's a lovely lad."

"I'm not sure whether that makes me feel worse about deceiving him and carrying out the robbery," Nancy said. She lifted her ringlets so that Maisie and Abigail could do up the tiny buttons on the back of the dress.

"Don't worry about that. He'll understand once we explain the only way this would work is if Dorian is caught red-handed in possession of the jewellery. Without that happening, he would only deny his involvement."

The tapping of a walking stick announced Ava Piper's arrival, and she hobbled into the parlour. "I have a little something to bring you luck tonight, my dear."

"I think I'll need it." Nancy suddenly felt nervous again.

The old woman pressed a tiny glass vial into her hand. It contained dried herbs and was sealed with wax. "Keep this in your pocket. I picked them on midsummer's eve." With a secret smile, she slipped away again. "I'll be thinking of you once the clock strikes ten. 'Tis a kind moon tonight, which will work in your favour."

"How did you..." Nancy wondered how the woman knew the time she and Arthur had agreed.

"Don't ask," Maisie said, chuckling. "She reads the cards and knows more than I'll ever understand."

"It's magic, that's all," Abigail said, throwing her arms around Nancy's shoulders. "Good luck, and promise you'll tell me all about it as soon as everything is over."

"I'm looking forward to it," Nancy said.

They spent another hour doing her hair, by which time it was almost dark. "Right then," Jack said, looking very smart in a frock coat when he came inside again. "It's time to go and give Dorian his just rewards."

As Nancy strolled up the drive between Maisie

and Jack, she had never seen such a beautiful sight in all her life. There were flaming torches dotted through the hotel gardens, and lanterns cast a soft glow on the terraces in the velvety darkness. The strains of piano and violin music drifted out of the open doorways from the ballroom, as well as the hum of all the guests talking and the occasional burst of laughter.

"What if Mr Smallwood and his wife talk to me? I know that I look like Abigail, but I'm afraid he might sense there's something not quite right."

"I don't think he will," Maisie said, giving her a reassuring smile. "You have to remember Horace has no idea that you have come back into our lives. Nobody would ever suspect who you are, and Jack and I will look after you. He and Lillian will be busy mingling with all the other guests."

They walked into the ballroom a few minutes later, and several people waved and called out greetings to them. There were at least twenty elegant couples swirling around the dance floor to a lively waltz, and out of the corner of her eye, Nancy saw Arthur weaving between some of the other guests, carrying a tray of champagne glasses. He looked dashing in his suit and thoroughly at ease, which gave her courage. As he approached, he gave her a discreet wink.

"A glass of champagne, Mr and Mrs Piper? And

one for your beautiful daughter, or perhaps she would prefer a cup of fruit punch?"

"Fruit punch will be fine, thank you," Nancy said quietly.

"Maisie, I'm glad you and your family are here," Horace Smallwood called jovially. He was making a beeline for them, and he shook Jack's hand enthusiastically. "The garden is looking wonderful, Jack. I don't think I've ever seen the roses bloom as well as they are this summer. How are your piano lessons going, Abigail? Remember that Lillian said you're welcome to play the piano here in the hotel any time you wish."

"Thank you, Uncle Horace." Nancy's hand shook slightly as she accepted the cup of fruit punch from Arthur.

Horace held her gaze for a moment, and she thought she detected a glimmer of puzzlement, but then a red-faced gentleman tapped him on the shoulder, and he excused himself as the two men fell into conversation about one of his other properties in Bath.

Nancy let out a breath she hadn't even realised she had been holding, and Maisie nodded graciously to two matronly women who scurried past to talk to Lillian Smallwood. "You see," she said quietly, "nobody is any the wiser."

A murmur went up from the guests as several

more new arrivals were announced. Nancy craned her neck to look around the ballroom and wondered whether the Ponsley-Mortimers had arrived yet.

"I think I'm going to stand near the potted palms in the corner of the room," she said behind her fan. "I'd rather not dance with any of the young men because I need to be able to look out for Arthur's signal."

"I'll come and stand with you," Jack offered. He grinned at Maisie. "I'm no good at dancing, as my dear wife will tell you. I stand on her toes too often, so I'm more than happy to accompany you and see off any young men with amorous intentions."

Maisie drifted away to talk to some of the other guests, and once she was hidden by the potted palms, Nancy started to relax.

"That's Lady Ponsley-Mortimer," Arthur whispered as he sidled up to them. He jerked his head towards a plump woman with tight, grey ringlets. Nancy had expected someone younger, but she looked to be about sixty years old. A glittering ruby necklace hung around her neck, with a large teardrop diamond resting on her décolletage. She wore a three-stranded bracelet over her elbow-length gloves, and the matching earrings sparkled in the candlelight every time she moved her head.

"I can see why Dorian chose her," Nancy whispered back. "Those jewels will be enough to set him up for life."

"Enough to send him away to prison for life, I hope," Arthur muttered with a slight frown.

There was a large grandfather clock in the corner of the ballroom, which chimed every fifteen minutes, although it was barely discernible over the sound of the string quartet.

"Have you seen the time?" Nancy's mouth went dry as she realised it was a quarter to ten, and the moment was almost upon them.

Arthur nodded and squeezed her hand. "I'm going to circulate one more time around the ballroom, and then, as soon as I see them coming towards this side of the room, I will spill the drinks. You steal the necklace, I'll take care of the other pieces, and then I'll give them all to you."

Jack shot them a glance, which, to Nancy's surprise, was one of respect. "You're a braver man than me, Arthur. I trust you'll be putting your skills to better use in the future if you're going to marry Maisie's daughter?"

"You have my word, Mr Piper," Arthur said, suddenly looking serious. "This is the last time I'll ever steal anything, I promise."

The next few minutes passed in a blur of music and colour as the quartet started playing a lively quickstep, and the dancers swooped and twirled.

Although the Ponsley-Mortimers were both rather portly, they were light-footed and clearly enjoyed dancing.

This is it. Nancy took a deep breath as Lord Ponsley-Mortimer whisked his wife towards their corner of the room. Just as they were right in front of Nancy, Arthur suddenly stumbled as a thickset gentleman inadvertently bumped into him. The tray tilted, and before anyone had a chance to stop it, two cups of fruit punch slid off, sending a splatter of the fruity concoction all over both of the Ponsley-Mortimers. For a split second, it reminded Nancy of that time, so many years ago, when the plum syrup had drenched her from head to toe.

"Goodness me, let me help," she sprang forward and started dabbing her shawl on Lady Ponsley-Mortimer's purple silk dress.

"Look what you've done, you fool!" Lord Ponsley-Mortimer cried, looking furious. He pulled out a voluminous, white handkerchief and also joined in, mopping the fruit juice from his white shirt.

As quick as a flash, Nancy took the necklace from Lady Ponsley-Mortimer as she bent over to examine what damage had been done to her gown.

"It's not too bad, my lady," Nancy murmured. She slipped the necklace into the secret pocket in her dress and hurried away.

"Mind that you don't stand on any broken glass,"

Jack said. He steered the Ponsley-Mortimers away, and Arthur hurried after Nancy.

"Did you do it?" Nancy's heart was hammering so loudly she thought she might faint.

"Yes. Quick," he whispered, grabbing Nancy's hand as they ran out onto the dark terrace. He slipped her the other pieces of jewellery, which she hid in her dress pocket with trembling fingers. "We only have a minute at the most," Arthur said urgently. "It's this way." They ran the length of the terrace.

"Help! I've been robbed!" Lady Ponsley-Mortimer's hysterical shout reached Arthur and Nancy just as they rounded the corner of the main house and sprinted across the gravel driveway towards the stables.

The music came to an abrupt halt, and more shouting ensued, but Nancy knew they couldn't afford to stop for even a second.

She picked up her skirts and ran faster, following Arthur as he weaved between the topiary box hedging. Just when she thought she couldn't go any further, the stables came into view, and Dorian stepped out from the deep shadows, his eyes gleaming with unbridled greed.

CHAPTER 26

"I believe you have something for me," Dorian said. His teeth glinted in the dim light from a nearby lantern as he smirked. He held out his hand and looked her straight in the eye.

"It's all here, this is everything." Nancy pulled the jewellery out of her secret pocket so fast that she dropped the bracelet.

"Take care." Dorian snatched everything from her and hastily bent down, scrabbling to retrieve the bracelet.

"Not so fast," a deep voice said. Constable Jenkins emerged from behind the stables and strode to Dorian's side.

"Thank goodness," Nancy gasped. She felt close to tears and blinked rapidly.

"Go on then, arrest him," Arthur said urgently.

Nancy shivered next to Arthur as they both looked at Constable Jenkins expectantly. "Quickly, before he runs away," she said.

Dorian smirked again, and Constable Jenkins slapped him on the back, chuckling. "That was a good haul, Dorian. Time for you and I to vanish into the night and leave Nancy and Arthur to face Smallwood and Lady Ponsley-Mortimer, don't you think?"

Nancy's stomach dropped. "You promised we would be safe." Her tears vanished, replaced by burning anger at how they had been used.

"I knew it!" Arthur's fists bunched, and he took a step forward. "You've been working with Dorian all along, haven't you?"

"Very astute," Jenkins said with a shrug. "I don't get paid much, and I already knew Dorian from some rather lucrative dealings we had in London. Getting you both to do our dirty work has been a stroke of genius, but now we must leave."

The shouts of outrage from the guests grew louder as they came out onto the terrace, and Nancy tugged Arthur's arm. "We have to scarper. Everyone is coming after us."

Dorian tipped his hat and gave them a thin smile. "It's been a pleasure knowing you. Do give Marigold my regards. I don't intend to write to tell her where I'm going, and I suggest you create one of your famous diversions, Arthur, if you want Nancy to get away. Constable Jenkins and I will be leading a very pleasant life with the money we get from selling this jewellery." He stuffed it in his pocket, and both men turned to run away.

Suddenly, the air was split by the sound of a whistle, and three men crashed out of the undergrowth. It was Constable Redfern holding a lantern, flanked by two other burly men carrying truncheons.

"Stop right there, you're under arrest!" Redfern shouted. "You might have got away with doing this in London, Jenkins, but we're not the bumbling country fools you take us for."

Without further ado, the two men sprang forward and wrestled Dorian and Jenkins into submission.

"Get your hands off me, you oaf," Constable Jenkins yelled, twisting and turning. He glared belligerently at Constable Redfern. "I was in the middle of arresting Dorian Holt and these two thieves. Wait until I tell my superiors about how you've treated me. You'll never work another day as a constable if I have anything to do with it."

"It's not true, Constable Redfern," Nancy cried. "They're in cahoots." A sob rose in her throat. "Please...you have to believe us."

The sound of running footsteps interrupted them, and she was relieved to see that the whole family had arrived. Verity, Bert, Dolly, Joe, and even Abigail.

"Did you get him, Harold?" Verity demanded,

elbowing past everyone to get to Constable Redfern's side. "I hope you believe our Nancy. And as for both of them treating Nancy and Arthur so badly, I hope you'll take that into account."

"What have I said about calling me Harold when I'm working, Verity? You're as bad as my aunt." He shook his head and gave the older woman an amused look. "It's Constable Redfern, remember, and yes, Jenkins and Dorian Holt are safely under arrest now."

"Quite right, too." Verity put her hands on her hips and looked at the two men. "Folk like you should know better, but nobody gets the better of our family."

More people appeared from the direction of the ballroom, and Arthur took hold of Nancy's hand as they realised it was Horace and Lillian Smallwood, closely followed by the Ponsley-Mortimers.

"What's going on?" Horace asked, looking shocked to see them all. "There's been a robbery in the ballroom." His gaze fell upon Arthur and Nancy. But then his eyes widened as Abigail hurried forward to stand next to Nancy. He blinked as though he couldn't believe what he was seeing. "Two of you? Who are you...what is this?"

In the dim lamplight, and both wearing green dresses, there was no mistaking the fact that Nancy and Abigail were identical twins.

"We can explain everything," Maisie said. She put

her hand on Horace's arm and gave him an earnest look. "We didn't want to deceive you, but we had to let the robbery go ahead so that Dorian would be caught red-handed. You remember that when I eventually got my memory back after the amnesia and found out that Abigail was my daughter, I knew I'd had twins but always believed one of my babies didn't survive being born?"

Horace nodded, still looking stunned at the sight in front of him. "Yes, my dear. You told me that Abigail's twin was buried in Frampton churchyard."

"By the grace of God, she lived, even though we never knew. She has been raised by another family, and then she came to stay at Kingsley House in Lower Amberley with Cressida and Marigold Kingsley."

Recognition flashed across Horace's face as he looked closer at Nancy. "I saw you in the park that time, didn't I? I mistook you for Abigail, but I couldn't work out why you looked slightly different, and you ran away before I could ask you."

Nancy nodded. "I'm sorry, sir. I didn't mean to deceive you."

Abigail stepped forward. "This horrible man, Dorian Holt, has been forcing Nancy and Arthur to steal things. He's behind everything that happened tonight."

Constable Jenkins tried to shake off his captor,

but Constable Redfern was having none of it and gave him a sharp jab with his truncheon. "I've had my suspicions about Constable Jenkins for a while, Mr Smallwood. There were rumours about him in London, but he thought he could get away with even worse here. Although he's pretending he was here to arrest Mr Holt, my men and I heard him quite clearly just now. They're working together. But worse than that, Constable Jenkins has been forcing Arthur and Nancy to do his bidding as well." His lip curled with contempt as he glared at his colleague. "You should know better, Jenkins. There's no excuse for your behaviour, and you will be treated like the criminal you are."

"But...but...," he spluttered.

"The jewels are in his pocket." Nancy pointed at Dorian's coat. "You'll probably find more in his rooms over the shop as well."

As Constable Redfern retrieved the jewellery from Dorian's pocket, Lady Ponsley-Mortimer pushed through the gathered crowd of onlookers, and Nancy's heart sank.

"I'm so sorry about what we did," she said in a small voice. "We didn't want to steal from you—"

Lady Ponsley-Mortimer held up a hand, cutting off her apology. Nancy started to tremble. There was no getting away from the fact that she and Arthur had stolen her jewellery, and they would surely have to pay for their crimes.

"I have heard everything the good constable has just said," she said, glancing towards Constable Redfern. "There is nothing I despise more than a bully. Or a gentleman who should know better than taking advantage of two innocent people." She walked up to Dorian and Jenkins with an imperious look on her face and rapped them both sharply on the knuckles with her fan. "If you think I was wearing the real jewels my papa gave me for our wedding, you're more foolish than you look. What you stole tonight are excellent copies, I grant you, but the real ones are safely under lock and key at home."

"Huh?" Dorian's face blanched.

"This is all just a silly misunderstanding," Constable Jenkins said, giving her an ingratiating smile. "It's all their fault, trying to make up some fanciful story about us making them steal things."

"He's right," Dorian chimed in. "Surely you must believe us over the ridiculous ramblings of these two." He gave Nancy and Arthur a scathing look. "I'm a well-respected businessman. They're just a couple of waifs and strays whose families didn't even want them. You only have to ask Cressida Kingsley. She'll vouch for me. If it weren't for my support, Kingsley House would have gone to wrack and ruin a long time ago. Cressida and Marigold don't have a shred of business sense between them."

Lady Ponsley-Mortimer drew herself up to her full height and quivered with indignation. "I know exactly what Kingsley House is and the marvellous work they do. I have been one of Cressida's benefactors for many years, and I won't stand for you running the place down."

A dull red flush crept up Dorian's cheeks, and he looked down and scuffed his toe in the gravel.

"As for you, Constable Jenkins," Lady Ponsley-Mortimer continued haughtily, "my brother is one of the highest judges in the land. He will take great delight in giving you a suitably long jail sentence to give you plenty of time to think about the error of your ways."

A ripple of applause went up from all the other guests as Constable Redfern bundled Dorian and Jenkins away to the awaiting police cart.

"Three cheers for the young lady and gent who saved the day," someone cried.

"Hip-hip, hurrah!"

The guests started to wander back to the ball-room, exclaiming about what an exciting night it had been, but that Constable Redfern had everything in hand.

"Goodness me, I don't know about you, but I think we all need a stiff brandy or perhaps a strong cup of tea." Horace Smallwood smiled at everyone, shaking his head in amazement. "It seems Lillian and I have a lot to catch up on, and we were only away for a few days. Not least, the fact that I now have two nieces, although I'm struggling to tell you apart."

As they all strolled back towards the hotel, the string quartet started playing again, and the strains of a more gentle waltz drifted out through the open doors into the warm summer air. Moths fluttered around the lanterns, and Arthur guided Nancy to the edge of the terrace. The moon was just rising, and it cast a creamy glow where it was reflected in the canal in the distance.

"We did it, Nancy. We're free of Dorian and his demands," he said with quiet satisfaction. "Can we just get on and live a normal life together now?"

As Nancy leaned against his broad chest and looked up into his blue eyes, she smiled. "That sounds like a wonderful plan, Arthur."

"Come on inside again," Abigail called from the doorway. "This is a ball; you're all dressed up, and you're the saviours of the hour. You should have a dance in the grand ballroom. It's the perfect place for a marriage proposal," she added with a twinkle in her eye.

"Give the poor pair a chance to catch their breath," Verity scolded as she bustled after them. She grinned as she said the words. "We do love a wedding, though, don't we, Bert?"

"We certainly do, my dear," Bert agreed. "But all in good time. I reckon they'm going to want a little while to get over all this business."

"I've never seen two people more suited," Dolly murmured to Maisie, who couldn't help but agree.

They walked into the ballroom, and Arthur put his arm around Nancy's waist with a bashful look on his face. "Will you do me the honour of having this dance with me, Miss Burton?"

"That would be perfectly charming, Mr Pittman." They shared a knowing smile as he swept her around the ballroom under the flickering light of the candles, and he thought she had never looked so beautiful.

UNTITLED

Epilogue, One Year Later...

"Thief! Thief! Mr Popinjay squawked and flapped his wings on his perch.

"Not anymore," Arthur chuckled back at the parrot. He strode along the hallway and stuck his head in the kitchen. "Do you know where Nancy is, Primrose?"

Primrose and Moira both looked up from their task at the large kitchen table. They were in the throes of putting the finishing touches to dozens of cakes for the Kingsley House Summer Fair, which was taking place that afternoon.

"She's finishing sewing the bunting in the front parlour." Primrose's face was pink with exertion, and she swatted Robert and Rick away, who were loitering nearby, hoping to lick the mixing bowl. "You two had better hop it. The chairs need cleaning from all the spider webs in the shed, and the trestle tables aren't looking too good either. We need everything set up in the garden within the next hour."

"Blimey, Primrose, you're more bossy than Moira, and that's saying something."

Arthur smiled to himself as he watched the two boys scurry away. He and Nancy had married in the autumn, and Primrose had come to visit them at Christmas. After much pleading with Margaret, Cressida had agreed she could stay and work in the kitchens as long as she was paid a proper wage and continued with her lessons in the evening. Primrose had settled in as though she'd always been there, and he knew how much it meant to Nancy that her younger sister lived with them.

"Is everything going to plan?" Arthur asked as he came into the parlour.

Nancy's heart lifted as she looked up from the string of bunting. She had just finished sewing the last piece, and she jumped up from her chair.

"I think so. If you can put the ladder against the apple tree, I'll go outside and put this bunting up."

"You'll do no such thing," Cressida said hastily. She was sitting at her small escritoire in the corner of the parlour, leafing through some documents.

Marigold put down the book she was reading and

looked over the top of her spectacles. She was meant to be preparing lessons for the children, but this was not a matter to ignore. "I know you like to be independent, Nancy, but climbing ladders is very ill-advised for someone in the family way."

Arthur slipped his hand around Nancy's waist and pressed a kiss to the top of her head. "If anyone's going up a ladder, it's me, my love." His eyes softened as Nancy's hand went to the gentle swell under her dress. It would be a wonderful Christmas at Kingsley House when they welcomed their new child into the world, and he gave her a proud smile.

"If you insist, but it's a long time until my confinement, and we have so many plans. I can't just sit inside all day."

"We don't know whether it might be twins," Arthur reminded her gently.

Cressida shuffled her documents with a thoughtful expression. "I'm just so happy for both of you, whether it's twins or not." She glanced across at Marigold and then stood up slowly and reached for her walking stick. Old age was starting to take its toll on both of them and Dorian's terrible behaviour the previous year certainly hadn't helped.

As if sensing her thoughts, Marigold snapped her book shut. "I had some news from Constable Redfern yesterday."

Nancy picked up all the bunting in her arms and

then squeezed Marigold's shoulder. There was no denying the fact that for a few months, Marigold had been quietly distraught by her husband's behaviour, but once Christmas had passed and spring had made a welcome appearance, she gradually got back to her usual cheerful self.

"What did he say?" Cressida prompted.

"It was just to let me know that Dorian has been moved to a different prison. Dorian and Constable Jenkins were discovered trying to bribe one of the prison guards, so it was decided it was better for them to be jailed in separate parts of the country."

"Do you think you will want to visit him at some point?" Cressida asked.

Marigold shook her head and gave them a rueful smile. "I don't think there's any point. With hindsight, I married too hastily. I allowed myself to be swept up by Dorian's romantic endearments instead of questioning why he was so desperate to rush into marriage." She glanced across at Cressida. "I'm sure that's why he didn't want you to meet him before our wedding. You would have seen through him straightaway, but I was blinded by what I thought was love." She looked sad for a moment but then brightened. "I have everything I want here, and what I'm most grateful for is that Constable Redfern fought so hard to make sure that no blame was apportioned to you,

Nancy. Or you, Arthur. I would never have forgiven Dorian if either of you had ended up in prison."

"I'm just glad it's all in the past now. Anyway, we'd better get on with the rest of our preparation for the summer fair," Cressida said, changing the subject. She looked through the window where Robert and Rick were arranging the tables and chairs on the lawn. The villagers would soon be arriving, and it promised to be an enjoyable day. A horse and carriage stopped just beyond the gates, and she smiled to herself. "Oh good, Horace is here," she said happily.

"I didn't know he was coming?" Nancy headed for the door. They still had a lot to do, and holding the summer fair to raise funds for Kingsley House had been her idea. She wanted it to go without a hitch.

"I invited him, especially." Cressida picked up her documents. "I know you're eager to carry on with your preparations, but if you could both come into the study, Horace and I have some important news that we'd like to share with you today."

Nancy looked at Arthur with a twitch of her eyebrow, but he shrugged. Neither of them knew what it was about, but it sounded serious.

"If you give me the bunting, I'll supervise Robert and Rick hanging it up," Marigold said. Her eyes sparkled with intrigue, and she wasn't going to take no for an answer, so Nancy agreed and then followed Arthur down the hallway.

The early morning sun streamed through the tall windows of Cressida's study, and there was a pot of coffee and four cups already waiting on the table, as well as a plate of ginger cake.

This is getting more mysterious by the minute. It seemed as though the meeting had been planned, and Nancy wondered what Cressida was up to.

"How are you, my dear?" Horace boomed. He strode into the study and took his hat off, laying it on the sideboard before giving Nancy a hug and shaking Arthur's hand. "In good health? I've just seen Abigail, and she's already declaring that becoming an aunt will be the highlight of her year. She asked me to tell you that she, Maisie, and Jack will be here no later than mid-morning so that they can help with the stalls. Jack has built a tombola and a lucky dip, which I'm sure will be in great demand with the villagers."

Cressida gestured for everyone to sit down, but just as they did so, the sound of singing caught everyone's attention.

"What a delight," Horace remarked. He tipped his head as the two voices rose and fell in sweet harmony.

"It's Anne and Sophie," Nancy explained. "The two sisters whose parents abandoned them when they emigrated to America. They adore singing with each other. They're going to be doing a few songs this afternoon, putting on a bit of a show."

"They have a remarkable talent."

"Marigold taught them to play the piano. The singing is just what comes naturally to them." Cressida tapped her fingers in time to the music, glad the girls were being praised.

"Never mind a show for a village fair. They're good enough to sing at the hotel." Horace looked thoughtful. "Would you consider allowing them to perform a concert for our guests sometimes? Lillian and Chester have been telling me we should offer the guests more entertainment."

"Oh, I'm not sure about that." Cressida looked across to Nancy. "Do you think they're old enough?"

"We could ask them. They never seem to get nervous. I'll pour the coffee, shall I?" Nancy added extra milk to her own cup because she didn't like it too strong now that she was expecting. She felt a stirring deep in her belly and smiled to herself. The doctor had told her that it would be impossible to know if she was expecting twins until they arrived, but Ava Piper had whispered something to her recently, which only confirmed what Nancy already knew in her heart. She was convinced that she and Arthur would be the proud parents of two babies before the year was out, but she had kept it secret for now, knowing that it might make Arthur even more protective. She loved that about him, but she also trusted Ava's prediction that the babies would be healthy and bonnie. Ava had never got anything wrong in the past, so there was no reason to doubt her this time.

Cressida took a sip of her coffee and then put her cup down again, looking across the low table at Nancy and Arthur. "I'm sure you would be too polite ever to say so, but it can't have escaped your notice that Marigold and I are not as young as we used to be."

"You still seem to achieve more than most women," Arthur chuckled.

"Horace and I have been talking about the future of Kingsley House." Cressida glanced in Horace's direction, and he sat up straighter in his chair to speak.

"Lillian and I had planned to open an orphanage when we were first married," he explained. "We didn't realise how popular the hotel would become, and the other hotel I opened in Bath as well. They took all my attention, which is why my plans for an orphanage never came to fruition."

"You never gave up on wanting to help poor, unfortunate children, though, did you?" Cressida looked fondly around the room. "Kingsley House has been a labour of love over the years, but everyone knows that such a place requires money and a great deal of determination to run it well."

"Since Lillian and I have got to know more about Kingsley House, we decided this is where we could help instead of trying to open our own orphanage." Horace stood up and walked to the window, clasping his hands behind his back. "I suggested that I would like to purchase Kingsley House, and to my delight, Cressida and Marigold agreed."

Nancy couldn't keep the surprise from her face. "Does that mean you're leaving, Cressida? I don't think Kingsley House would be the place it is if you're not here."

"No, my dear. But we do want things to change. Horace, Marigold, and I would like you and Arthur to run Kingsley House from now on. We will still help, of course, but it's time for Marigold and I to step back a little. We all feel that you two are the best people to continue what we've started and make Kingsley House even better for all the children we want to help in the future." She leaned forward. "Will you say yes? I do hope so."

Arthur reached across and squeezed Nancy's hand, looking at her with nothing but happiness in his eyes. "What do you say, Nancy? Reckon we're up to it?"

"It's a lovely surprise to be asked." Nancy suddenly felt emotional, remembering the first day she had arrived. She exchanged a smile with Arthur, nodding. "I think it would be a great honour, Cressida. You gave Arthur and me opportunities and an education that neither of us would ever have had without your generosity and steadfast belief in us and other children who had fallen on hard times."

"We'll ignore the opportunities Dorian foisted on you," she replied dryly.

"This is home." Nancy looked around the room and to the garden beyond. "There's nowhere else I'd rather live than here, with Arthur, and to watch our children growing up with all the other little ones."

Horace rubbed his hands together and grinned at Cressida. "Your instincts were right. I'm glad that's all settled. Lillian and Chester should be here soon, and we'll be able to enjoy ourselves at the fair, knowing that the future of Kingsley House is secured."

The sound of laughter drifted through the window from the garden, and Nancy jumped up from her chair, closely followed by Arthur.

"Ma's just arrived with Papa Ezra and Josiah," she said as she spotted another horse and cart in the lane.

"We're hoping to persuade them to come and live in Lower Amberley now that Ezra is almost of an age to retire from the railway company," Arthur said.

Horace chuckled. "Nancy and Abigail have an uncanny knack of getting what they want, and I'm sure with Nancy's powers of persuasion, they won't be able to say no,"

He picked up his hat again, preparing to leave. "How do Margaret and Maisie get on, my dear? Well, I hope, but it must have felt a little strange knowing that you have two mothers, so to speak."

Nancy shook her head. "They're as thick as thieves," she said, laughing. "Between Abigail, Maisie, and Ma, I'll barely get a look in when the babies arrive." She clapped her hand to her mouth as Arthur's eyes widened with shock.

"Did you just say babies? As in..."

Nancy laughed again as they strolled along the hallway and went outside to stand in the sunshine. "Ava might have mentioned something to me the other day about twins. And since Abigail and I discovered each other, and I now have the best twin sister I could ever have dreamt of...I suppose it was only to be expected."

Some of the younger children were playing tag, weaving between the trees, and shrieking with excitement. The once-overgrown garden was slowly turning into something more beautiful under Jack's care as he taught Robert and Rick gardening skills, and Kingsley House was returning to its former glory.

Arthur sighed contentedly and put his arm

around Nancy. "We didn't do too badly for two children who fell on hard times, did we, Nancy."

She leaned her head against his shoulder. "We might have thought we were the forgotten ones, but in truth, it was the opposite. Coming to Kingsley House and having you as my friend turned out to be the best thing that ever happened to me."

She waved as Ezra ushered Margaret through the gate, and they walked up the gravel pathway. The bunting flapped in the apple trees, tugged by the breeze, and Josiah raced across the lawn to help Robert and Rick with another pile of chairs. It was going to be a wonderful day...the first of many she and Arthur could look forward to. She had her family here, old and new, and good friends. It was everything she had ever hoped for and more.

READ MORE

If you enjoyed The Forgotten Girl, you'll love Daisy Carter's other Victorian Romance Saga Stories:

The Snow Orphan's Destiny

As the snow falls and secrets swirl around her, Penny is torn between two worlds. Does a gift hold the key to her past, and will her true destiny bring her the happiness she longs for?

Penny Frost understands that she's had an unusual start in life. Taken in by a kind-hearted woman, she becomes part of the close-knit Bevan family of Sketty Lane.

Poverty is never far away, but they manage to scratch a living working for the miserly Mr Culpepper in the local brickyard.

Penny dreams of something better and never feels as though she quite fits in. And the fact that her mother never mentioned her own childhood only adds to the mystery of who she really is.

When she is bequeathed a piece of jewellery, Penny wonders if it might unlock the secret to her past. However, before she can find out, a shocking event one dark and snowy night brings her to the attention of the wealthy Sir Henry Calder.

Suddenly she finds herself swept into a world of privilege and comfort, far away from the Bevans and her best friend, George, and it seems as though her future is finally secure.

But not everyone wants Penny to succeed and will go to any lengths to get their own way, even if it means leaving her destitute.

Will the mistakes of the past be repeated and snatch Penny away from her true destiny?

Can she reclaim what is rightfully hers even though the odds are against her?

Torn between two very different worlds, Penny must decide whether to follow her heart or put duty first if she's to have a chance at love and happiness...

The Snow Orphan's Destiny is another gripping Victorian romance saga by Daisy Carter, the popular author of Pit Girl's Scandal, The Maid's Winter Wish, and many more.

* * *

**Do you love FREE BOOKS? Download Daisy's
FREE book now:**

The May Blossom Orphan

Get your copy by clicking here

Clementine Morris thought life had finally dealt her a kinder hand when her aunt rescued her from the orphanage. But happiness quickly turns to fear when she realises her uncle has shocking plans for her to earn more money.

As the net draws in, a terrifying accident at the docks sparks an unlikely new friendship with kindly warehouse lad, Joe Sawbridge.

Follow Clemmie and Joe through the dangers of the London docks, to find out whether help comes in the nick of time, in this heart-warming Victorian romance story.

Printed in Great Britain
by Amazon